THE

SURVIVORS

'THE most remarkable living writer' — that is what such diverse critics as Leon Daudet and Ford Madox Ford unite in calling René Béhaine. With this novel, he begins the history of a fantastic society, the world of the French provinces.

Catherine de Laignes's parents carry over into the twentieth century, of which they are hardly aware, a way of life which has not changed since the eighteenth century, and which even then had begun to be outmoded. At her convent school, Catherine learns only to repeat prayers, as, at home, she learns only a serene politeness. Thus armed for the modern world, she marries.

Besides all the absurdities of this society, M. Béhaine makes his readers feel its richness and solidity. He writes with an austerity which serves to emphasize the dignity of the picture he presents.

THE
SURVIVORS

RENÉ BÉHAINE, 1880-

*

TRANSLATED BY

EDWARD CRANKSHAW

PREFACE BY

FORD MADOX
FORD

BOSTON AND NEW YORK
HOUGHTON MIFFLIN COMPANY
1938

From the French original
"LES SURVIVANTS"

FIRST PUBLISHED IN ENGLISH
IN 1938

RENÉ BÉHAINE

By FORD MADOX FORD

FOR MANY YEARS NOW—for ah, how many!—M. Léon
Daudet and this writer have cherished one belief. It is
that the novelist whose name stands at the top of this
page is the most remarkable living novelist. Flaubert
said that if France had read his *Education Sentimentale*
she would have been spared the horrors of the *Débâcle*
of 1870. One may say of M. Béhaine that if the world
would read his books—his one immense book in many
parts—the world would be spared its next Arma-
geddon . . . because it might know France.

Conrad spent the whole of his writing life in trying
desperately to find a new form for the novel. He used
to say that the writing of novels is your one occupation
for the proper man, because with the novel you could
do anything . . . provided always that you had your
New Form. M. Béhaine, who has something akin to
Conrad's smouldering and passionate contempt for
the imbecilities of common humanity, has, without any
of poor dear Conrad's writhings as to form, consum-
mately given the novel at least a new status. There is
about his writing not so much a smouldering contempt

i

as a passionate austerity. Beside it, as if on a height giving on to the whole world, you view a usually imbecile and almost always disagreeable humanity. But when you have read Béhaine you will know France.

And knowledge of France is the sensitive spot of the Western Hemisphere. Sooner or later in your life you will find yourself fighting either to preserve or to destroy France. That has been the fate of humanity with almost exact regularity every half-century since first the hordes of Brennus thundered down, through the Gaul which is France, to the sack of Rome and the destruction of a mighty civilization. It has been the function of their successors periodically to thunder down towards the Mediterranean, passing through, or staying to plunder the Gaul of the moment, thus putting back the clock of our Mediterranean civilization—of our civilization which is a civilization only in so far as it is Mediterranean—a decade or so every half-century. Nevertheless, through those millennia of armed inundations, France has always come up again—not always smiling, nor even with the complacency of races who can count on always muddling through. No: grimly. For France is always grim. She has to be. She has her five annual saturnalia, the Fourth of July, the Assumption of the Virgin, and the rest, during which over all her broad acres you will hear the sound of Browning's drum and fife . . . and in some of them the lovelier *cornemuse*.

But, once those days are over and the street dancing places restored to the traffic of the automobiles, and all her toiling millions return to the grim task of making France fit to withstand the whole world.

It is difficult to understand how France has contrived to do this for centuries when any other people must have given up the task if not in despair, then in pure weariness. For in her functions of guarding the shores of the Mediterranean and so keeping some line of contact open between Western Europe and the sources of her civilization, France for a millennium and a half has had continually to face our invasions, sporadically those of the Spaniards, Austrians, and Italians, periodically those of the Germans, and once at least for over a quarter of a century the onslaughts of the entire Western World. That is matter of fact, not of opinion. It is one of the most astonishing of facts.

You begin to account for it when you see the great mountains of the Central Massif of France, terraced right up, on their steepest of escarpments to the very summits that are clear of snow for only six or eight months of the year. Compared with those monuments, the Pyramids or the vast, vulgar buildings of the Romans are mere whimsies. What then gives this people that desperate persistence that has lasted for centuries and still lasts? You answer: Only one thing can have done it, an immense sense of rectitude. If you added: and an unparalleled love of the soil, you would have the correct answer.

From where does that immense sense of rectitude come? That desperate persistence? You get the answer in M. Béhaine's tremendous series of meticulous works. For M. Béhaine's vast labours are produced in the spirit of an austere and conscientious judge of appeal writing a judgment. There is about him none of the careless bull-charging of a Balzac or even of the support in his attack on human problems that Flaubert got from the enraged disappointments of his native optimism. There is in M. Béhaine no optimism to be disappointed. He watches his characters with the grim amusement of a man looking at beetles trying to climb up the slippery sides of a bath.

There is one of M. Daudet's characters in, I think, his *Les Kamtschatkas* who, whenever he comes upon a particular instance of unimaginative human barbarity, says: *Cela vous donne une fière idée de l'homme!* But I cannot imagine M. Béhaine saying that in that negative sense. There is little that is negative about him. Once, years ago, when I lived on a Mediterranean hill particularly difficult of access and he was coming to see me for the first time in that place, he arrived late. And his first remark to the lady of the house as he hurried down the precipitous garden path was: "Madame, under a king I should not have put you to this inconvenience." He meant that under a king the posts of France would be efficient and he would have received the letter containing a plan of our approaches that she had sent him— thirty miles or so away—three days before. So he would not have been delayed. He *meant* that. For him the Third Republic spells inevitably unthinkable graft, unparalleled inefficiency of public services, unimaginable slothfulness of un- or under-paid public servants; and a complete indifference to all public complaints of the mandarins in the Paris ministries, the one concern of the Ministers of l'Infâme being how they may get diamond tiaras for all of their several mistresses before the fall of their Ministries. But, not knowing what was going on in the brain of that figure of the *ancien régime* with the supremely serious expression, that speech, before the lady had even been presented to the Master, gave her a *fière idée* of M. Béhaine among the wild roses of the Mediterranean.

M. Béhaine in short is, first, a royalist: after that an atheist; after that a Pacifist. And then he holds the singular, and to most serious Frenchmen repulsive, belief that a young man should be a virgin on his marriage. Into this last article of his creed we need not go, Anglo-Saxons presumably sharing it with him. But the other three beliefs we may consider a little.

Almost every normal Englishman and American, forgetting that tastes in governmental forms change and then return almost as completely as tastes in books, will tell you that monarchism in France is as dead as the taste for, say, the novels of Sir Walter Scott. But if you will read to the end of M. Béhaine's book you will see the groundlessness of that belief. A very great number of the serious French believe that a king alone can save France. The more serious they are, the more seriously and with the colder tenacity they will cherish that belief. They will cherish it indeed with such icy passion that unless you are likely to be able to help the Cause forward, they will neither speak about nor expound it. Amongst themselves it will be the one continuously canvassed topic. But it is because of their taciturnity to strangers that the stranger much underestimates the strength of the movement in France.

How deeply seated it is in France, and how comprehensible in the end that fact is, you may judge from *The Survivors*. This particular book occupies itself almost entirely with the class from which the real royalists are recruited: the whole series of half a score works occupies itself with the union of a daughter of the aristocracy of the *ancien régime* with a son of the family of the *haute bourgeoisie*. . . . Les Varambaud; and it is as it were through the eyes of that young couple, once their difficult union is effected, that we survey the currents and movements of French life at all social depths and heights.

The Revolution, if it did nothing else, added another to the ruling classes of France—that of the *Haute Bourgeoisie*, which to all intents, if concealedly, acts on public life as the Supreme Court does in the United States and the hereditary Second Chamber in England. It consists of all the members of the Senate, all the great judges, all the higher permanent officials, all the considerable lawyers, professors, surgeons, physicians and pharmacists, the forty French Academicians, the members of the other Academies, and, as if by courtesy, such representatives of commerce as are sufficiently long established to have founded families and to be unshakenly "serious" . . . and at the other extreme a few Dukes who by devotion to mineralogy, biology, or the collection of the lepidopters have proved themselves to be completely without the sense of humour and the perils that a sense of humour entails on the incautious. I once heard a high French official whose position entitled him to inscribe on his cards the portentous title "Controller of Asia," explain why he had become incurably Anglophobe. He had gone to call on Lord Strachey, Viceroy of India, then in Paris, I think, on his way out to India by way of Marseilles. When M. X. was introduced into the Viceroy's drawing-room he found that representative of the King looking humorously at his visitor's card which had been sent up to him. And:

"H'm," said Lord Strachey, " 'Controller of Asia?' . . . I thought *we* had something to say to that."

It was useless to try to persuade M. X. that the Viceroy was merely indulging a quite friendly sense of humour. M. X. remained bitterly hurt—as if he had been reproved for assuming a vainglorious function. He said that if Lord Strachey had been a serious and educated public figure, he ought to have known that the title he derided merely indicated that its bearer was permanent chief secretary of the Asiatic department of the Colonial Ministry.

Indeed, nothing remotely approaching a sense of humour is to be found in any of the characters in *The Survivors*, except in the case of several very old maids, nuns, and ancient priests who retain sufficient of the eighteenth-century tradition to make extremely innocuous jokes about the bodily functions of humanity—jokes that have the air of having been wrapped up in lavender for a generation. That is not to say that M. Béhaine himself possesses no sense of humour. On the contrary, he is full of it. The later volume in which the adventures with domestic helps in Brussels of Catherine de Laignes and Michel Varambaud are grimly rendered will make you laugh enough, if you are of the type to laugh at Breughel's picture of the blind leading the blind.

Certainly outside the pictures of Breughel it would be hard to find a more fantastic collection of mentally and physically crippled, malignant, thievish, and inefficient beings than those with which M. Béhaine afflicts that unfortunate young couple. But M. Béhaine, grimly indifferent to whether you laugh or not, has merely there set himself the task of showing how Michel Varambaud, instinct with the sense of order and efficiency, shudders as if on the rack at being brought forcibly into contact with the disorder and want of efficiency that are the distinguishing characteristics of the majority of to-day's humanity. And in the

tragedy of the admirable but helpless Catherine faced
with furniture that will not let itself be forced into too
small rooms, with smashed tureens, unwashed rags
stuffed into corners, with the thefts, greed, and continual
truancy of completely undesirable female helps . . .
in that tragedy M. Béhaine is no doubt intent on making
us feel his malign condemnation for the upbringing of
Catherine at the hands of her mother and the swarms
of female and male religious and old maids with whom
her youth was surrounded. And into that, too, creeps
his almost Satanic hatred for Catholicism as affecting
the young . . . and the grown-up young in all the other
ages of man.

It is an amazing affair, that education as it is here
presented . . . as if the young Catherine went on her
pilgrim's path towards adolescence in a perpetual
shower of little papers stamped with prayers, scapulars,
papier-mâché images, imitation flowers for the
decoration of shrines, and all the devices invented by
the lesser members of the Church for continually
drawing back the pilgrim's mind towards the affairs
of that Church and instilling into her an otherworldliness that makes her completely ignore everything
connected with housekeeping or the regimentation of
the household and the control of its helps.

On the other hand, that education—which, however
you look at it, was an education rather than instruction
—was admirably calculated to impel you to regard
the prospect of your ultimate dissolution with equa-

nimity . . . to lead up to the frame of mind in this book where the Comte de Laignes in the family vault without any emotion indicates to the remaining members of his family where they shall finally lie. . . . To his sister: "You shall lie there, over Mother"; to his two cousins: "You there and you there"; to his wife: "You beside me, if you like" . . . the whole transaction being taken both on his part and that of his relatives with the quite serious indifference of persons arranging before going on a journey where a party shall sit in the already engaged seats of a railway train.

How that frame of mind is produced we may tell by listening to M. Béhaine. In Catherine's convent, as in every teaching convent in France, the day's business is brought to an end, after a faint veneer of lay wisdom has been applied to the child mind, beneath the endless shower of tiny religious observances, in this way:

. . . Gradually night came on. In the pulpit the curé knelt and prayed. His quiet voice echoed mournfully in the dim silence of the church, and down in the shadows a muffled and uniform murmur rose in response, hardly audible, and ceasing abruptly.

After the Litany at the close of prayer there came the meditation on Death. And the sombre majesty of the words they heard awoke in those childish minds a sort of terror that haunted them till they were safely back in the class-rooms, half an hour later, each in her own place. But in bed in the dormitory at night those words, like a solemn warning, echoed again in the depths of one's soul.

x

> *"Let us always remember that we may die to-night, let us see if we are ready to appear before God. . . . O God! O Moment! O Eternity! A God that is all, a moment that is nothing, an eternity that can deprive you of all or bestow all upon you for ever. A God whom you serve so ill, a moment that you turn to such little account, an Eternity that you leave to chance. . . ."*

And adroit artist that M. Béhaine is, he checks the effect of that solemnity with:

> Some of the little girls, afraid of dying in the night, recalled Sister Edmond's advice and traced the names of Jesus, Mary, and Joseph on their forehead with their thumbs.

That is not the guffawed anti-climax of Mr. Shaw, nor the sedulously machined antithesis of Mr. Galsworthy. It is the fainter and more delicate substitute for comment by the author that is all M. Béhaine's own. It is hardly even humorous. Yet it is as if the tremendous meditation—fit, as someone has observed, only for the mouths of saints, and hardly for common men or children—is made to be a little ridiculous since its only effect is to make children scrape their thumbs on their foreheads, in the night.

You might say that is all M. Béhaine were it not that he is a greater artist and a man more scrupulous than to let it go at that. The Catherine that that training evolves is a human being entirely desirable, of a high conscience that is yet bewildered by the terrific antitheses between which she finds herself as soon as her individual passion begins to work. She finds herself that is to say, in the volumes subsequent to *The Survivors*, between the immovable cliff of her parents' opposition and the irresistibly harsh passion of her suitor, Michel Varambaud, so that she has as it were two consciences, each diametrically opposed to the other. That is the fate of poor humanity of a to-day in which so many exactly opposing causes are apparently incontrovertible.

In any case the effect of her religion-ridden education on Catherine is to render her at once singularly helpless when she comes to marry Michel and to have to face rather straitened circumstances. She has been used to a household where everything under her mother's masterly handling has run as on wheels, to furniture that always, as if automatically, shone with beeswax and turpentine, to immense linen presses filled, as if by Providence. In all this she has taken no part. Three of her four chatelaine's duties Catherine's mother, the Comtesse de Laignes, performs with the admirable rectitude demanded of her position. She is the master housekeeper, the consummate organizer of all the charities of her neighbourhood, and incomparable at her social duties. She "calls" indefatigably, to the point of physical and mental exhaustion, and that perhaps is the most important of her functions, since the Cause of a class practically excluded from public service and subject to many political disadvantages is almost exclusively kept alive in salons whose communications, like creeping root-stocks, run under the whole soil of France. So that, exhaustively performing her other duties, Madame de Laignes, with every warrant from her point of view, entrusts the education of her daughter to the good nuns and secular and lay clergy who swarm in her neighbourhood. The result is to emphasize in Catherine her natural sense of rectitude and to give her that strong contempt for the things of this world that the nightly recital of the terrible meditation on Death has conferred on her. Because, paradoxical as it may seem, the French-woman of the class of Catherine de Laignes goes through what to the ladies of all other nations to-day would seem fantastic household operations, not with a view to the comforts they might be expected to produce, nor with much desire of ostentation, but simply as a matter of maintaining whole and unflawed the great tradition of harmony with the infinite that is the chief glory of France. She more than any other being of to-day would agree to the rightness of the poem of George Herbert's that I never tire of quoting:

> Each servant with this clause
> Makes common things divine:
> Who sweeps a room as for Thy cause
> Makes it and the action fine.

With his remarkable and delicate art in his *History of a Society*, Monsieur Béhaine make these things apparent. His art is indeed so delicate that unless you keep your awareness functioning very actively you will be apt to miss the fact that there is any design in his books. His great master was undoubtedly Flaubert, but he has advanced on the sage of Croisset to the extent that his more austere, Gallic temperament makes him eschew at once the immense horse-laugh and the recurrence to coincidence and antithesis that were part of the strengths of the author of *Bouvart et Pecuchet*. Monsieur Béhaine would never *entamer* a whole intrigue that was to embrace and blast all the accepted ideas of science and the world with the exclamation of one of his characters to another of: *"Tiens, nous avons eu la même idée, celle d'inscrire nos noms dans nos chapeaux!"* He carries, nevertheless, each of the books of his series to its double climax with all the exact observance of *progression d'effet* of Flaubert himself. The screw of minute and breathless religious observances is turned and turned in the case of Katherine with a gradual implacability until there is nothing to be found in the way of development but a breaking down into a complete aimlessness, and then in the void appears the already slightly sinister figure of the young Michel Varambaud, who in the subsequent volumes is to turn into her distracting fate.

Similarly, alongside the career of Catherine in her convents goes the apparently aimless gradual decay of the great house and the disruption of the unnumbered acres of Laignes. So that on the occasion of the last visit of Monsieur de Laignes to the deserted home of his childhood you seem almost physically to see the great mansion give, like an old horse, at the knees and sink for ever to the ground. And as you read that scene in its muted poignance you realize that the ambition of Monsieur Béhaine to be the historian of his day has been fully realized. Later on, when he comes to deal with that most disastrous of the only disaster to France whose disruptive effects are not even yet exhausted, you will have him rendering, through the eyes of Michel, a far more loud historic note. And with such verisimilitude that this reader at least who passed much of his youth in the Paris of the *Affaire* can vouch for the fact that in it Monsieur Béhaine brings to life again the crowds in the night, the shafts of light in the darkened boulevards, the innumerable cries, the very feel of the damp night air on the face of that half-century ago. For the Dreyfus Case seems always to have been transacted in a sort of darkness.

But in this particular book our author is the renderer of that smaller, but always active history that gnaws away the shapes of monuments, renders streets, once crowded, impenetrable with the great branches of brambles that will never again be cut, and over the names of the mightiest of the earth casts the cloak of oblivion.

> His eyes fixed at random on an epitaph, he (M. de Laignes) would read over words from another age, words which his ears were long unused to hearing and of which the very sound was no longer familiar to anyone:

CY DEVANT SOUS CETTE TOMBE

REPOSE LOUIS CHARLES ANTOINE AMÉDÉE
POTHON DE LA TRENOYE, COMTE DE LAIGNES.

NÉ LE 18 AVRIL 1743, IL FUT REÇU PAGE DE MADAME
LA DAUPHINE LE 13 AVRIL 1757, FAIT CORNETTE AU
RÉGIMENT ROYAL-LORRAINE CAVALERIE EN JUILLET 1760,
POURVU D'UNE CHARGE DE LIEUTENANT DES MARÉCHAUX
DE FRANCE EN 1772, CHEVALIER DES ORDRES DU ROY

Between this date and the next there was a long
interval of time. It ended:

MORT EN SON CHÂTEAU DE LAIGNES LE 9 MARS 1825

But before this calm succession of honours and titles,
one following another, and in face of the empty space
destined to receive his own inscription when he was
dead, Monsieur de Laignes would sometimes find
himself thinking with secret bitterness that beneath
his name his children would read nothing.

So passing and divested of the last shreds of active
political power, these aristocrats gave place to the
Haute Bourgeoisie, a class which to this day remains
the continuous check on public impetuosity in France.
A constant factor and one almost unknown to the
outside world, they continuously colour French life
and thought. And they are the factor with which either
the political friends or temporary invaders of France
should most count—with their incredible cold serious-

ness and their terrifying tenacity of purpose to keep alive and dominant in the world not so much France as what France and they stand for. . . . To turn from that sublimity of phrase, Mr. Dreiser has observed in France a symptom that stands for that side of her activities. "What madmen you Parisians are," said he once to an interviewer. "You have in Paris the finest night life in the world. Yet the whole city is in bed by nine o'clock." . . . That is because next day at dawn that city must be up and about its unceasing task of keeping on the map what France stands for. With the wonderful efficiency of the French *ménagère* she keeps herself furbished up: that is the face she presents to the stranger. But with the otherworldliness of that same housewife who daily throughout her childhood recited at nightfall the meditation on Death and whose place in the family vault has been long since settled, she coldly ignores the splendours she keeps untiringly going.

It is this tenacious side of France that Monsieur Béhaine gives us. For that we cannot be too grateful to him, for you will find such a presentation in no other author as far as I know. The *Comédie Humaine* of Balzac is a mere fairy tale, and the vast disillusioned optimism of Flaubert, even in *Education Sentimentale*, is mere *défaitisme* beside the portrayal of bitter industry with one sole purpose that you will find in this History of a Society.

And indeed, what better illustration of his theme

could you have than Monsieur Béhaine himself! A man of some property, the Germans burned his manor-house, cut down all the fruit trees which gave him his income. They gone, the priests, he being an atheist, saw to it that he received none of the reparation funds; because he was a royalist, Labour saw to it that no workmen would work at rebuilding his house; because he was a pacifist, the royalists—except for Monsieur Léon Daudet, who devotes to any new book by this author on its appearance nearly the whole of the next number of *L'Action Française*—give him no support, and every disaster known to humanity has since showered itself upon his head. . . . But Monsieur Béhaine built for himself a house with his own hands, planted himself a new garden—and with a miraculous tenacity went on—and goes on—unceasingly evolving this history of his time. Do you not recognize in that, *in petto*, an epitome of those marvellous workers with whom we started—the men who in spite of invasions, wars of religions, avalanches, droughts, pestilences, murrains, have gone on through the centuries terracing the great mountains of the centre of France—terracing, manuring, sowing, harvesting, and having to carry pocketfuls of dung and seeds up the sides of slopes as steep as the dome of St. Paul's Cathedral, whilst down below them as often as not their houses, byres, fruit trees, and gardens, lay levelled to the ground as symbol of the passage of one type or another of Visigoth or Hun. . . .

Mr. Crankshaw in his translation has made a valuable experiment. Possessing as he has amply shown us a smooth, musical style of his own, he has recognized that smoothness and music are not the appropriate vesture for the raven-voiced, metallic truths of his original. It was not a case for the usual listlessness of the translator of commonplaces. He has therefore of set purpose adopted a number of Gallicisms and inversions sufficient to make you have all the time the sense that it is "matter of France" that you are reading. I don't say that he uses as many of these cross-channel devices as adorn my own pages, but he uses enough. The consequence is that if you read on through the pages without halting meticulously to question the advisability of this word or that phrase you get—or this reader certainly does—the sense that it is actually French that you are reading. It is a most singular effect. And, since it is completely without the barbarity usually attendant on literal translations, and since in its long cadences you seem to hear the bitter equanimity of the very voice of my friend Béhaine himself, you may regard it as an experiment of the greatest value and success. I wish other translators would study his effects.

PEOPLE are only beginning to do justice to the great novelist René Béhaine. His entire work constitutes a document of the highest merit as to the events of our time, and there is no literary attitude more noble than that of this writer. . . . His literary position much resembles that of Marcel Proust on the eve of his receiving the Goncourt Prize. He is recognized as a remarkable and sometimes astounding analytical writer—by his brother writers and by a hundred or so of persons of discrimination. But he has not yet been accepted, as he well deserves to be, amongst the world's elect. . . . Placing him very high I wish him success as deeply founded as he deserves. For an analogous achievement Jean Paul Richter was accorded such success in Europe and in Germany, though he remains unknown in France. Béhaine might well receive it here . . . and all lovers of literature will rejoice.

LÉON DAUDET,
de l'Académie Goncourt.

CONTENTS

ANTOINE DE LAIGNES

1

ON SUNDAYS THE BARONESS DES MENULS often went to Monthuis to see her daughter, who was being educated at the Convent of the Annunciation there. She was allowed to see her in the parlour after vespers, but only in the presence of a nun and behind a grille: through the bars she could be seen as a well-grown girl, strongly built, with a pale, aquiline face, standing there a little awkwardly in her narrow frock and her short cape of dark cloth barred with the blue ribbon of the Children of Mary; even the regulation bonnet—a crochet affair which entirely covered her hair, cut short at the neck —could not subdue those proud and angular features.

The Baroness would ask about her health, her marks, and whether or not she was happy; the girl answered briefly in her quiet and level tones. Then she in turn would inquire as to her mother's health, and her father's and her grandparents'. The ringing of a distant bell would terminate the interview. Before leaving, Madame des Menuls would surreptitiously slip her daughter a little packet of cakes.

Only for the long vacation did Anne-Marie des Menuls go home to her parents, whose estate lay some twenty miles out of town. At three o'clock, after the prize-giving, the carriage would come to fetch her. And beside the mother who had not kissed her for ten months, and afterwards back in the great house where there seemed to be no place for her, she would feel sullen, lost, and almost hostile.

When she finally left the convent she spent several months at home, helping her mother in charitable works which involved their going once a week to town together. Then she married. The bishop arranged it all, and the marriage united two ancient families of Laonnais, that part of the Île de France that borders Picardy—a hilly, wooded country, from the narrow cultivated heights of which one looks out on to range after range of little valleys, with a village in every hollow.

Shortly before the date fixed for the ceremony those girls in Monthuis who worked for the charities patronized by Anne-Marie (daughters of tradesmen or small officials) received a letter from Mademoiselle des Menuls informing them of her marriage, to which they were not invited, and asking for their prayers at such and such an hour on such and such a day—"the hour at which," the letter ran, "His Eminence the Bishop of Monthuis will celebrate in the chapel of the Château des Menuls her marriage to the Comte Amédée Pothon de Laignes de la Trenoye."

In the first few years of their married life Monsieur and Madame de Laignes made the round of their friends and relations, often setting out in their carriage in the morning and not returning till night, or, if their destination was too distant, remaining away from home for two or three days together. Some weeks of every summer they spent at Menuls. Then Madame de Laignes became pregnant, and once the child was born—a son, called Antoine—they lived entirely at home.

It was an old house, isolated in its park at the bottom of a little valley hung round with woods, and some distance from the village; one of those old mansions with extensive frontages and tall windows, designed to hold large families, whose unpretentious grandeur astonishes and annoys latter-day parvenus, who scorn it as evidence of a past from which they are excluded and a spirit they have been able to destroy but not to replace.

Apart from his mother's and father's rooms, which remained exactly as they had been when they died and in which nothing was touched, Monsieur de Laignes had the château completely renovated for his marriage. The old panelling in the dining-room was replaced by new mahogany panelling; the bare beams of the ceilings were plastered over. And if the two great reception rooms were left untouched it was simply because their remodelling would have been too expensive; only the furnishings there were renewed. Madame de Laignes chose new upholstered furniture; the old settees and armchairs with their carved knobs and ribbons and tufts of feathers were relegated to the attic. Festoon-blinds were put up in all the windows, and much of the château now took on a comfortable, bourgeois appearance. The entrance-hall, opening on either side into the two reception rooms, was likewise transformed; mosaics depicting classical myths replaced the huge flag-stones from the original château on the foundations of which the present building had been erected a century before.

When Antoine was four years old his nurse's husband died. Her parents took charge of her own son, her place at home was forgotten, and henceforth all her care and love was bestowed on the child of her employers.

In the evenings, when the child grew peevish as night began to fall, she would take him on her lap and, sitting by the window, soothe him by singing one of those old, gay, light-hearted songs which have gathered a certain melancholy with the passing of the years. If she paused in her singing the child, who had seemed asleep, would start crying. Unweariedly the nurse would begin again:

> Three little drummer boys
> Were coming home from war.

And all the while she sang her eyes would wander over the scene outside, the broad meadows, and the road beyond them stretching away, lined with apple-trees.

She would tell him stories, too, fantastic tales and legends often based on centuries-old memories of doings of the de Laignes in that part of the country; some were very old, some comparatively recent, and she jumbled them all together in an indeterminate sort of past without perspective. There was the story of Trembling Piot, and the story of the White Lady de Laignes, an ogress who lived on little children and whose neck was so white and so fine, they said, that you could see the blood pulsing beneath the skin. Then there were the adventures of the Chevalier de Laignes: he had been forced to take to the woods at the time of the Revolution and had remained hidden for a whole fortnight in an oak quite near the highway; a mattress had been fastened in the topmost branches, and every day an old servant and his nurse took it in turns to bring him food and drink.

After six years of married life (in which period two other important events also occurred, the death of her father and the death of her mother), Madame de Laignes had five children, three boys and two girls; but she left it entirely to the nurse to carry out her minute and careful instructions for their upbringing, assured that everything possible would be done for them and that they would lack neither care nor attention; she was thus able to forget such details and, secure and untroubled, arrange her own life in the way she meant it to go.

Her marriage, by assuring to her the position to which she had been born, had, without altering the way she ruled her life, merely added new duties to those she conceived already hers. She believed that her leisure should be devoted to those who had none, and accepted as a matter of course what seemed to her less a wearisome burden than a voluntary obligation, which indeed she took as a prerogative, almost as the mark of her rank.

She visited the sick, tended them and took them medicines and linen, comforted the dying, made the newly born and their mothers her especial care, and never omitted to stand as godmother to the poorest of the children, whom she invariably presented with a hundred francs. Sometimes she would go and sit in some low farm-house room to cheer a poor old woman with her conversation. And conscious of the rôle she had imposed upon herself, easy in the assurance of her own position, she always—whether giving advice, administering a rebuke, asking some small service, or inquiring into the little happenings of the humble lives she had linked with her own—retained the same tone of tranquil authority, the same easy familiarity, which was possible because the gulf between her and her charges seemed to the latter as great as it was natural, and she knew they would never dream of overstepping it. Her mind, moreover, dulled and warped by the education she had received, put her almost on a level with those with whom she dealt: to her, as a Christian, the world meant nothing, and she could look upon the greatest as upon the most trivial happenings with an interest which was at bottom no more than indifferent contempt.

Every Saturday, as much to set a good example as from a habit of piety which she had kept up since her marriage, she went to church and took her place among the six or seven other devout ladies who knelt or sat on the benches beside the confessional, awaiting their turn to confess. All at once a sound of heavy footsteps would be heard outside, and a swish of skirts, and Abbé Rousselot, the curé, would appear in the side door, hat in hand. Saluting the altar in passing with a profound genuflexion, he would disappear into the sacristy, to emerge a few moments later in a white surplice that accentuated his corpulence and made his broad red peasant's face look redder than ever.

He would open the door of the confessional, his burly figure seeming to fill the narrow box, take down his violet stole which hung on the wooden partition, and lift it mechanically to his lips, as ritual prescribes, before slinging it round his neck; his resigned gaze, which he tried in vain to make severe, would dwell on the pious, kneeling ladies. He seemed to be reckoning them up, calculating the time each would take him and the hours he must spend on his spiritual judgement seat. At length he would sit down heavily, the Comtesse de Laignes would kneel in one cabinet and another exalted lady in the other, and he would close the door with its grille lined with green baize. Thereupon one of the wooden shutters within would immediately slide back with a dry scraping sound to reveal a small opening allowing confessor and penitent to communicate; and in the silence of the church voices began to whisper.

As summer drew to a close Monsieur de Laignes would begin to receive the guests who came for the shooting, and life at the château would change a little. These guests were mostly local landowners or town gentry, the Marquis de Fourcy, the Comte de Lafont, the old Duc de Gessin, Monsieur Bréant. They would arrive overnight and set out early next morning, Antoine, who was already allowed to accompany his father on these shoots, going with them. And all day long the sound of their guns told those at home of their whereabouts from hour to hour.

Posted at intervals along a road or ditch or bank on the outskirts of the wood the beaters were working, they waited in silence, motionless, gun under arm, ears stretched, while the line of beaters advanced at a steady pace through the wood, putting up the game and driving it towards the guns. Soon one voice after another would be heard announcing the approach of game. Suddenly a large bird would burst clumsily out of the undergrowth and fly up with a great crackling of foliage. The sportsman would raise his head and take aim, and the bird, its wings abruptly failing, would change in that moment from a living creature into an inert mass falling to earth of its own weight. Or perhaps, if the gun in question were looking elsewhere, Antoine would catch sight of a rabbit, its long, alert ears almost on a level with the red earth, humped, preoccupied, anxious and cunning, its eye staring sideways, its cheeks bulging like those of an old woman munching sweets. Suddenly, catching sight of the man with the gun, it would prick its ears, hesitate, remain motionless for a second, and then with a leap and a violent swerve plunge back into the wood: accelerating its jerky course, its white scut flickering at every bound, it would head through the undergrowth to its secret home, all unaware of the weapon that now kept pace with its flight. A shot would bring it up short; a sudden somersault and it would drop motionless, paws outstretched.

At home in the evening the keepers would empty out the bags and sacks of game before the guests assembled on a lawn near the château, tumbling them out pell-mell before arranging them in neat rows—rabbits already cold and stiff, that could be picked up all of a piece by those broad, horny hands grasping them round the loins, astonishingly rigid, as though supported by an inflexible inner core. And the birds, the colour of autumn leaves, would fall on top of one another soundlessly, their heads dangling, their eyes often still alive, while from the tip of a half-open and feebly gaping beak there hung a tiny drop of blood.

From day to day one guest would depart and another arrive, and all through November there was company at the château. But every evening they came back earlier from the shoot as night came on more quickly. The woods reddened, the avenues in the park were thick with dead leaves. Through the thinning trees the mortuary chapel of the château, built by Monsieur de Laignes' great-grandfather, began once more to be seen.

The last guests departed, the drawing-rooms were shut up, and the great dining-hall. And one evening Monsieur and Madame de Laignes would find their places laid again at the round table in the small and characterless room which was their usual dining-room.

2

RIGHT UP TO THE END of autumn Monsieur de Laignes
would be busy with his accounts. There would be rents
to receive, sales to arrange; then a journey to town to
see his lawyer about investments. Meanwhile, the rains
coming on would render the roads almost impassable,
and the château seemed more isolated than ever;
sometimes it was impossible to go out for weeks on end.

At such times, if there were some document he had
been wanting which might be supposed to be among
his papers and which he had put off looking for from
day to day, or if there was some grant, some dispensa-
tion or service the origin of which he wanted to ascer-
tain, Monsieur de Laignes, taking advantage of this
enforced winter idleness, would often spend whole
afternoons shut up in his study going through the
family archives. All sorts of papers of varying ages were
crammed into five large trunks, normally relegated to
the attic, among which parchments predominated,
since they were tougher: marriage contracts, notifica-
tions of baptism and death, documents relating to past
transactions between a Comte de Laignes and the
inhabitants of some village, title-deeds and inventories,
papers or copies of papers relative to law-suits, safe-

conducts, passports, some of these very old indeed with a dab of wax at the end of a silk ribbon; a voluminous will, even, which Monsieur de Laignes came across in the course of his investigations and stopped unnecessarily to read through with complacence from beginning to end.

Or a letter, folded obliquely and across and still preserving besides its address traces of the wax or wafer that had sealed it, would suddenly turn up between two leaves of the document into which it had slipped, and Monsieur de Laignes would immediately look for the signature and sometimes even glance through the letter with a vague curiosity. Next it would be family letters, intimate or formal, tied up in bundles of varying size—old letters whose polished turns of phrase recalled an ampler and more ceremonious age, or little affectionate notes in large hand-writing, the spelling mistakes of which in no way detracted from their nobility of expression; indeed, their contempt for the rules seemed less a matter of ignorance than of deliberate indifference, as if those who had traced these tall and unevenly slanting characters had scorned in advance that age of easy revenge which was to come, when the multitude would struggle weakly and in vain to acquire what is not to be won but is simply inherited.

Of all the names his eyes chanced upon, however, the majority meant nothing to him at all. Apart from various anecdotes or incidents concerning certain members of his family, Monsieur de Laignes knew nothing about any of the others. And although he had inherited from his ancestors a pride of name which consorted ill with his indifference to those who had borne it before him, he experienced no least desire to come in contact with the past or make the smallest effort to learn anything about it. Living from childhood among the portraits left behind by generation after generation of Comtes de Laignes, he had never shown the slightest interest in them or thought to discover whom they represented. For a generation each picture in turn had been, as it were, the evocation of a living being, and while waiting for the inevitable moment when the annihilation of the man is followed by that of his image they had already passed through two degrees of death; first that succession of deaths which deprives those who no longer exist of all who once knew them; then there comes a time when nothing is left in human memory of all the people depicted. Little by little they lose all associations and fall one after the other into the anonymity of mere pictures; until at last they are less portraits of ancestors who were once alive than so many decorative paintings.

There they were—apart from a few chosen for his study by Monsieur de Laignes and others disposed here and there among the hunting trophies in the hall or on the staircase—hanging from the walls of the two large drawing-rooms and the great dining-hall, wherever there was room for them, at various heights, isolated above a doorway, or in groups of three or four between the ornamental sculptures of the panel below a niche. Some were copies of originals which had been dispersed. Several, rubbing shoulders with the work of mediocrities, were signed by illustrious names.

The oldest of them, darkened by time, had the age of the figure portrayed painted in in a corner of the canvas next to the name and beneath the invariable crest which reappeared in every picture. Gradually that solicitude for reality which had ruthlessly revealed the dominant traits of all these faces gave way to a more conventional style, in which all wore the same aspect of stately majesty and easy authority; and this in turn was succeeded, in the following century, by an air of lively and smiling grace which shone in the brilliant, speaking eyes and on the mobile, shaven mouths. But towards evening, when dusk merged clothing and background and only the pale shapes of the faces remained visible, there were no longer courtiers or bishops or soldiers or magistrates in this long succession of individuals, but only men descended one from the other; then, under all the various head-dresses, and in spite of the diversity of their careers, a similarity of countenance in them all could be discovered, more and more distinctly as the racial character strengthened, a similarity of attitude, even, caused by the disposition and shape of the nose which, set firmly beneath the narrow, arched forehead, and leaving a considerable space between its peak and the slightly protruding lower lip, gave one and all the appearance of holding their heads well back and of looking down from a height.

There were two or three portraits of children, too, and several of women, most of these with alien features, whom marriage had brought into the family—women in full dress with low-cut gowns and jewels, or, at the painter's whim, in fancy dress accompanied by mythological emblems. And suddenly and with astonishment one would realize that this one, with the fresh complexion and fair curls, was the grandmother of this other whose hair was white. Among these infrequent portraits of older women was one showing bony cheeks, a colourless skin, thin lips darkened by thick down, and a forbidding appearance under the high ruched bonnet; tradition had it that this was the Ogress herself.

Every evening after dinner the children would spend a few minutes with their parents in Monsieur de Laignes' study before going upstairs with their mother to bed. Madame de Laignes would return to find her husband playing patience while he waited for her, seated at a little card-table with the cards spread out before him. His patience finished, he would suggest a game of piquet or bezique; and on Sundays, which was the Abbé Rousselot's day for dining with them, they would play three-handed whist.

More often than not, however, seated alone by their fireside, Monsieur and Madame de Laignes would wait in dignified boredom until it was time to go to bed. They talked very little. Their conversation, interspersed with long silences, was nothing but a repetition of things already said earlier in the day. Sometimes they would discuss acquaintances of whom they had recently had news, and about whom one or the other of them would call to mind some little anecdote or happening. Never, however—and in this they were different from the majority of men, who live in hopes and in dreams—never did they turn to what was yet to come, but only to what had been: perhaps they felt that the past, obscure as it was in their eyes, belonged to them more than the future could ever do, and perhaps they felt too a certain responsibility for this uncertainty and decline.

Every week, and several times in the week, Monsieur de Laignes went down to the village to attend to his duties as mayor. On other days he would shoot, or perhaps the course of his walks would take him over to one of his farms, or to a wood to see the wood-cutters and inspect the trees to be felled, or he would visit Rossignol, his keeper, who lived in one of the first cottages of the village high street. Often, setting out for a walk or returning, he would pass close by the chapel in which his parents were buried. Occasionally he entered it.

Built on a little mound, it was exactly like those edifices one comes across occasionally in city cemeteries, though larger. An inscription on the lintel of the doorway called attention to its purpose: *Ossa patrum*. Unlike most of those who have died, whom those who best loved them are eager to banish from their lives and relegate to a carefully selected anonymity, the de Laignes dwelt still in their own home, a stern and venerable centre to that family life of which they were still a part. And this proximity of the dead inspired in the living neither fear nor repulsion, as much because they were accustomed to it, perhaps, as because these Christians saw in death no more than a moment of waiting.

As he pushed open the door Monsieur de Laignes would see at once precisely what he had seen when he had last closed it. At one end the tiny altar with its violet lambrequin, its candlesticks and copper crucifix; in front of this prie-dieu and chairs, neatly aligned; between these and the door an empty space, brightly illumined by the light which poured through the stained-glass windows on to the black and white flagged floor. Right and left along the wall were flowers arranged before the long marble plaques, each with its epitaph, each surmounted by the same emblazoned coat of arms—wreaths and bouquets, put there as a rule to mark some anniversary and then left to fade, pervading the damp atmosphere with a faint breath of corruption.

As one glances round a rarely visited room to make sure that all is as it should be, so Monsieur de Laignes, standing on the threshold, and sometimes even without uncovering, would glance sharply round to make sure that nothing had been disturbed and then almost at once withdraw, his mind busy with the small matters which filled it at the moment, and without thinking particularly of what he had just seen. But if something had recently occurred to sadden him by stirring forgotten memories, or if there had been a service lately to the memory of his dead parents, or if he had been ill at all, then he would become oppressed by feelings normally foreign to him. He would brood over the idea of death, recalling those of his parents. And with a characteristic and melancholy egotism he would stand suddenly lost in meditation, struck by the silence and the utter stillness. Beneath him, in the vault which he had seen opened and the shape of which he knew so well, were his father, his mother, his grandfather, his grandmother, and two uncles who had never married. And little by little in the midst of this mute assembly whose voices he still seemed to hear he would forget his ordinary preoccupations and the busy life outside; prey to a strange feeling of mingled confidence and pride, he would for a moment become aware of all that was implicit in the heritage handed down to him. His eyes fixed at random on an epitaph, he would read over words from another age, words which his ears were long unused to hearing, and of which the very sound was now no longer familiar to anyone.

CY-DEVANT SOUS CETTE TOMBE
REPOSE LOUIS, CHARLES, ANTOINE, AMÉDÉE
POTHON DE LA TRENOYE, COMTE DE LAIGNES.
NÉ LE 18 AVRIL 1743, IL FUT REÇU PAGE DE MADAME
LA DAUPHINE LE 13 AVRIL 1757, FAIT CORNETTE
AU RÉGIMENT ROYAL-LORRAINE CAVALERIE EN JUILLET 1760,
POURVU D'UNE CHARGE DE LIEUTENANT DES MARÉCHAUX
DE FRANCE EN 1772, CHEVALIER DES ORDRES DU ROY

Between this date and the next there was a long interval of time. It ended:

MORT EN SON CHÂTEAU DE LAIGNES, LE 9 MARS 1825.

But before this calm succession of honours and titles, one following on another, and in face of the empty space destined to receive his own inscription when he was dead, Monsieur de Laignes would sometimes find himself thinking with secret bitterness that beneath his name his children would read nothing.

3

ONE OCTOBER MORNING the boys and girls playing round the church porch as they waited for their lesson in the catechism saw the château carriage turning into the square. The Comtesse de Laignes alighted, preceded by her eldest son, and swept between the little groups, subdued now and suddenly dumb. And when, a little later, they streamed into the church in the wake of the Abbé Rousselot, they found Antoine already seated there and reading a little book like those they had themselves, while Madame de Laignes, come to help her son through his first lesson in the catechism, knelt a few rows farther back.

Twice a week from now on, at eleven o'clock in the morning, the carriage brought him to church just as the children were coming out of school, straggling along the village street. The whitewashed houses all had a bourgeois air about them, with their steps up to the front door and their neat windows behind nearly every one of which, summer or winter, stood a pot of flowering geraniums on the sill between glass and muslin curtains. Singly or in little irregular, chattering groups, the children came hurrying up the street, carrying their school-books at the end of a strap or in a leather satchel. In the midst of these boys with their patched clothes and their clumsy friendliness Antoine felt more at ease and less isolated than the difference in their appearance might seem to indicate.

Boys on one side, girls on the other, they took their seats in the first two rows of the nave. After a hymn which they all joined in singing, the curé, who had been kneeling at the altar, would turn round and immediately call out some child by name and ask him a question. Anyone chancing to enter the church at such a time, or glancing through the great door which always stood open in summer, would have seen at the far end of the nave the Abbé Rousselot, catechism in hand, standing in front of the seated children or pacing up and down before the screen. His great resonant voice, raised above the sing-song of the childish piping and drowning for a moment the ceaseless murmuring from the pews, would begin the answers to his own questions, continue them, and often enough conclude them too. When the fidgeting became too great he would grow angry, and taking a ring-leader by the arm lift him out of his seat like a sack of flour and roughly dust his ears with the closed catechism; and until the end of the lesson the culprit would remain in a corner in disgrace, kneeling on the edge of his sabots. On the other hand, any child who was good and had learned his lesson properly would be called out, and, supreme honour (but dreaded as much as any punishment), the curé would hold out his snuff-box for you to kiss the lid, which was painted with a skull and cross-bones.

Shortly before noon the church door would open; a little man in citified clothes would enter noiselessly in cloth boots and take down the bell-rope which was caught up on a great nail. All heads would be raised: it was Monsieur Hotte, the schoolmaster, come to ring the angelus.

As though the title of schoolmaster had conferred on him also the title of jack-of-all-trades, he employed the leisure left him by his principal career in five or six other public functions or minor careers with which he did not scorn to swell his income. And according to the time of day and the day of the week he might be seen in this or that character, each different, but all alike in Monsieur Hotte's conviction of their importance. Successively precentor, clerk to the Mayor, public scrivener, land-surveyor, on feast-days he was also to be seen at the head of the firemen, beating a big drum, his cloth boots keeping step with military precision; then again, a latter-day Cincinnatus, far from the hurly-burly of public honours, he would be found in the churchyard mowing the grass on which he fed his rabbits; and at dusk he might be met on the road pushing his loaded wheelbarrow, from the front of which stuck out the handle of the scythe laid across it. And three times a day, with a punctuality which regulated the whole life of the country-side, he appeared in church to ring the angelus.

He would start pulling the rope with short, jerky movements; these gradually strengthened until one could hear the scraping of the hemp on the edge of the circular opening in the vaulted roof. High above in the belfry the bell, balancing on its pivot, would grate, and abruptly the first stroke of the angelus would sound. The curé would slap his book with the flat of his hand, there would be a scraping of clogs, and down they would all go on their knees, and to the same tune that they had sung before they would now sing a hymn of praise.

Often Monsieur Hotte would still be ringing as they went out. Alternately bending and straightening his knees, his hands clutching the rope one above the other, his nose pointing skywards (a bony nose, surmounted by spectacles and brushed by a short moustache yellowed towards the centre by too much snuff-taking), he would let the rope swing him up and down, while from a distance the motionless children watched it rising and falling, seeming alternately to shrink and stretch.

In the afternoons, until it was time for Antoine and his two brothers, Bertrand and Philippe, to return to their lessons, which were given by the schoolmaster or the curé according to the day of the week, the children would go for a walk with their nurse. Sometimes they took a country road, sometimes they went up into the woods. Occasionally, on Thursdays, they would come home by the village, and then the nurse would stop at her parents' house to see her own son, whom otherwise she often only saw for weeks at a time on Sundays coming out of church after Mass.

When Antoine had been confirmed, Monsieur de Laignes engaged a tutor to take charge of both his and his younger brothers' studies. From now on the nurse had nothing more to do with them but tend them when they were ill and look after their clothes.

They spent all their time now with the Abbé Bornet, their tutor. His room adjoined theirs and he never left them, being always at hand to intervene in all the circumstances of their lives as pupils and children. Humble of birth as he was, mediocre of intelligence, and far from refined, he yet, without allowing them more initiative than they had already acquired, knew how to improve and develop their natural excellences of character and bearing simply by rigidly applying those supple principles of education which the Church inculcates in those whose duty it is to teach. He ruled them with easy authority, and disciplined these rough and independent little boys so adroitly that they were unaware of any change in their life or any curtailment of their liberty.

Away from their studies he was a gay and ingenious companion, gifted in amusing them, and still young enough to take part in their games without any suspicion of condescension. From her bedroom window Madame de Laignes would see her three sons tearing about the lawn after a large ball hurled by the sturdy fist of their tutor, who, bareheaded and gown flying, would direct the game with gesticulations and shouts in a loud voice that betrayed his peasant origin. Or they would take long walks together, sometimes far afield, and make expeditions to some church or sanctuary hidden in the woods. And the goal of their walks was always sufficiently distant to necessitate their hurrying.

Indifferent to the charms of nature, as much from innate insensibility as from a kind of acquired contempt, he continued his lessons on these walks with a series of statements, observations, questions, posed with exact knowledge of the character of each of his pupils and nicely calculated to turn their eyes and thoughts from anything that seemed to him capable of inspiring them, even for a moment, with any emotion over which he could have no control—never at a loss to distract them with his talk when he saw them plunged in thought and inclined to brood over an idea or trying to theorize and get to the bottom of things.

A year after the tutor's arrival, when he was thirteen, Antoine took up shooting seriously. The lower animals are in the charge of man; he guides their destinies almost as he wishes, allowing them to live only that they may die at his own pleasure and in his own time. Antoine in his turn learnt all the various ways of killing every sort of living thing; it seemed to him quite natural and pleasant. He could contemplate such slaughter with indifference; it would never have occurred to him that anyone's heart might be troubled by it, so accustomed was he—and this intensified a certain hardness and insensibility of expression, handed down from a long line of like-thinking ancestors—to considering coldly from the height of his own exalted position the whole ordering of life and its tangle of cruelties and iniquities, which may not be questioned since they are the will of God. There is, in fact, deep down in the soul of man, beneath his Christianity, a sharp revulsion against this universal injustice; nevertheless, without wishing to, and perhaps because this internal revolt is in practice a submission, man has personified and long adored in the God who was at first the incarnation of his dream, the inexorability of nature.

Once, when they had been out ferreting the day before, Antoine came across a rabbit leaping eccentrically about round one of the buries they had worked. It let itself be taken easily, and the explanation of this curious behaviour was at once apparent: the ferret, the day before, had eaten out its eyes.

It was in the marshes below the woods in the valley bottom that he saw the death of his first wild boar. Hit from a good way off, the animal had run towards him before collapsing. And hurrying to the spot Antoine discovered the great, tawny-sided beast lying on its side in the midst of the reeds, blood-spattered now, in the shelter of which it had passed its strange and savage life. It lay on its side, its long snout covered with earth, its jaws feebly opening and closing, its eyes fixedly staring; and on the other side, a figure of dumb ecstasy and undisturbed tenacity, the dog had seized its stomach and now pulled at it jerkily, all smeared with rosy blood, furiously worrying and tearing at this flesh from which the life seemed already to have fled —retreating, as it were, before the immensity of this catastrophe to which it must submit, indifferent to all else but the approach of death.

4

EVERY AUGUST THE TUTOR went off for his holiday, first to stay with his family, then to enter the seminary for a short retreat. A little later the de Laignes would set off for the Château des Menuls, where they sometimes also spent a few days at Easter.

At the edge of the great plain, cut up by long, rectangular stretches of water by the side of which dark heaps of peat were stacked with geometrical precision, the landscape changed. Low hills now appeared. The carriage, following the baggage-wagon sent on some hours in advance, would pass through village after village, all alike, with their meadows, hedgerows, orchards, horse-pond by the church, and low cottages whose reddish clay walls were striped with the dark lines of beams and on whose great Ardoise roofs doves perched and preened.

The journey would end towards evening. Entering the village the road made a bend, and as soon as one rounded this one saw the château, more clearly now as one crossed the wooden bridge over the broad stream which bounded the park; a short but lofty avenue of planes led to a garden bright with flowers, and through their blotched and peeling trunks one had an oblique view of the squat mass of the château itself and, straight ahead and at right angles to it, shutting in the garden on that side, the regular line of the outbuildings dominated by an ancient, storeyed dove-cote.

On the first Sunday after their arrival the whole family would attend High Mass. Up the three roads converging on the church, which stood opposite the château in the centre of the village, the peasants would come strolling in their Sunday-best, and from far off they could easily pick out the tall, lean figure of Cottenceau, a farmer and old tenant of the Baron's, as he marched with huge strides down the steeply sloping roadway from his house, invariably crowned with the same small and curious top-hat and clad in the same frock-coat, an ancient garment whose short skirts stopped half-way down his thighs, leaving a long expanse of leg encased in skin-tight trousers.

He would approach them with an embarrassed and delighted eagerness, and holding his hat in his finger-tips, his great freshly shaven chin quivering with emotion and bashfulness, touch with his large bony hand the hands extended to him one by one. He inquired after everybody's health, thanked them for the interest they took in him, and hastened to agree with every remark addressed to him almost before he could have taken in the words; then, as he was turning to go, he would announce his intention of sending the first hare he killed up to the château. On that day, regularly, he was invited to dinner.

45

He was never at all sure of how he should behave during this meal. He did his best to watch what the others did and do the same himself, all the while trying to please them in his capacity of guest, and guest of inferior station at that. But if anything they did seemed to him too informal to warrant his copying it he did nothing, divided between a fear of not doing the proper thing and a fear of seeming too familiar. Thus, the most embarrassing problem of all was provided by the little bones which he saw the others all round him leaving on their plates. First he contemplated them long and anxiously; then, after a moment's further hesitation and a hasty glance round, he threw a bone quickly and stealthily behind him. Monsieur de Laignes, all amiability, assured him he might leave the bones on his plate, but he protested politely that he would not dream of doing such a thing!

Every day while they were at Fontaines Monsieur and Madame de Laignes went for a long walk with their children. Like all townspeople in the country they would always follow the sun-baked main road, finding neither interest nor pleasure in their progress, simply intent on spending so many hours out of doors. Sometimes Antoine would go shooting with Cottenceau in the early afternoon, and not return until it was dark. Then the sudden barking of the house-dogs would come through the drawing-room windows to the assembled family waiting for dinner, and almost at once Antoine would appear in the doorway carrying some bird which he would gaily hold up to show them, the dog at his heels running in as though the room were a fresh hunting-ground, blundering about amongst the furniture with his loping, springy gait, brushing against it with his sandy coat and sniffing excitedly, and wagging his tail mechanically all the time.

As October drew near they began to think of departure. The countryside now, parched by the strong summer suns, was beginning to soften beneath the first autumnal rains, and as the men worked the fields ripe apples fell from the trees in the hedgerows and buried themselves in the rich earth of the furrows. Before they left Fontaines they would see the first cart-loads of apples being driven in, and Antoine and his brothers would taste the fresh cider; then one morning, at the foot of the château steps, Monsieur and Madame de Laignes and their children would all get into the carriage which two months earlier had brought them there. They were always back again at Laignes some days before the feast-day of the patron saint, the last Sunday of October.

On this day it was the custom to throw the park open to the peasants, and, if the weather permitted, to hold a dance just inside the park-gates under the trees of one of the avenues.

At eight o'clock in the evening, by the light of large paper lanterns festooned about the trees and about the four corners of the garlanded platform upon which sat the fiddler and his son (an urchin of twelve), the dance,

which had been broken off for supper, would start up
again. Until the candles were put out the almost
uninterrupted sound of the two violins was carried
abroad by the strong, fresh gusts of a wind which
heralded the first approaching frosts; their tones were
shrill, for the boy, still unskilled, more often than not
contented himself with letting his bow wander aim-
lessly over the strings, making an irregular and dis-
cordant bass to the airs played by his father with
much spirit and a tapping of the foot to mark the beat.

In the intervals between the dances, while the
dancers strolled round arm in arm, all alike in couples,
between the benches which formed the enclosure, the
fiddler would amuse them by imitating on his violin
the braying of an ass.

5

When winter arrived there would be days of hunting
with the Duc de Gessin's stag-hounds. Antoine himself
was old enough now to hunt; and in the spurred and
booted figure who rode off with his father on the
morning of a meet, his horn slung from his shoulders,
the Abbé could scarcely recognize his pupil of the day
before, who would turn into a schoolboy again next day
with no difficulty at all.

After a hurried lunch, which they took at a roadside
inn to rest the horses, Antoine and his father—and
sometimes Madame de Laignes, the Abbé, and the
other children as well, who would all have gone direct
by carriage—would arrive at the rendezvous somewhere
about one o'clock. This was usually a keeper's lodge
or a cross-roads in the forest. Many people would be
already waiting there, and there would be a ceaseless
dismounting of horsemen, and a drawing up of fresh
carriages behind those already in place. A little to one
side and in front of the bored and silent pack held in
leash by two hunt-servants, the piqueurs* waited on
horseback, whip in hand, horns slung across their

* The French term is retained since it cannot be translated accurately either as "whip" or "huntsman."

chests, in their hunting dress that carried out the national colours—white breeches, blue coat with scarlet revers, great three-cornered hat.

In the midst of the followers in their red coats and the members of the hunt—gentlemen and landowners of the neighbourhood, rude gallants with fair moustaches and faces burnt red by the sun, and a sprinkling of habited women—the Duke, an upstanding old man with an aquiline nose and a prominent chin, welcomed his guests as they arrived; his carefully arranged hair appeared from under his cap in white curls on the nape of his neck—one almost expected a pigtail. Stooping a little, his face relaxed in a smile which brought a thousand tiny wrinkles round his eyes, he listened to their compliments or gossip with an air of benevolence and shrewd good nature.

At last everybody had arrived, and the Duke approached his piqueurs. One of these urged his horse a few paces forward and, hat in hand, bowing his dark, square, priest-like head, made his report. The Duke decided on the programme for the day.

Then in ordered array the cavalcade rode off between the tall, leafless trees on either side of the road and plunged into the forest: first, side by side, the three piqueurs; then, behind them, alone and a little ahead of the members of his own hunt and the rest of the field, the Duc de Gessin, horn slung across his chest and whip held upright against his thigh in a white kid-gloved hand. Some way ahead of the cavalcade the forty-five hounds—held on three leashes by a hunt-servant who looked very small beside all these mounted figures—trotted down the road in a confused mass of black and white surmounted by forty-five identically agitated tails.

At the spot where hounds were to be cast off a halt was made, and the hunt servant tied the ends of his long leashes to a tree. And then for the first time that day the muffled and raucous notes of the horns burst out above the vociferations of the hounds—a melancholy fanfare designed to make the stags raise their heads as they browsed in the depths of the wood; and the servant bent down in the midst of the suddenly frenzied pack and slipped the rope collars as fast as they came to hand. The leaping, floundering, yelping dogs streamed off one after another as soon as they were released, nose to the ground, breaking into the music of the chase and answered by mournful howlings from their un-leashed companions and those purposely held in reserve. And behind the rapidly vanishing pack the piqueurs set off at a long, loping canter through the trees.

First by paths, then again through the underwood—and once, suddenly emerging on to a road, they came upon the carriages again—the field followed. And almost invariably the same things happened now as in any hunt—the hounds were at fault, the stag had rejoined his herd; or, alone before the hounds, he sought to escape by those unchanging ruses common

51

to all his kind and employed by generations of stags before him—ruses so unvarying that the whole thing seemed like a game all the moves of which were regulated in advance, though these ineffectual and easily foretold feints were in each case the final and supreme efforts of a creature at bay; and when at last the stag, worn-out with running, turned to face the hounds, it was hard to realize that beneath the heaving, tawny flanks of the beast now brought to stand there throbbed an individual anguish.

Meanwhile those hounds which had gone astray would have returned and gathered dejectedly round a wrathful piqueur halted at a cross-roads and listening intently as he lashed out at random with his whip. Or two or three might be encountered hunting on their own through the trees, and without slackening their pace lapping a few mouthfuls from the surface of the puddles lying in their path, splashing up the water as they ran, and each following precisely in the footsteps of the other, as though following an invisible path. And watching the hunt from a distance as it wound its way through the vales, the Duke, from time to time accosted by a piqueur, galloped unhurriedly up and down the rides, hat in hand, his left arm giving easily to the movement of the horse. Or again, alarmed by the baying of the hounds and the rallying of the horns and the ceaseless cries of the whips resounding wildly through the forest, there would suddenly appear a little group of timidly straying hinds, trotting along and pausing, then all turning their heads together in the same direction and making off to another part of the wood, a fearful and scarcely dangerous little band.

The day advanced and the stag still kept his distance and ran. The aspects of the forest changed incessantly. Now a deep lane would suddenly become a bog, now there would be a slope to be climbed and new prospects to be revealed, and the rider would see the whole purple forest stretched out at his feet. Or sometimes, through a clearing, he would glimpse the open countryside with its villages and church towers. Men would be working in the fields nearby; or a little girl would be standing guard over a flock of greedy turkeys scratching in a field beside a house. Suddenly the notes of a horn would come down wind; the stag was viewed. And the scattered field would make their way back into the forest and join up again. At last, straight ahead, and only a little way off, they saw emerging from the undergrowth the long-expected silhouette, delicate and tall.

The stag, sighting his pursuers, stood for a short moment undecided. Motionless, his head held high, he considered them one by one, astonished and fearful, turning his head to the right, turning his head to the left. Then, after a last hesitation, he made a sudden violent plunge to the side where least danger seemed to threaten, the pack surging at his heels.

Suddenly, as if shot from a cannon, a single hound burst out of the seething undergrowth, all four feet extended, back arched, nose still held low, followed by the whole pack in full cry—oblivious of the stag ahead of them, whom they could easily have overhauled. But now, hard pressed, it made off, and was soon glimpsed some distance away scudding along on its delicate hooves, its antlers lying back. The light patter on the dry leaves grew fainter as it sped away through the underwood. Suddenly, at the place where it had last been seen, a solitary hound emerged; then, after a moment when nothing at all happened, there was a sudden irruption from the trees, from the bushes, from every side at once, and the swarming black and white of the pack in full cry came tearing down the slope, in and out of the hillocks.

Now, when victory seemed sure, the old Duke, who had been worried, became quite excited. Bending low over his hunter's neck, he forced his way through the trees; other riders galloped after him; raising his voice he shouted joyously into the wind. At the cross-roads they came to a halt, and the horns were turned in all directions to sound the gone away : the stag was breaking cover. All his ruses foiled, every avenue of escape cut off and the space narrowing round him, there was only one choice left him now; it seemed to him his own choice, taken of his own free will; but actually men working from afar had driven him infallibly to take it.

The hunt would emerge from the forest into a clearing or a field, or on to the brink of a narrow ravine on the edge of the forest where the stag had sought safety. Stumbling on the stones, feeling the pack at his heels, he would turn on the slope and face them alone; the hounds would watch him without moving, baying all the while, and he stood there, coloured like the earth and the rocks, motionless, his head held high. One or two of the hounds would come up from the rear, but more to sniff at him than to kill; and in this respectful waiting for man's arrival on the scene there was something strange. It was up to man now to play his part; they had done theirs.

Meanwhile the field had dismounted. The Duc de Gessin advanced, pistol in hand (though sometimes he might use a knife). At this the stag, taking his eyes off the pack, gently turned his head to face the newcomer. In silence the master raised his arm and took aim; the stag still gazed at him steadily. There followed a brittle report; and for a moment the fallen beast struggled amidst the leaping hounds. When the ladies came up, their long skirts caught up over their arms to show spurred riding-boots, they would see one of the piqueurs in his red waistcoat kneeling by the great body as it lay on its back encircled by the whipped-off hounds; and hear the soft, dull sound of his steel as it ripped the still warm flesh.

When the carving was at an end the entrails were wrapped up in part of the skin with the head attached. Then the Duke advanced into the circle formed by the hounds; the members of the hunt were drawn up facing him, and little groups of peasants watched silently from a distance. And as in the finale of an opera the tenor, supported by the chorus, will launch into an aria celebrating his own valour and the happy ending of the drama, so the Duke, standing there erect, a tall and dominating figure above the little heap of bloody flesh, put his horn to his lips and very seriously and proudly sounded the Morte, which the others then took up. And in this theatrical scene following on a victory so disproportionately tame, there was something a little shabby, which rendered still more striking the fanfare sounding over those poor remains in celebration of a heroism so facile, a triumph so inglorious.

6

THE TWO GIRLS, Agnes and Clotilde, were also beginning to grow up, and since their mother did not want to send them to a convent yet it was decided to employ a governess. This involved Madame de Laignes in several excursions to Monthuis, but at last her choice fell on a young girl of seventeen, Mademoiselle Marie Pigeotte, who had been recommended to her by the arch-priest of the cathedral.

She arrived on the evening of the appointed day, a little before dinner; and the two little girls, following their mother out on to the terrace at the sound of wheels, saw a very slight and youthful figure alighting from the coach, enveloped in a great cloak and wearing a shallow bonnet over a mass of blonde braids. She was taken almost at once to her room, and did not come down again until dinner-time, when she was introduced to the Comte, the sons of the house, and the Abbé. Madame de Laignes tried to put her at ease by talking of Monthuis and the convent she had just left and the priest who had recommended her; but she lowered her eyes whenever addressed, responded with the briefest words, and fell silent again immediately, confused by the sound of masculine voices, by the strangeness of the customs she would have to adopt, by the frigid kindness of Madame de Laignes, and even by the stares of Agnes and Clotilde, who were studying her curiously.

The daughter of a Catholic workman, she had been educated as a day-scholar at a religious boarding-school. Being studious, docile, and devout, she had been taken into the school at fifteen. Two years later she had passed her examinations, and this was her first post: without any period of transition she had changed from pupil to mistress, passing from the tranquillity of the convent to this worldly life which had been painted to her in such lurid colours.

The day after her arrival, in consultation with Madame de Laignes, she drew up a curriculum of studies and a plan for the employment of the day: rising would be at such and such an hour, then prayers and ten minutes' meditation: the times for lessons and the times for walks were all laid down. There was also a paragraph concerning herself—*free time*—and this free time she spent in writing long letters to her parents and the Mother Superior of her convent and in keeping up her diary. Or she would re-read various books given her as prizes, or old sermons which she had written down from memory and which filled several large copy-books. On Sundays she played the harmonium in church.

During her first winter at the château she was several times taken to meets of the Duc de Gessin's hounds. From these she would return in a state of over-excitement, prey to a complex of emotions whose conflicting elements she was unable to resolve.

Indeed, in spite of her Christian upbringing, she was not without some vague and confused presentiment, gained from books and the repercussions of life itself, of the existence of that higher conscience which man has formulated for himself in opposition to the natural order of things against which he rebels, tortured by the need for an absolute justice impossible to realize and therefore invalid. And seeing these animals dying at her feet—impotent victims of the sportsmen whose amusement they had been—she was filled with mingled pity and revolt; and this, expanding within her into an unconscious sense of kinship, all at once brought home to her an awareness both of her own feebleness and of its extent. But her Christian upbringing disposed her towards the acceptance of all natural laws, and—modest link in the universal chain of beings—she regarded with instinctive respect just those whom she was beginning to hate but who represented in her eyes a natural authority impossible to resist. She revered them as pitiless forces, to which she came to attribute all powers and all rights; and in the presence of Monsieur de Laignes she would be overcome with a feeling of timidity beneath which there lurked something of defiance, at once a kind of aversion and an admiring submission.

Often nowadays as she was giving her lessons she

would see Monsieur de Laignes come in and sit down to listen, saying nothing. The lesson over, he would stay for a moment's chat, or ask her to do him some small service—check an account or copy a letter. And he who in company addressed her in tones of mock-serious irony now spoke with easy friendliness.

She happened to confide to him once her fondness for reading, and he offered to lend her some books. Opening for her benefit the long-disused library (for Monsieur de Laignes no longer read, and Madame de Laignes subscribed to a library at Monthuis which kept her supplied with the Catholic reviews), he gave her the various novels as they turned up here and there, scattered indiscriminately among the great works of earlier centuries; nobody could remember how they came to be there, or what choice, what fleeting fashion or idleness, had brought them there.

One day Madame de Laignes observed to Mademoiselle Marie with ill-concealed displeasure that she was still somewhat young for that kind of reading, and reproached her husband on the matter in the young girl's presence. But when the embarrassed governess came to return the books he reassured her, discounting his wife's remarks as excessive scrupulousness, and persuading her to take them again: he nevertheless advised her to keep the books as much out of sight as possible in future. For some time she was deeply perplexed, hesitating between curiosity and fear of wrong-doing; later she returned the novels without having so much as opened them. Then, accustoming herself to the idea of doing something only half permitted, she took up her reading once more, half troubled and half excited by the secret she now shared with Monsieur de Laignes and by a tacit understanding which seemed to have brought them closer. She read secretly at night in her room, sitting up until late. And unsettled by the astonishing vistas which now opened up before her, vistas which disclosed vital motives hitherto unsuspected and very different from those that had hitherto upheld her, she would dream at great length of the lot of the portionless young girl who marries a nobleman or an officer.

In her free periods, or when she had to take the children for a walk, she would put a novel at the bottom of her little work-bag and take the road behind the château which led to the summit of the hill, a wildish kind of place, where pines had pushed up through the rubble of ancient quarries. She would sit down on a rock, and the children would gather flowers around her; one would run up with a nosegay, or the other ask a question, and she would raise her eyes and let her book fall to her knees as she answered them absently, remotely, her eyes wandering unseeingly over the familiar prospect spread out beneath her, which she saw only vaguely, as the habitual background for her reveries. And suddenly, down in the valley still filled with light, with its long village at the bottom creeping a little up the further slope, unstirring with its square-towered church, the angelus would ring out. And this ringing, slow and spacious, might have been the signal for another, for there rose up as if in answer to it from the trees in the park the hurried pealing, shrill and jerky, of the château bell sounding the first warning for dinner. It was time to go back. Near the iron gates of the park they would pass the new buildings being put up by Monsieur de Laignes and now beginning to rise above the level of the earth.

As if all the activity which now surrounded him at home had made his own idleness insufferable to him, Monsieur de Laignes had been seized with an access of energy, but of a somewhat aimless sort. First he was full of the idea of transforming the whole château, the new plans for which he had drawn up himself in consultation with several architects. But these vast projects had ended in nothing more than the construction of twin lodges at the park entrance, one to the right and one to the left of the great iron gates, on the foundations of the two original ones which had been demolished. At any moment of the day Monsieur de Laignes would be off to supervise his workmen. And when he went out in the broiling hours of the early afternoon he would see through an open window at one end of the château the Abbé pacing up and down as he dictated to his pupils from the book in his hand; and at the other end Mademoiselle Marie would be half closing a venetian blind or adjusting a curtain to lessen or increase the light in the room where her pupils were drawing.

Nowadays, when it was warm enough, dinner was taken out of doors on top of the little grassy mound above the ice-house; and after the meal—while the children, together for the first time in the day, chased each other shrieking round the clumps of trees close by—a move would be made to the terrace, where the evening was brought to a close. At nine o'clock the château bell would ring for prayers; for ever since he had been at the château the Abbé, at Madame de Laignes' request, had said prayers every evening before the assembled family and servants. These latter would be grouped at the far end of the great drawing-room, round the double-doors which opened into the dining-room. The Abbé would kneel and everybody follow suit, his voice alone raised in the complete silence, until he came to the Paternoster, in which they all joined. A little to one side stood Monsieur de Laignes, his crook'd knee resting on a chair, impassive and absently attentive; only when they came to the prayers for the dead did his face take on an air of grave interest.

Immediately after the final blessing the nurse would lead the two little girls from the room, and after them Madame de Laignes herself would retire. Antoine, Bernard, and Philippe usually played billiards with the Abbé, and Monsieur de Laignes would accompany Mademoiselle Marie out into the garden, where, insensibly, the conversation of the afternoon would be renewed. He would ask about her reading, and passages from novels he had not read for years would suddenly come back to him. Or he would discuss the convent where she had been educated. And she who had formerly avoided whenever possible the least chance of being alone with Monsieur de Laignes now actually found courage to enjoy these conversations. She told him all sorts of little things about the life there, and about the nuns, often quoting Sister Marie, an authoritative sort of person whom she greatly admired. She had even caught certain of her gestures, and one of these little tricks eventually became very familiar to him—a way of shutting her mouth and compressing her lips whenever she uttered any emphatic or would-be conclusive remark.

By this time the Abbé would have come out and joined in the conversation; the young girl would be faintly shocked to hear him talking suddenly like any other man and passing judgement on his fellow priests with what was meant to be a humorous irony. But the conversation would grow livelier, as it never did when Madame de Laignes was present, and Mademoiselle Marie would become quite animated, raising her voice in defence of her own half-formed ideas, then abruptly falling silent, confused at having dared speak thus openly before a priest.

Sometimes Monsieur de Laignes would let himself be persuaded into a game of billiards with his sons. From the wide-open French windows Mademoiselle Marie would watch them; or perhaps she would stroll out on to the lawns, never wandering far from the house. Monsieur de Laignes would quickly win his game and leave the others to continue playing; pausing for a moment by the doors to breathe in the night air, he would stroll out casually, slowly descend the terrace step by step, and turn in the direction of the park. When he returned to the house the children and their tutor had often gone.

One evening as the Abbé was sitting out on the terrace before going up to his room, he saw Mademoiselle Marie come running towards the house. She passed quite close to him without seeing him; he spoke to her, but she did not hear. A moment later Monsieur de Laignes also appeared from the same direction. The Abbé let him cross the terrace without speaking a word; for a few moments he waited, then he too went silently indoors.

For some days after that the governess took no part in the common life of the house, and for a whole week she never left her own room or the schoolroom except for meals. She pleaded that she was tired or unwell, that she had a lesson to prepare or an exercise to correct, every evening a fresh excuse for retiring early. But imperceptibly she returned to her old life, and soon the evenings were so prolonged that Monsieur de Laignes himself used to see to the locking of the doors and the closing of the windows. It was at this time that Madame de Laignes observed with some surprise that Mademoiselle Marie was abstaining from communion. And then, a month later, the young girl asked permission to go in future to Monthuis for confession. This request seemed perfectly natural to Madame de Laignes, for the Church directs that one may choose as one's confessor whomsoever one wishes.

Then came the holidays, which she cut short; and from the moment of her return Madame de Laignes noticed a change in her. Her energy flagged, she became moody, betraying a melancholy and an impatience for which Madame de Laignes several times had to rebuke her. Further, she seemed to distrust them all, and her antipathy, which Madame de Laignes thought unjust, was turned particularly against the Abbé. It was at this period that her two pupils surprised her weeping one day, with the Abbé addressing her severely, as though blaming her for some sin or threatening her with some punishment.

As the winter advanced her health deteriorated from day to day, and Madame de Laignes, imagining her to be sickening for a serious illness, confided her fears to her husband. Monsieur de Laignes declared he had noticed nothing wrong; but often now he would watch her surreptitiously and uneasily.

Then, towards the close of winter, she fainted one evening at dinner—she had come down with a face even paler than usual and despite a very visible distress. When she had been carried up to her room and had recovered somewhat Madame de Laignes began to question her, and the suspicions which had begun to take shape in her mind were suddenly confirmed. After long and repeated denials the young girl confessed that she was pregnant. Madame de Laignes accused her of lying, and in the same breath, ravaged by a sudden jealousy which she made no attempt to resist, demanded to know how such a thing could possibly have happened and all the details of it; in a flood of tears Mademoiselle Marie related all that had passed between her and Monsieur de Laignes. But she stopped short at that day when the Abbé (she would have died rather than confess this) had first forced his way into her room and threatened her, as he had done each time he visited her, with the revelation of what he had seen if she dared call for help or denounce him afterwards.

It was not horror at what she called sin that inspired Madame de Laignes, so much as the desire to avenge herself and humiliate this woman who had so unexpectedly crossed her path and stepped into a place which she herself had disdained, which she still in fact really scorned; with unconscious subtlety she mingled religious admonitions with her invective and reproaches, crushing her rival both as woman and as Christian. She threatened her with one thing after another, spoke of damnation, her guardian angel, the wrath of God, her parents' horror, her own dishonour, ingratitude, Hell, the sort of asylum provided for lost girls, and the fact that no matter how long she lived she could never expiate her sin. She regained her self-control at last to think out the best way of avoiding any scandal.

Making the girl swear never to say a word to anybody, she decided that she should go away next day—on the pretence of her father's having been taken ill—and withdraw to a convent.

Suddenly, about one o'clock in the morning, the dogs began to howl. Antoine, awakened by the noise, got out of bed, opened a window, and leaned out. The night was pitch-dark; he could see nothing. Nevertheless, a few moments later, he thought he heard a faint sound of footsteps over by the lake, followed almost at once by a muffled splash. He called out, but no one answered. So he went back to bed; but for a long time he could not get to sleep again because of the persistent howling of the dogs.

Next morning, at daybreak, the gardener found the body of the governess in the lake.

7

AFTER THIS OCCURRENCE the children were sent away:
the boys to Paris, to a religious establishment run by
the Jesuit Fathers, the girls to Monthuis, to the convent
where their mother had gone before them. The château
relapsed into silence, and nothing further occurred to
disturb the lives of those it sheltered. But in the spring
of the following year the district was swept by a sudden
epidemic, and Madame de Laignes, deciding that her
place was in the midst of danger and that she was most
needed there, once again took up her village visiting.

She brought to her tending of the sick a cold and
fanatical ardour; she sat with the dying in her arms,
she watched over them at night, made their beds,
shrouded them when they were dead; all of which filled
the peasants more with dismay than gratitude. Then
she too in her turn fell ill, and soon they knew she was
dying. Monsieur de Laignes, having dwelt by the side
of his wife for so long in a state of hostile indifference,
now abruptly changed his attitude. He had imagined
until then that he could look forward to many more
years of life with her; and now, seeing the span of years
before him shrink, he felt a sudden need to draw nearer
to one who would soon be no more—not so much

genuinely moved, perhaps, as upset by contemplation of this death which, appearing so swiftly, was obliging him to hasten on with what he had imagined time itself would bring about.

Before she died Madame de Laignes sent her daughters out of the room (her sons had not yet come) and told her husband that she pardoned him. She charged him with various instructions about her pensioners and the Masses she wished said for her soul, and reminded him that she had been going to provide dresses for the children who were being confirmed that year. Then she spoke of the old nurse's son who was being educated at the seminary at her expense, and of the nurse herself, expressing the wish that she should be allowed to live out her life in one of the newly built lodges. Some moments later—day was drawing to an end—being told that a countrywoman had just arrived to inquire after her, she had the old woman sent up to her room. And, as the departing traveller charges himself with messages from those who must stay behind, so she asked, in a voice which had lost nothing of its tranquillity, though from minute to minute it grew feebler, what messages she should take to those whom she would so soon be rejoining.

"I shall be seeing your daughter to-night," she said, "and your mother. Is there anything you would like me to tell them?"

In accordance with her wishes she was buried in the costume of the Third Order of St. Francis. All her life

70

she had worn its insignia beneath her clothes, the girdle round her loins and the hair-cloth, or cilice; and that evening when her sons were brought into the room they could hardly recognize their mother in this nun in the rough serge habit and black woollen veil. Then over these humble relics the coffin-lid was screwed down: in the centre, surmounted by a coronet, it bore the two supporting coats of arms of the Menuls and the de Laignes.

On the eve of the funeral members of the family, relatives, and connections began to arrive from all parts of the department and the province; some so distantly related that the name alone gave substance to their claim. The intercourse which Monsieur and Madame de Laignes had had with their relations in the early years of their marriage had gradually dwindled and ceased, and now Monsieur de Laignes found himself surrounded by faces he had scarcely seen since those early days, and then only at ceremonies of a similar kind. Some, prevented by illness or by other causes from attending, had sent their sons instead, and frequently some young man coming up to Monsieur de Laignes and calling him "cousin" or "uncle" with easy familiarity had to explain who he was. Every lunch and every dinner found them more and more numerous. And in a sort of involuntary animation resulting from the presence of so many people all together, the meals were passed in discussing in great detail—always with genuine interest, and with none of that distrustful coldness found in families where alliances are dubious—such events as had taken place in all the various households: births, marriages, deaths —all those matters which form, continue, and modify the progress of a family; these being considered less from the point of view of the individuals concerned than as events in themselves, as if in their eyes the family was a living whole, in itself of absorbing interest, with the individual existing only in what he brings to it—to this family which they still respected, although they were no longer capable of carrying it on.

With the children back at school Monsieur de Laignes was horrified to find himself face to face with a solitude which nothing, it seemed, could ever end. He lapsed into a state of boredom which grew deeper the more he surrendered to it. Always inclined to melancholy, he now became moody, suspicious, and difficult. And soon he had sunk into a state of utter demoralization, broken only by periods of sudden reaction; now wishing to see nobody at all, now seeking out the company of no matter whom. In such moods he would invent excuses for descending on the servants or the nurse and holding them in conversation, drawn in spite of himself to wherever there were people about or work being done. Indeed, to have someone on the spot whom he could always be sure of finding, he engaged a carpenter by the year, keeping him busy with odd jobs. Whole afternoons he would pass sitting with this fellow and watching him at work.

One morning, quite unexpectedly, and unpreluded by any warning on the day before, he did not come downstairs; and for several days he did not leave his room. His meals were taken up by the old nurse. He spoke only in signs, never answering her questions.

And the nurse, worried and unhappy, always ended by sending for Rossignol, the keeper, who with the years had become a sort of inferior friend to his master —a type no longer to be met with now, whose qualities of heart and bearing were bred by the peculiar circumstances of his station, at once intermediary and independent, forming the ground on which his master could meet him freely without demeaning himself.

"Up you go, Narcisse," she would say. "Think of something to amuse him."

And up he would go to relate some story or other. Once he had made his master laugh his task was ended.

Meanwhile his affairs, so long neglected, were falling into confusion. He no longer gave orders, no longer answered letters. Leases had expired and the properties were not let again; his farm-buildings were left unrepaired. And neglecting all that could possibly be neglected without causing him immediate inconvenience or annoyance, he invariably put off all decisions, even the most urgent, to a future day, reassured by the thought that all this would at least last as long as he would, and incapable of taking any interest in a patrimony which after his death would come to be divided. Such cases as absolutely demanded a letter or a visit he had taken to leaving to Monsieur Hotte, on whom he soon laid entire responsibility for all decisions, provided his own peace of mind was not disturbed or he himself called on to do anything.

At the end of three years Antoine left college, leaving his brothers to finish their education there, and, on the pretext of choosing a career at leisure, stayed on in Paris under the eye of a remote cousin who exercised a very mild and distant surveillance over him. But the allowance he received from his father was no longer adequate, and further, the more calls there were on his money the more irregularly was it doled out to him, so that he was almost invariably forced to beg for credit. There were difficulties, too, about his share of his mother's inheritance, which Monsieur de Laignes continually put off settling. Rather than make a fuss Antoine began to run up debts.

From time to time, suddenly smitten in the midst of his round of pleasures by the desire to see his own country again, or by the wish to pay his respects to his father on certain yearly occasions, he would return home. And one evening the villagers behind their closed doors would hear the château carriage rolling over the cobbles and know that Monsieur Antoine was back again.

As soon as he arrived at Laignes he would forget all that he had left behind him, feeling, without in the least knowing why, a sort of peaceful satisfaction in the thought that while he had been doing so many different things nothing here had changed, neither the country nor those who dwelt in it, and that all was as he had left it in this little corner of the earth where life evolved so slowly that it seemed not to move at all. And his eyes were grateful for the unchanging shapes of fields and woods, only varying in colour as the seasons changed, and which, while he had been at school, he had only seen in a single aspect.

Occasionally, either alone, or with his two brothers if they were home for the holidays—for since the death of his wife Monsieur de Laignes had never cared to revisit the Château des Menuls—he would go over to Fontaines for a few days.

The old farmers were gone, their places filled by strangers to the district whom Monsieur de Laignes had engaged by post on Monsieur Hotte's recommendation, without so much as exchanging a word with any of them. Careless and incompetent, they were not too scrupulous either, as if determined to recover somehow or other, even by shady means, what their own lack of industry and care had cost them. The fields were no longer maintained in their old condition, dying apple-trees were not replaced, rents were in arrears. And when Antoine and his brothers went to call on Cottenceau the old man would bemoan the state of affairs; it seemed to him a terrible thing, not merely because he was devoted to the de Laignes family but also because his peasant instincts hated to see the earth falling into ruin. And in the great room which served him as sitting-room, dining-room, and bedroom all in one— a bed draped with flowered curtains stood at one end— seated opposite the three young people at a round table covered with spotless oilcloth on which stood a bottle of old brandy and four little glasses, he would unburden his mind to them—how the property was no longer being cared for as it should be, and how different it all was from in the time of Monsieur le Baron; how it was only too clear that a guiding hand was lacking; how Monsieur le Comte was too good, believing everything anyone cared to tell him; how what was really wanted was a man on the spot to be there all the time . . . And so he would go on, inspired by a secret hope that one day one of the three brothers would decide to come and live at Fontaines.

Soon he would suggest taking them round the estate, and they would all go out, Cottenceau very proud and quite cheered up again, and beaming all over his face. Without ever hastening or checking his progress, treading the earth with that solid, unvarying peasant's stride which defies all interruption, he would point out to them, one after another, without comment but in a tone which betrayed both his pity for the earth and his secret disapproval of those who let themselves be so easily deceived, unlet meadows, dead trees unreplaced, trees fallen by the roadside, left to rot where they lay, which he kicked in passing with the toe of his great boot; and everything they saw would lead him on to fresh asides about the owners of the lands they were crossing, or the tenants, or the neighbours; or perhaps it would be a story of sharp-practice, or a tale of low tricks played on Cottenceau himself, all of which he related in a low voice never pausing in his scrutiny of fields and thickets. He would talk of surveys and landmarks, sketching with a thumb on his broad horny palm incomprehensible diagrams which to him perfectly conveyed the features of the ground in question; this finger would be a tree, that one a stream. And in the middle of his explanations he would stop at some ditch, or at the edge of a field, or beside a boundary-stone scarcely discernible under the accumulated soil and dead leaves but immediately plain to his peasant's eye, exclaiming: "Yes, that belongs to Monsieur le Comte," or, "Yes, that's yours"—for he used either term impartially. Sometimes he would add, desiring it understood that here he himself had been the farmer: "Yes, I had this bit of ground a long time myself," while he had a casual way of saying, "Yes, this belongs to somebody or other." And his tone would change again as he said with assumed modesty, "Yes, this bit's mine"—unable to supress a feeling of pride, despite his affection for the family he had served so long, and a visible joy in being able to show that at last he was independent and no longer needed anyone. Out on the open stubble little heaps of manure might be already ranged in rows, and when

Antoine congratulated him on the pains he took with his land he would smile silently, with a happy, proprietorial air.

He would give them detailed information, too, about the doings of their own bailiff. In addition to his own affairs he was familiar with every transaction and sale that took place and knew the value of every harvest and the receipts from the sale of grain and wool, leaving the young people to add up the total for themselves and leading them on, without comment, to draw the inevitable conclusions. In certain matters, discreetly, he would compare the revenues of to-day with those of yesterday. And as if he felt a kind of superiority, even in the midst of his genuinely respectful thoughts, in knowing details of which the young people were so ignorant and in having lived in days which seemed to him so far superior to present times, he gave himself up to his memories, exclaiming at every other moment: "Of course, that was before your time, young gentlemen. . . ."—happy in his own knowledge and full of a secret pride in his ability to instruct them. Dates he never cited, preferring to designate the years by their various peculiarities: thus, this had happened in the year of the great frost, that in the year when the walnut-tree up at the château was struck by lightning, this other in the year the bell was consecrated. And never on any account did he fail to remind them of the time when every spring, in the early years of their mother's marriage—he still occasionally called her Mademoiselle Anne-Marie, quickly correcting himself, however—he used to go off to Laignes with cider for the children from the Baron des Menuls. These were the only occasions on which he had ever left his village. And the memory of these journeys, made laboriously on foot, and forming for so many years a regular break in the monotony of his life, remained in his mind as something of extreme interest which he delighted to describe whenever opportunity occurred, invariably in the same terms and without ever changing the order of his recital:

"I would set off with my four horses early in the morning," he would begin, "and get to Laignes in the evening. They'd make me sit down to dinner with them, and after dinner Monsieur le Comte would go and play billiards with Monsieur le Curé or some of the other gentlemen. He'd want me to play too. 'Come on, Cottenceau,' he'd say. 'You'll have a game with us, won't you?' But I'd say. 'Well, Monsieur le Comte, I hardly know how.' But that was no good, for the next thing he'd say would be, 'Come all the same and watch us play.' So off I'd go with them, not daring to refuse, and stay and watch them playing. But really I was asleep on my feet, and longing to get to bed. All day long I'd trudged beside my horses, and I had those forty kilometres in my legs."

8

THEIR SCHOOLDAYS OVER, the two young girls came home to Laignes. Agnes, the younger, intended to enter a convent, and only returned to obtain her father's consent and because it had been stipulated that before taking her vows she should return to the world and remain in it for a year. The elder, Clotilde, intended to take her mother's place and run the house.

But almost at once she came into conflict with one of the chamber-maids, a girl called Delphine. This girl had been only a few months in Monsieur de Laignes' service, but she had quickly contrived, little by little edging out the old nurse, to exercise a despotic authority over the whole household; and now she saw her power being threatened. To the orders given her by Mademoiselle de Laignes she replied with invariable respect, never raising any objection, but obviously determined to have her own way in the end. When the conflict became too evident Monsieur de Laignes would intervene, flying into a passion and shouting at the girl— one day he would treat her with extreme rudeness, the next with circumspection—and commanding her obedience. But afterwards he would sulk with his daughters. More than once he even put the blame on his elder daughter, guided by a muddled determination to be fair that took no account at all of the difference between her and Delphine.

Little by little, hurt and humiliated in this way at every turn, saddened moreover by what she divined, Clotilde assumed a kind of lofty indifference. There was something chilling in her manner, which concealed a deep shyness and a passionate desire not to appear complaining; and this was emphasized by her tall, angular, not very attractive figure, and by the carriage of her head, which she held always very high, as though in defiance. This lack of ease and cordiality resulted in few people liking her; she was considered proud.

Her year over, the time came for Agnes to bid farewell to the world. She had been awaiting that day in cheerful tranquillity, only vaguely disturbed by what she saw going on around her; for already she contemplated such matters with the dispassion of the nun—an egotism more complete than any other, beneath which, nevertheless, there persists a remnant of inactive affection for parents or other loved ones. The world to which she now said farewell consisted for her only of her father, her sister, the curé, and perhaps her brothers.

It was very soon after this that the Mother Superior proposed a husband for Clotilde. She accepted with confidence and with indifference. All she had ever asked of marriage was that her husband should be a good and practising Christian.

Her wedding was celebrated with great pomp. The Bishop of Monthuis himself gave the blessing, and there were also present eighteen curés from the county round about, all dining in the presbytery at Monsieur de Laignes' expense. In addition to this a banquet was spread in the orangery for the villagers and farmers, and when dessert was reached the new Madame Villedieu and her husband came out to drink with the oldest of their guests.

His daughter's marriage had done something to stir Monsieur de Laignes from his apathy, but he soon relapsed into his usual state, and even the homecoming of Philippe, his second son, did not rouse him. For several years now he had fancied himself ill, and, looking for diseases, soon found them. More for something to do than with any idea of a cure he followed a variety of regimens. He wrote for medicines, looked forward to their arrival, had them unpacked in his presence, and meticulously read the directions, almost delighting in the rules to which he subjected himself and which kept him occupied in their observance. All this gave him the illusion of leading a real life, with real satisfactions and boredoms, without, however, ever being obliged to think about anyone except himself.

He died of a disease he had never dreamed of having. Once more the great painted coat of arms was brought down from the attic; it was only used for funerals, and never appeared above the lofty château doorway save as a centre-piece to mourning emblems. The coffin was placed in the great entrance-hall, transformed into a funerary chamber by hangings which reduced its size but did not deaden its echoes; and there, half visible at the back, seated at their prie-dieu covered with black housings, two Sisters from the school kept vigil over the catafalque all night long.

As soon as he arrived at Monthuis, where the carriage had been sent to meet him, Antoine, with a sorrowful sense of shock, heard himself addressed as "Monsieur le Comte." And it was only this which really brought home to him what he had known all along. As he left the town he skirted the walls of the convent in which his sister lived. Of all the five children of Monsieur de Laignes she was the only one who was not coming to the funeral; but she had written him a letter, as to the new head of the family, which he found that evening at the château with many others. In it she said no more than that her superiors were excusing her from all work until after the funeral (she was now in charge of one of the higher forms at the convent), and that thus in her great sorrow she would have the consolation of praying for the repose of her father's soul as long and as often as she wished.

The very next day—and their first act was to dismiss Delphine—the children of Monsieur de Laignes found themselves faced with a material situation of which they knew almost nothing, and which it was almost impossible to disentangle. Indeed, whenever one or other of them had tried to find out anything about their affairs from their father, asking for specific information or explanation, Monsieur de Laignes had always disingenuously evaded the subject with the air of a man resenting any attempt to supersede him or encroach upon his rights, but in reality afraid of exposing the disastrous state of his possessions and thus laying himself open to the risk of having to receive advice from his own children, advice which would have been at once a reproach and a lesson. And now that their father was dead, they felt that to do what he had never done himself would be almost like setting themselves up in judgement upon him. Moreover, inheriting as they did much of his irresolute and apathetic character, they preferred to wait, as he had done before them, for some accident to settle matters and take any decision out of their hands. They felt, too, that since their father's possessions were now to be divided among all five of them, to act in any way might be to injure an inheritance which chance had hitherto preserved intact but which would now have to be run on entirely new lines, and the consequences of this new management faced. An unconscious respect for the past restrained them on the one hand; but on the other they were all of them selfishly eager to enter upon their individual shares of the paternal inheritance —an arrangement that appears on the face of it to be so equitable, so in accordance with the most enlightened justice, but which, in reality, fosters the lowest kind of greed, fatal to the continuity of the family. Hesitating thus between contradictory feelings which they could not resolve, they ended up by doing nothing at all, not in the least knowing how to profit from their conflicting advantages.

They did not sell any lands, but divided what could easily be divided, that is to say, the actual cash. Since Philippe had in the meanwhile married, it was agreed that he should keep on the château, which otherwise would have stood empty, in return for a rent to be paid his brothers and sisters. The estates themselves remained intact; Philippe looked after them, and all the responsibility rested on his shoulders; yet he was allowed no freedom of action whatever, for at every turn his brothers or his brother-in-law, each jealous for his own shred of authority, would wield it haphazard and withhold their consent from this or that project under the most far-fetched pretexts, although they usually knew far less of what had to be done than Philippe himself, who was on the spot and in a position to decide.

And since it was soon felt throughout the country-side that he was not the true master, but simply a deputy for the family, a sort of steward, he soon began to lose the position his father had held. It became only too evident that he had to ask permission before doing anything at all, and was really dependent upon others. What had been possible for the father was no longer so for the son. And in the midst of this network of rights and obligations which his ancestors had formulated he was now leading very much the life of an ordinary bourgeois, subject to the same needs and the same expenses as of old but without now the same resources. The villagers, however, offended in their conception of the manner of life incumbent upon the lord of the manor, preferred simply to say that Monsieur Philippe was close-fisted.

As time went on, moreover, his whole appearance changed. His weather-beaten face and carelessly arranged hair, and the ordinary sort of clothes he now wore, all combined to give him a rough, countrified air from which all refinement had fled. His whole manner, his very gestures and ways of speech, were those of a peasant's. But the more his appearance seemed to approximate to theirs, the more, in reality, he grew away from them.

Ill at ease in a countryside where the spirit was beginning to change, incessantly crossed by his brothers and sister, he realized at last that the day would soon come when he would have to leave; and for several years he dreamt of going, incapable of bringing himself to the point of making a sudden and decisive break with all the past.

But the death of his wife's parents confirmed him in this resolution. Being an only child she inherited the family estates, and there they now went to live. At his departure he took with him his agreed part of the furniture, to which he quietly added several pictures and a large part of the library.

He left, and the château was shut up: Monsieur Hotte kept the keys. From time to time, through him, news of the family still came to the village. Antoine, often at first, then less and less frequently, wrote to say that he was coming: but he never came. The tall iron gates, which were never opened now, took on the colours of rust, like the railings round neglected graves. And very soon, for the village, all that remained of the château was the little lodge where the nurse lived out her days.

MARIE-ARMANDE
DE CHAPPES

1

THE GREAT DOUBLE GATES of the de Chappes mansion
swung open: an old-fashioned closed carriage driven by
a coachman in black emerged from the vaulted porch,
and the horse broke into a steady trot as though for a
long drive, setting off up the rue de la Vicomté, a short
street leading in to the cathedral square. Almost at
once it pulled up in front of the church; and the
proprietors of a number of shops forming one angle of
the square looked on curiously as the two ladies
alighted from it, the Marquise de Chappes, and her
daughter-in-law, who had come to be churched. Half
an hour later they left the cathedral again, returning
as they had come. The gates opened quickly for them
and shut as quickly behind them, and the carriage
drove into the cobbled courtyard of the mansion;
although the evening was drawing in no light appeared
in the grey stone façade.

This was the first appearance of Madame de Chappes
since her confinement, and thenceforth she resumed her
normal life with the dowager Marquise and her husband,
a life of social duties and good works. She started the
day always by attending early Mass with her mother-
in-law in a small side-chapel of the cathedral; and

once a week at least this would be a foundation, sometimes of great antiquity, for some past member of the family. After this they would visit their pensioners. Then, in the afternoon—while the Marquise attended a meeting of one of the numerous municipal or Catholic charities in which she was interested or of which she was a patron—Madame de Chappes would dress with great care and go and call on the bishop or on some relative who might be expecting her. But scarcely ever did she venture beyond the old quarter of the town, that part of Saint-Loup clustered round the cathedral, a complex network of damp and dark little streets with gabled houses and ancient mansions affording sudden glimpses of the irregular roofs of hospice or convent, each dominated by the belfry of its chapel.

These calls would be returned after due notice had been given. She would receive her visitors wherever she happened to be, in her own sitting-room, in the drawing-room, or even, if it was fine, in the garden. This was overlooked by a smiling, peaceful frontage, which one would never have suspected from the other side of the house which looked on to the courtyard, cold, dark, and gloomy; it was a house with two faces, protected from the curiosity of the street by the mystery of its great windows with curtains invariably drawn.

Unlike other children, who are taken out into avenues and public gardens in elaborate prams, Marie-Armande passed the whole of her infancy in the house or the garden. There she was pushed in her pram, there she took her first steps, and behind those peaceful walls, so like a convent's, she led her childish life, that regular and regulated life which is generally watched from day to day by neighbours, but which in her case was lived far from the eyes of the world in the midst of her own family, yet not for that reason restricted or confined. They gave her what time they could (now her mother, now her grandmother), and were chiefly concerned to instruct her in one after another of the religious practices usually taught small children. If she went out at all, it was to be taken to a convent, to the bishop's palace, to a Christmas-tree party on Christmas Eve, or to see one of her cousins, Olympe de Trannes, some years her senior and one of the very few little girls she ever met. Then one day her parents took her to High Mass; and those who had seen her from time to time in the streets of the old town, walking hand in hand with her nurse, were quite astonished to see such a big little girl instead of the baby they seemed to remember from only the other day. She sat soberly by her mother at a prie-dieu which had been turned round for her. Later she had an ordinary chair. And from the way she followed the service in her prayer-book it was plain that she could already read.

Their seats in church (although on certain feast-days Monsieur de Chappes, who was a member of the committee for the preservation of the cathedral, went over to sit with the other churchwardens in their special pew) were facing the pulpit, and at the side of the block reserved for the seminary and for the clergy who sat there during the sermon. Not far from them sat Mademoiselle Aurore de Polyso, an elderly relative, familiarly called Aunt Aurore. After Mass they always exchanged a few words with her, and sometimes Monsieur de Chappes would offer her his arm home. In the evening, after vespers, she would go back with them to their house.

Every week, indeed, Sunday dinner united the whole family. This was a meal in the old style, luxurious and carefully chosen, and, though only a family affair, prepared with a care reserved to-day for the benefit of strangers. The cook would be some fat old woman in a white linen apron and a black ruched cap, whose sole preoccupation was to cook a dinner for guests who would appreciate it and be as pleased with her for succeeding as she herself would be pleased with them for finding it to their taste.

There were always two dishes of choice fruits on the table, chosen from the store in the fruit-loft reserved for such occasions, or perhaps sent by a relative; and between them, in the middle and at either end of the long table, in chafing-dishes which gave off an odour of wax and hot metal, were the main dishes of the meal; dishes at once simple and complex, their quality derived, perhaps, from the fact that they had been long and carefully cooked, and that in their preparation neither time nor pains had been spared. Among the old recipes preserved in the family was one handed down from Mademoiselle de Polyso's mother for a very special stew to be simmered on the fire for forty-eight hours and cooked to the point when a straw would go through the meat without bending. Pélagie, the cook, two days before the dish was required, would announce, "I shall start Madame Polyso's stew to-night," and if Marie-Armande happened to slip into the kitchen after dinner she would find Pélagie banking up a glowing fire with cinders to keep it in all night. And then, very carefully, she would put on the great copper casserole, with a dish instead of a lid containing an infusion of spices in Burgundy with a squeeze of orange juice.

On entering the dining-room there was always some minutes' confusion while the Marquis de Chappes sorted out his guests. When the others were all seated Aunt Aurore would remain standing for a moment with clasped hands, murmuring a grace, which some of the ladies (and even a few of the gentlemen) managed to murmur too as they unfolded their napkins. Then, with a final and triumphant Latin word, and an emphatic sign of the cross, Aunt Aurore would take her first spoonful of soup with a coquettish air and plunge straightway into the general conversation—to which, in spite of herself, she had been listening all the time.

With urbane good-humour, and without ever lapsing into anything like an argument, they would talk of trivial matters over which it might safely have been conjectured they would never disagree—perhaps because they never so much as touched on anything like an idea. They bandied compliments rather than opinions, and were as skilled in elaborating these as others are their own pretensions; for them wit took the place of argument. And among these people, whose fortunes were sometimes so sharply disparate, the question of money, if it chanced to come up at all, was taken no more and no less seriously than any other subject. Nobody seemed unduly concerned about it: cropping up casually, and then as casually dropped, it did not occupy in this conversation the dominant place accorded it by those who have only recently acquired it or by those still struggling to acquire it— labouring to increase their possessions so that each child may receive his inconsiderable portion, with the result that each of these, with no leisure for refinement, is obliged to continue that painful effort necessary in the beginning of all families but in this case bound to be sterile.

After dinner a move would be made to the drawing-room, a large room difficult to warm, and always rather chilly and smelling of wood-smoke, which they entered with that slight shiver experienced on leaving the table at the conclusion of an excellent meal The senior members of the party would at once make up a four for whist. The other ladies took their seats in the semi-circle of armchairs ranged round the room, their voluminous silken gowns spreading in stiff folds around them; some would hold embroidered fire-screens in their hands. Then Madame de Chappes would sit down at the piano, and Monsieur de Chappes, in that fine churchly voice which might be heard two or three times a year in the cathedral, on Christmas Day or at a wedding, would sing a fashionable ballad or an air from the latest opera. And someone would implore him to sing again, recalling, perhaps, the opening words of some light or witty song he had himself composed in bygone days (for he possessed a great facility for writing light verse or turning a witty couplet), based on some family incident, some unlucky accident or ridiculous misadventure which had once inspired his fancy, and had been remembered, perhaps, during dinner.

On anniversaries the guests would be more numerous than at other times, and on such evening⟨ Monsieur de Chappes never failed to make a little speech over the dessert, a little complimentary address or tribute in verse composed for the occasion, which he delivered standing up, glass in hand.

Among the religious feasts which divided the year into its familiar, unvarying periods there was one, the Fête-Dieu, which was celebrated at Saint-Loup with especial pomp and ceremony, and with a procession through the town. Some time before the day the bishop would designate the gentlemen, fifteen to twenty in all, who should take it in turns to bear the canopy. The Marquis de Chappes invariably took his place in this privileged group, which, indeed, was composed almost exclusively of his own relations.

Some days before the actual feast the scaffolding used in the construction of the street altars would be brought out of the sheds and lofts of the various churches and erected, as a rule at a cross-roads or in a little square. Late into the warm evenings the hammering of mallets and the sound of voices would be heard; groups of people stood about in the streets; and on doorsteps or in open courtyards men might be seen working backwards, like rope-makers, busy binding ropes with the moss prepared by the women and girls around them; and as they worked they stuck in here and there a posy. Between the different parishes there was a great spirit of rivalry. Those who could boast of a Musical Society retained its services for their particular altar. The day before the fête Madame de Chappes would put her chandeliers and hangings at the disposal of the cathedral vicar, and he would be seen walking back beside the gardener with a hand-cart loaded with laurels and orange-trees in tubs. Then, on the day itself, some of the tapestries which usually hung in the hall would appear on either side of the gateway of the de Chappes' mansion, tapestries with green flowers on a grey ground, chosen from among those which had no figures on them.

And on the Sunday, after Vespers, to the pealing of

bells, the procession would emerge from the cool shade of the cathedral into the dazzling sunlight of the outer sanctuary. The flames of the tapers appeared then as little yellow points, smoky and wan, and the glass of the triangular lanterns carried on staves by the older acolytes flashed as it caught the sun. Crossing the square, the procession wound its way down the rue de la Cité, escorted by a double file of soldiers in full-dress, rifles at the slope; at its head, preceded by their drums and bugles and a gigantic drum-major twirling and tossing his long tasselled staff with its knob of gleaming copper, marched the bearded sappers with their bear-skins, hatchets, and aprons of white leather, two abreast, with short, slow, even tread.

Right and left along the swept and empty street white sheets hung like tapestries, covering the shutters of the shops and the ground-floor windows of the houses, and decked here and there with flowers and sprays of foliage gathered the night before in the surrounding fields—poplar boughs, mostly, whose metallic leaves shivered at the slightest breath of air. Slowly, heralded from afar by the intermittent sound of brass and drums, the procession advanced; slowly this elaborate and immense cortège wound through streets momentarily transformed and lent a flowery and unusual aspect by their decorated houses; a cortège at once military, civil, and religious; the gold-brocaded vestments, the silken banners, the specimens of goldsmith's art, seen usually in the dim effulgence of stained glass, sparkled oddly in the strong light of the sun. In every window groups of people stood watching, bowing their heads and crossing themselves as the Host went by.

If the military band stopped playing for a moment some other brass band would soon start up, and high above the town the house-tops echoed gaily with the pealing of the bells of the cathedral, which never ceased their ringing; and all the while, beneath all this, the dull trampling of the crowd filing by was heard.

One after the other, always with the smallest children in front, came the boarding-schools, the convents, the orphanage, the boys' school, the college; finally, behind the scarlet band of acolytes and a little in advance of the clergy, came the choir, hybrid creatures, more than lay and less than clergy, bearded and moustached, striding with measured tread and almost entirely enveloped in their immense flowered and heavily fringed cloaks; holding their great books on a level with their mouths they sang their hymns in sonorous tones which the warm air all about them seemed to muffle.

Next came the canopy of the Host, its plumes nodding high above the crowd, escorted by a sombre and ceremonious little band of gentlemen in black, bare-headed despite the strong sun, and followed by a row of worthies—that is to say, the general, the chief magistrate, the prefect, and the mayor. Parish by parish, each grouped around its vicar, the faithful followed. According to the width of the streets they had to pass through, the ranks closed up or broke and faltered, and sometimes the procession, completely dislocated, would take a short lane overlooked by nothing but garden walls and the backs of houses with only attic windows to be seen and a sudden occasional glimpse of a lower window with drawn blinds.

The procession made its last halt at the altar outside the de Chappes' mansion. Standing on the pavement in front of their own house, together with a few relatives and a crowd of servants, the two ladies, the Marquise on her daughter-in-law's arm, awaited the coming of the Holy Sacrament as they would have awaited any distinguished guest. The head of the procession would already have reached the outer sanctuary of the cathedral when the bishop stopped. Ascending the altar steps he blessed the crowd and the house, and the procession moved off again. The two ladies, still accompanied by their relatives, their rosaries dangling from their fingers, now joined in the march; and lost in the crowd they went with the procession up the rue de la Vicomté, devoutly escorting to His home the God they had just received, ceremoniously, like a guest.

2

EVERY THURSDAY AFTERNOON Marie-Armande went to
see her Aunt Aurore. She lived alone in the rue du
Grand - Cloître - Saint - Pierre, not far from the de
Chappes', in a great old rambling house which had been
her parents' home; she was looked after by a servant,
Jeannette, and her life was almost exclusively given up
to working for a certain charity, the Tabernacle
Charity, designed to provide poor parishes with the
ornaments necessary for worship. She worked for this
charity alone, employing all her leisure time in embroidery, in creating filet lace from the finest net, or
in fashioning raised designs in gold or silver on silk—
true works of art, which would have cost a great deal
to buy. But her chief occupation was the refashioning
of old artificial flowers into fresh ones to be used in
the composition of those dreadful stiff and insipid
bouquets which stand on altars in tin or china vases.
Her friends and acquaintances everywhere would send
her their own old flowers—ancient hat-trimmings,
posies from ball-dresses, bridal wreaths. She had a large
store of these, all sorted out into colours; and after
pulling them to pieces she would collect together all
the petals, all the centres, all the leaves, all the stems,

and arrange them in the cupboards of the narrow little drawing-room where she spent most of her time—cupboards opening at a man's height from the floor, divided one from another by fluted columns whose capitals still bore traces of gilding, and with curved latticed doors backed by curtains of yellow silk. Beneath these, reaching to the tiled floor, were other cupboards with plain doors.

Seated by the window at a small mahogany table littered with florist's paraphernalia, she would work away delicately and patiently with her little steel tools, gumming, carding, reshaping, and then, to finish off the stems, twirling the great freshly painted roses in deft fingers as she wound a strip of green paper effortlessly round the wire. From time to time, without pausing in her own work, she would bend down a little to see how Marie-Armande was getting on, she being installed at her feet on a tapestry footstool and doing her best to knit, all entangled with her wooden needles and her ball of wool. At dusk they would lay aside their work, and to please the little girl Aunt Aurore would sing to her or tell her stories.

Despite her dawning infirmities, her age, her stoutness, which rendered movement difficult and which she always made fun of, as she made fun of everything, gently and good-humouredly—in spite of all this she retained that ironical and mocking spirit which is dying out nowadays, a light-hearted way of looking at life which is gradually being superseded by a habit of reasoning, and which finds the main subject of its epigrams in the imperfections of the human body, that body which Christianity, by confusing the physical aspects of love with the baser necessities of man, has for long past credited with a blemish against which our ironical race protests. A garment, it might be said (and for Christians the body is but a temporary envelope), in any way defective, inconvenient, or absurd, is but a momentary nuisance; so isn't it best to laugh at it? Many people, even if this servitude revolts their reason, attach no implication of disgrace to what is only one of Nature's littlenesses, but the rest of the world pursues these tattered garments of ours with mockeries; the real cause is lost to view; until at last, beneath the weight of these continual sarcasms— expressed in the most varied forms, in anecdotes, in proverbs, or reduced to the crudest terms—there arises a whole attitude of mind which comes to extend even to those who are capable of reflection, and these find beneath their laughter the very subject against which they rebel.

In all the stories which Aunt Aurore liked to tell, stories which she had had from her mother, who herself had had them from hers, the central figure was invariably a priest or a monk, a ridiculous figure at that, and this in spite of her profound respect for their ministry and her deep piety. It was as if, without her realizing it, the priest, man by nature and angel by profession, hearing everything, seeing everything, yet apart from everything, occupied a lonely and conspicuous place in the world which made his life scandalous if he failed in his vows and gave him if he kept them a ridiculous appearance of having to try to convert everyone else into the bargain—this being the aspect which has given birth to the central figure of our ancient tales, a figure, indeed, whom we meet to-day in all stories of priests, to whom men like to attribute the very opposites of the qualities they are supposed to possess, such as gluttony, ribaldry, lechery, and vanity. Often, when the story culminated with some droll or improper word, Aunt Aurore would lower her voice at the end, or roll her shocked and mocking eyes, or pull a little face, as though to say: "But my dears—what have I said!"

A little shocked and very much entertained, Marie-Armande would listen to the tale of the priest whose pulpit some boys had smeared with—well, Aunt Aurore would say, you know what! And he began his sermon by placing both hands on the desecrated velvet: "The world, brethren, the world . . ." he cried, lifting up his hands, "the world is only . . .!" And her grimace expressed the word she would not say. In another tale an acolyte had half-sawn through the board on which the priest sat during his sermon, and as he proclaimed the text of his discourse in the following terms, "A little while, and ye shall see me; and again a little while, and ye shall not see me . . ." he disappeared abruptly into the depths of the pulpit as the board gave way beneath his weight. And this malicious irreverence would be extended also to that higher type of clergy, with whom we are so freely provided, the blessed company of saints.

"In the porch of a certain church," Aunt Aurore would begin, "there stood the statues of the four Evangelists. St. Mark was standing like this" (and she rested her left elbow in her right hand and held her hand to her nose); "St. Luke, behind him, was like this" (and she held up her hands on a level with her shoulders); "St. Matthew was standing like this" (and she pointed with her left arm, frowning); "and St. John stood like this" (she assumed an air of bewilderment, half spreading out her hands). "St. Mark said, 'There's a bad smell here!'; St Luke replied, 'It isn't me!'; St. Matthew said, 'It's him!'; and St. John replied, 'It must have escaped me, then!'"

To end up with, for Marie-Armande's special amusement, she would relate a tale which, she declared, was true, since she herself had known the Abbé concerned —a certain village priest. One day this Abbé inadvertently locked his donkey up in the church. The donkey rubbed himself against the trestle-table where the fine chasubles were kept—rubbed so vigorously that one of them slipped off and on to its back. And when the villagers, startled by the noise, ventured to open the church door, what did they see but the donkey parading up and down in a gold-embroidered cope, loudly braying!

106

One day, not long after Marie-Armande's sixth birthday, she was told she was going to have a little brother. Jeannette came to fetch her, and for a fortnight she stayed with her Aunt Aurore.

They had put up a bed for her in Mademoiselle de Polyso's own room, an enormous apartment which one had to pass through to get to the drawing-room; in one corner was an alcove draped, like the windows, with white muslin over yellow-striped blue repp curtains, and here there stood a rosewood bed; above it hung a large crucifix, and its eiderdown of yellow silk was covered with a large, fringed square of tatting. On the herring-bone parquet floor was a thick hand-made carpet with a pattern of foliage and birds.

Marie-Armande went to bed early. For some while Jeannette would move to and fro getting Aunt Aurore's bed ready; finally she would take out the warming-pan —an apparatus consisting of a wooden batten shaped like a carriage-spring, from the centre of which was suspended an earthenware pot filled with cinders and hot ashes, and which in winter was often put into the bed as early as three o'clock in the afternoon. All this while Aunt Aurore would be sitting in a plush arm-chair at the head of her bed saying her office. Having, as her last duty, banked up the fire for the night, Jeannette would withdraw, taking leave of her mistress every night in words that never varied and which seemed like the conclusion of her day's toil: "Well, Mademoiselle, I wish you good night." And Aunt

Aurore, without interrupting her office, but raising her voice a little at this point, would slowly incline her head in reply. When she had finished she would go and kneel at her prie-dieu to say her prayers. Then she began her toilette for the night.

Marie-Armande, pretending to be asleep, would watch her take off her bodice, her skirt, and her corset; beneath this, like a hygienic breastplate, hung a broad scapular of brown material symbolic of the brown habit of the Franciscans (Mademoiselle de Polyso was actually Superior of the Third Order of St. Francis). This she would kiss. Then came the false front—and her head, as bald as a turkey's, looked very odd without it. Then she would put on her nightcap and her bed-jacket and, still half-dressed, climb up on to her high bed; and there, standing in the billowy mass of feather-mattress, she would slip off her petticoats one after the other, stuffing them under the eiderdown to keep them warm for the morning. At length, afraid of seeing herself in her chemise, she would hurriedly slip between the sheets. Finally she would blow out the lamp; and then, with her head in its starched cap lying well back, her chest well out, and her hands folded, looking rather as if she were lying in state, she would fall asleep almost immediately, never stirring until Jeannette came in (winter and summer Mademoiselle de Polyso got up at five) to make up the fire. Then, leaving Marie-Armande, all unsuspecting, alone in the house, the two would go off to Mass, always getting back well before the little girl was awake.

In the afternoons they would go into town to buy something for Marie-Armande, or perhaps because Aunt Aurore wanted something for her work from Madame Balavoine-Pincemin's, the draper's.

This was in the rue Notre-Dame, in the business part of the town, a very ancient street, irregular and winding, with tall, narrow, gabled houses with great beams, some still with overhangs and steeply sloping roofs, and others with oriels projecting at the corners. These houses had never more than two windows on each floor—and on the topmost floor, in the sharp angle of the gable, the windows were so close together, separated only by a wooden upright, that they seemed to be only one, larger than the others and of a different shape. The shops on the ground-floor were very deep and badly ventilated, with a single room at the back, usually the dining-room, looking out on to a tiny courtyard and lighted from the shop side by a curtained glass partition.

As soon as she knew it was Mademoiselle de Polyso, Madame Balavoine-Pincemin—a large, dark, majestic woman, invariably dressed in black silk with lace cuffs —would herself emerge from the parlour where most of her day was spent and from where she organized her docile army of assistants, and appear in the gloom at the far end of the shop.

Before coming to the real purpose of the visit there

would always be a little preliminary conversation—
mutual inquiries about the health of their respective
families, a remark or two about the weather, an
exchange of news. But at length Mademoiselle Polyso
would ask for what she wanted, and then, with a jerk
of her head, Madame Balavoine-Pincemin would
mobi ize the squadron of young ladies who had been
waiting in silence throughout the conversation. Goods
were brought out, cardboard boxes got down, and
heavy bales of material let fall upon the counter with a
dull thud, to be unrolled by one of the young ladies and
displayed by Madame Balavoine-Pincemin herself.
With carefully measured gestures she would indicate
confidentially what she herself recommended, and at
every movement her earrings—long pendants consisting
of two balls of blue marble linked by a golden chain—
would click against her starched collar. Sometimes
her husband, a handsome gentleman with side-whiskers
and a pink complexion, precisely like one of the
dummies displaying ready-made suits across the road,
would appear to add his opinion. And then, one by
one and in order of importance, the smiling young
ladies behind the counter would add theirs in fluting
tones.

Once a week, after Mass, Mademoiselle de Polyso
received her poor pensioners. The day before Jeannette
would provide herself with a good stock of bread.
Then, soon after they were home from Mass on the
appointed day, there would arrive by the great gate-

way which was opened specially for the occasion a lamentable procession of cripples, senile derelicts, and women with children hanging round them—all coming from the cathedral where they had been attending the arch-priest's catechism; for Mademoiselle de Polyso's poor, like those of all right-thinking people in the parish, were drawn from those who attended the arch-priest's catechism. And now in the covered way from street to garden which normally echoed with the modest tread of formal piety there arose a continually increasing din, with everybody talking and shouting together at once, often ribaldly enough. One day, for instance, Marie-Armande heard one of them calling out to a poor woman known as *Ouin-Ouin* because of the hare-lip which made her snuffle, who was also invariably pregnant, something that was received with shouts of laughter. But when Marie-Armande asked Aunt Aurore and Jeanette what they had been laughing at she asked in vain.

"Look at her"—that was what it was—"she's like the coaches: always full up inside!"

At the sight of Jeannette opening the kitchen-door with a large basket filled with hunks of bread, calm was at once established. There was an immediate return to the draggled bearing of the professional beggar. Crutches which had shown some signs of independence suddenly subsided, tremblings grew into convulsions, backs were bowed lower, bodies leaned still more heavily on sticks, rosaries were surreptitiously

111

dragged from pockets, and they all began shuffling towards the end of the passage where Jeannette, dutiful but quite unsympathetic, equitably doled out the bread as they filed before her.

Then, at ten o'clock—a little before or after—and quite alone as was his habit, the Drummer would appear. The one beggar who did not go to catechism (and Jeannette secretly favoured him for that), he was a genial old fellow with a white goatee, some sort of uniform jacket with blue facings, a plumed képi, and a drum which he beat about the town. His drum would first be heard several streets away. It came nearer, receded, grew again in volume, all of a sudden stopped, and then, when it was least expected, all at once broke out afresh right under the kitchen window. Bringing his roll to an end he would at once start up a song in his tremulous old man's voice. But first he would announce the title. It might be, for instance, "The Song of the Little Man," which began: "There was a little man who went to gather sticks . . ."—and when he got home with his faggots on his back he found his wife in bed with a monk. Then Marie-Armande, who would be watching from the window, would demand another song; the one about Cousin José, or the one about the Drunken Man—who wanted to be buried under the biggest hogshead in the cellar, on the understanding that the tap should be left turned on; or perhaps the one about the Unhappy Husband. With a little gesture of assent the Drummer would begin:

112

I lie in bed o'mornings and my husband works instead,
He sweeps my room when I get up and then he makes the
     bed.

And when I'm going to a ball my husband runs about
To fetch my cloak and lantern and see me safely out.

At nine o'clock my husband comes and goes down on his
     knees,
Saying, Will it suit your ladyship to come home now,
     please?

And at this point the old man would kneel down and imitate the unhappy husband's timid tones.

When he had finished his song he would be given two sous, a glass of wine, a bit of bread, and often odds and ends of food as well, which Jeannette had carefully put by for him. With a final roll on his drum by way of farewell he would march off, crying: "Till next week!"

3

IT WAS AT THIS TIME of the year that the annual fair
at Saint-Loup took place, and of course Aunt Aurore
took Marie-Armande to see it. And from then on, at
the same time every year, the old lady took the little
girl once if not twice to the fair.

Feeble echo as it was of the whole wooden town
which used once to spring into being for so short a
time, even now it extended for nearly half a mile along
the old fortifications on the right bank of the river in
two unbroken rows of flimsy, hastily constructed plank
booths which lined both sides of the road. All kinds of
things could be bought there, often quite valuable
things. And in the space in front of the college, where
the old ramparts had been cleared away, were clustered
the stands of the wandering showmen; circuses,
menageries, roundabouts with wooden horses (the old
sort of roundabout, with floor and balustrade), theatres
of every kind presenting comedies, melodramas, or
fairy-plays, performing animals, and even a conjuror's
show—Mademoiselle de Polyso always referred to him
as "the doctor." Elsewhere there was a marionette
show—articulated mechanical figures set in motion by
a steam-engine, the incessant noise of which made a

thudding accompaniment to the scenes from prison-life which were represented: work, rest, escape, execution: there, under the muzzles of cannon and surrounded by stiff and melancholy-looking soldiers, the close-cropped convicts, cap in hand, knelt round the scaffold. And then, all jumbled together, were waxwork shows, lotteries, games of every description, monstrosities (such as giants and dwarfs), elaborate games of skittles (with dolls for ninepins dressed up like a wedding-party—which of course included a mother-in-law), and panoramas, that is to say, daubs on canvas which one looked at through a peep-hole bringing them up to life-size, and which depicted scenes of horror—generally St. Bartholomew's Night or Catherine de Medici in royal purple and crown, surrounded by her courtiers, and walking superbly over the half-flayed bodies of her victims.

On Sundays, and particularly on that Sunday known as "Fine Sunday," the town would be overrun from early morning by the peasants who came streaming in from every corner of the department, and who would go back at night laden with parcels of clothing and tools and household utensils of every kind. Through the midst of this crowd in which the townspeople were temporarily submerged, Aunt Aurore would make her way, anxious and rather frightened, holding Marie-Armande by the hand and accompanied by Jeannette. At every other moment Jeannette would find herself marooned in the flood of people; dark and wary, she looked suspiciously about her and kept her hand in her pocket all the time; every now and then, with an exclamation that was hardly even surprised, she would recognize acquaintances from her own part of the country whom she hailed by name and stopped with for a moment's gossip. And all the while, through the deafening racket of whistles, showman's howls, organs and blaring bands, rolling drums and hurriedly clamouring bells, the crowd flowed placidly up and down. There was an incessant forming and reforming of groups; some would stop to stare at a burlesque, or at a woman in tights, supposedly fast asleep and reclining horizontally and rigidly in mid-air, to all appearances supported solely by an iron bar projecting vertically from the platform. And all the time, close at hand, clear and precise above the general tumult of the fair, came the dry clop of bullets on the sheet-iron plates of the shooting-gallery, and the hammer blows which sent the Turk's head flying up its wooden post, and the grating of the revolving platforms laden with crockery and glass round which the crowd continually pressed, tickets in hand, in the hope of winning a splendid flower-vase, but generally getting a tiny spunglass pigeon instead, bobbing on the end of a wire. And then, suddenly, a new band would blare out, isolating with its din a stand raised higher than any of the others, a band composed of two cornets, big drum, and sidedrum. This was the quack.

Dressed in unrelieved black, like a doctor or a lawyer

in formal attire, he stood high on the front seat of his cart, a very high cart with shining brass-work, beating the huge drum painted red and gold. Holding up a bottle or packet he would vaunt the virtues of his remedies—remedies primarily directed at the peasants' two most common ills: tooth-ache and indigestion. In due course the moment came for tooth-drawing, and he would invite all sufferers to come and be operated on, pointing energetically, to the accompaniment of a formidable burst of music, first to the dentist's chair, then to the narrow ladder giving access to his stand.

At last some peasant standing with a group of friends would seem to be making up his mind to go. Encouraged by the others, who egged him on as much for their own amusement as in his own interest, and who jeeringly exhorted him not to be afraid, he would take a tentative step forward; and then, pushed forward by those behind him and fascinated by the kind and welcoming gestures of the fine gentleman leaning down from on high to catch him up, as it were, and help him to ascend, he clambered timidly up the ladder and sat down in the chair with his back to the onlookers. For a moment the band stopped playing, as it will at the circus when the gymnast is about to drop to the net from the top of the dome or the acrobat to perform his most perilous turn. The fine gentleman brandished on high a glittering pair of pincers, had the bad tooth pointed out to him beyond mistake, and with a nod

117

to the musicians perched on the top of the cart let loose another burst of deafening noise. And in the same breath, as it seemed, without any apparent movement but the double flash of steel, the tooth he had removed with a conjurer's dexterity was graciously held aloft in the jaws of the shining tool.

Then it was proferred to its owner, who got up and stood there staring silently at it for a moment, took it, instinctively wrapping it up in a corner of his handkerchief, and descended from the cart bewildered and spitting and seeming to find his mouth suddenly much too large. Once safely down he would protest that it had not hurt at all, and slyly advise others to follow his example.

Then there was the singer of laments who while he sang displayed a canvas on the end of a long pole depicting the different stages of a crime long famous in the district, each stage of which was the subject of a separate verse. The moral was always of a very pious kind. It seemed that the wrong had been done to God Himself rather than to the victim, for when the murder had been committed Christ Himself appeared in person to reproach the murderer with his sin. The melancholy hero of this drama was called Placide, and Christ, calling him familiarly by his name, asked him:

> What have I done, Placide,
> That you persecute me so?

Expiation followed in due course; and that itself

was rounded off with some good advice to parents, invariably listened to in a deep and attentive silence:

> Fathers and mothers all
> With little children dear,
> Take heed to bring them up
> Jesus Christ to love and fear.

And, since there was no accompaniment, at the end of every verse the singer's wife would imitate the twanging of a guitar.

Among the booths which Mademoiselle de Polyso always made a point of visiting with Marie-Armande was a certain marionette theatre. The show never varied. Mixed up with the tableaux created by past generations of proprietors there were—although it was impossible to say how they had survived—unexpected traces of those ancient medieval mysteries in which the last vestiges of the old mythology are seen merging into the newly risen Christianity.

When the booth was full, the showman would turn round in his pay-desk, stick his head and shoulders through an aperture in the canvas, above which hung a gong, and, with one eye on his takings and the other on the show, begin his commentary on the action.

The curtain went up to reveal a stage on a level with the heads of the audience, quite like the stage of a proper theatre, with wings and backcloth. First of all, down the semblance of a river winding through a wild and rocky landscape, palely glimmering (doubtless

119

Styx or Acheron, since the dog Cerberus was chained to the bank), a boat came floating, steered by Charon and loaded with shades. And there it all was, the thing great nations have believed in and dreaded! . . . Then, without a pause, and doubtless to avoid a waste of scenery, another boat appeared, rowed gaily by a child with wings, while in the stern sat an old man with a scythe; and the showman, lounging in his window, would announce: "Love makes Time pass!" Then the boat reappeared, crossing in the opposite direction now; and this time the old man was rowing, and the child sat sadly in the stern: "Time makes Love pass."

Then, to hide the change of scene, a white curtain was lowered for a moment, reducing the depth of the stage; and against this screen satirical scenes were shown in silhouette: a rich man's funeral, with a plenitude of priests; a poor man's funeral—a modest bier followed by a dog. When at last the curtain rose once more it disclosed a black hell of horrific aspect, shot with bright lights.

Beside an enormous cauldron stood a great devil, all red, taloned, and horned. His eyes, jaws, arms (these grasping a pestle) were all articulated. The damned filed before him (and during this scene the showman himself addressed the judgement seat, calling the devil "Messire Satan"; and the devil worked his jaws as he dispensed his judgements): the false magistrate, recognizable by his cap and gown; the drunkard, still hiccoughing; the wicked rich man; and then, unexpectedly, preceding Dom Basile (the discreet image of a wicked priest, whose misdeeds were left to the imagination), a little pastry-cook came sliding along the invisible grooves of the stage, one hand clutching a cake, the other—oh, irreverence!—scratching his behind; and finally, the most popular figure of all for whom the crowd had been eagerly waiting: Mademoiselle Crinoline, the picture of elegance, the personification of feminine coquetry and fashionable absurdities. Then a very tiny devil's acolyte took an enormous pitchfork and with it removed, one after the other, her beautiful hat, her wig, the padding of her breast, and finally her superb crinoline, beneath which—and how the children laughed!—a young student was found hiding. And then one by one the various figures were tossed into the cauldron with the cry: "Into the copper you go!" each dispatched to the accompaniment of vigorous bangs on the gong, which made everybody jump. And the devil, Messire Satan, setting all his jointed parts in motion, simultaneously rolled his eyes, ground his teeth, lashed his tail, and pounded at his cauldron from which fierce flames were leaping.

After a short interval there followed The Temptation of St. Anthony. This opened with the hermit, a marionette worked by strings and intended to be seen only in profile, praying outside his hermitage, his pig by his side. Then he got up and walked; and every time he raised his leg there also rose into the air, slightly trembling as it did so, an arm bent at a right angle and ending in an open hand—for leg and arm were operated by one and the same string. Then ensued a conversation with the pig. And when at last Prosperpine, the Devil's wife, the Queen of Hell, appeared upon the scene, she would frequently arrive back to front by mistake; she always emitted a curious kind of neigh, partly to terrify the hermit, partly because what she had to offer him was more than a little awkward to put into words. She would retire almost at once, however, and when she had gone a group of six imps would appear, and all sing teasingly and persistently, though actually only with one voice, of course (and every now and then all six would hurl themselves in concert at the pig, or St. Anthony, or the hut, their soft, inanimate legs just brushing the stage):

> Let us demolish, let us demolish
> The hermitage, the hermitage;
> Let us demolish, let us demolish
> St. Anthony and his pig!

At last, unexpectedly, the pig's tail would burst into flames and set fire to the hermitage; St. Anthony would flee in desolation only to return at the moment of his apotheosis. Then, upright in a sort of skiff entwined with flowers, he soared slowly heavenwards, dispensing blessings as he went.

This would be played alternately with the Passion Play. Here not one of the famous traditional scenes was omitted. Pontius Pilate, Pilate's wife, the traitor Judas,

St. Peter (and the cock to crow three times), all were there; and, to finish up with, the good thief and the bad thief crucified on either side of Christ.

Sitting in the front row of the reserved seats between a very serious Aunt Aurore and an attentive Jeannette, Marie-Armande, feeling rather as she felt in church during a Good Friday sermon on the Passion, was really moved when Jesus on the Cross cried out in piteous tones: "I am thirsty!" and a Roman soldier held up a sponge on the point of his lance, saying: "There, take a drink of that!"

4

ONCE A WEEK the ladies of the Tabernacle Charity
would meet in the work-room at the bishop's palace.
Marie-Armande would often go too, usually with her
mother, but sometimes with her governess—for now
she was having lessons from an elderly spinster called
Mademoiselle Cazotte, who also taught two or three
other little girls from the pious families of the town.

They would make their way down by the side of a
small courtyard overlooked by the outbuildings and
containing a chicken-house. Thence, by way of broad
wooden steps which later turned into a spiral staircase
leading up to the attic floor, they arrived at the work-
room. This was a large mansard attic, roasting hot in
summer, in winter always cold despite the stove; the
walls were quite bare and the only furniture consisted
of chairs, foot-stools, four cupboards, and a long trestle-
table. Round this table, in small groups of two or
three, with marked intervals between the groups, sat
the ladies at their needlework, while at the far end
Mademoiselle de Polyso, who presided over these
meetings, sat surrounded by the ladies of her committee. Behind her on the wall was a bracket with an
image of the Virgin garlanded with roses.

Here the work begun at home was finished off, some of it sent in by members living in the country or in small neighbouring towns. Here they hemmed, lined, mounted, sewed on braid. And nothing could have been stranger than to see these devout and sombrely apparelled ladies handling great piles of silks of a richness and magnificence forbidden us to-day, and which might have been destined for some fête or masquerade: brocades, satins, damasks, all in the strongest and most sumptuous colours—crimsons, purples, greens and blacks and whites. Here too they made ordinary Communion-cloths and altar linen—that is to say, corporals and purificators, batiste squares used respectively for receiving the chalice when it is placed on the altar and for drying the hands when Communion is over, these being trimmed with cheap narrow lace.

The mistress of the works, Madame Quoniam, accompanied by her adjutant, Mademoiselle Chantriot, would walk round the long table carrying stuffs, thimbles, reels of silk of every colour, heavy balls filled with lead beneath which the material was slid to smooth it, and gold and silver braid. With an air of great importance she would answer the inquiries of some humble-looking person, sitting solitary and apart, and plying her needle assiduously without ever speaking all through the session, like a daily needlewoman, and now murmuring her question in a low voice as though ashamed of being forced to ask. When any article was finished, Madame Quoniam would come and remove it, fold it up, and place it in a cupboard.

The ladies would often already be at work when Mademoiselle de Polyso arrived. At once they would all rise and hurry towards her with affectionate cries of welcome: "Our dear president! . . . How are you, dear Mademoiselle?" She would walk down the room, answering them all, and looking round to see who was present. And if she saw someone who had not been for several weeks, she never omitted a gentle reproach:

"Here's someone who's been unfaithful to us!"

Or she would jokingly pretend not to recognize her, because, as she said, it was so long since she had last seen her. Then they would have a prayer, and set to work and conversation again, exchanging views on the latest preacher, or on a retreat, or paying each other compliments which either party would receive with becoming modesty:

"But you are so good, so devout!"

"No, no! I do it all for Our Lord!"

Or—"Don't praise me. Poor things, I do it for them!"

And the gentle murmur of conversation would continue uninterrupted save for an occasional sound of footsteps on the stairs or the bang of a door slamming. From time to time a cock would crow in the silence outside. Or there would be a sudden crunching of wheels on the gravel of the main courtyard; the bishop was returning. Madame Quoniam, whose dumpy silhouette might have been seen continually passing and

126

repassing the curtainless windows, through the tiny panes of which one caught a distant glimpse of the great grey bulk of the cathedral, would stop to look down into the courtyard, where the bishop had now been set down at his own door and where the carriage was now driving away. It was a large courtyard, planted with trees and surrounded with high battle-mented walls: in the centre, melancholy wooden stands bare of plants surrounded an old and mossy stone basin from which the water had long since drained away.

Half-way through the afternoon Mademoiselle de Polyso would rap her knuckles on the table for silence and announce that they would have a little reading; some lady would then read aloud from the *Lives of the Saints*, choosing the saint appropriate to the day, or perhaps a few pages from a devotional work of a piety so exalted that it seemed intended only for those already in a state of grace. The reading over, Mademoiselle de Polyso would beg̱ to say her Rosary and the ladies would all respond as they sewed away.

As the afternoon drew to an end and the ladies prepared to go Jeannette would arrive to help tidy up. Mademoiselle de Polyso would see each lady to the door, and as soon as one had gone she would remember something particular she had meant to say to her; and, talking to one and clutching another in reserve by the arm, she would send Jeannette hurrying off after a third whose departure she had overlooked.

As the winter wore on the piles of finished articles in the cupboards grew ever larger and the beautifully written lists nailed inside the doors longer. Finally, sometime in March, they would hold an exhibition of work in the diocesan hall, before sending it off to any clergy who had appealed to Mademoiselle do Polyso or the head of the Charity in the course of the past year. The various articles were displayed round the walls on sheets hung over the grey, moulded panelling, or else set out on muslin-covered tables; and every year there was one example of what the ladies called "church adornments"—that is, a complete set of chasuble, stole, maniple, chalice veil, and burse, which, embroidered in violent colours, never failed to excite remark. This was the work of an old nobleman, the Chevalier de Jausselin, who lived on the outskirts of the town, an invalid and not quite right in his head, who spent his whole life in embroidery. On the day of the opening ceremony, as the bishop passed from table to table blessing the work to right and to left, the ladies and guests in his train would point out the famous "adornments" to each other and smilingly commiserate the unhappy curé to whom they would be allotted. After the blessing they would go round again at leisure. Sometimes Mademoiselle de Polyso would halt in front of a chasuble or stole of white silk and explain in a low voice that it had been made from a wedding-dress, and name the young girl who had offered it thus to the Charity.

Next day—and on these occasions Marie-Armande's

co-operation was always in request, so that she generally brought a friend as well, or her cousin, Olympe de Trannes—Mademoiselle de Polyso would return to the bishop's palace to do up the parcels and send them off. But actually all she did was sit and chat placidly with a little group of ladies while Madame de Quoniam, Mademoiselle Chantriot, and Jeannette turned themselves into packers and snipped, wrapped, and tied, every now and then putting a knee to a parcel to pull the string tight. At intervals Madame Quoniam would consult a list and read out a name and address; and then Marie-Armande, seated at a little table before a large bundle of labels, would write:

"Monsieur le Curé . . . . . . Care of . . . . . ."

It was the retreat, however, even more than the exhibition, that kept Mademoiselle de Polyso busy and caused her worry. This took place for one week in every year, and always in the same church which, complete with beadle, acolyte, and *Suisse*, was lent for this period to the Tabernacle Charity in accordance with the terms of a convenient parish legacy: here were held all the different services which go to make up a retreat (Mass in the morning, followed by a sermon, and in the evening another sermon, followed by Benediction), all designed for the spiritual improvement of the members of the Charity. All day long between services, but particularly on the last day but one, the priest would hear confession; and on the last day, which was always a Sunday, there was a solemn

Benediction in the cathedral after vespers. On the success of the retreat depended the success of the collection taken after this final ceremony; and this was the Charity's principal source of income. Thus months beforehand Mademoiselle de Polyso would start trying to decide which ladies should be asked to take the collection, each of whom, moreover, had to be accompanied by a gentleman. She would tire herself out with calls and inquiries. The importance of those she asked depended largely on her desire to secure them. There were some with great reputations as collectors: such-and-such a lady, for instance, was simply wonderful, and if she went round with such-and-such an escort a rich harvest might safely be expected—for the gentleman in question never put less than a hundred francs in the plate. Then there were the vocalists to be decided on. Sometimes, at Communion Mass, Monsieur de Chappes would consent to sing the Credo. But the most important thing of all was to secure a really good preacher.

Mademoiselle de Polyso would confer with the director of the Charity, the Abbé Tourasse, one of the cathedral vicars, and he would advise her to interview such-and-such a priest in their own diocese, or to write to such-and-such a monastery. And every year, to provide fresh interest, the preacher, who was nearly always one of the regular clergy, was chosen from a different order: according to the state of the Charity finances he was a Jesuit, a Capuchin, a Lazarite, or a

Dominican—for the remuneration offered the priest who preached the retreat (presented as a gift in the sacristy after the final sermon) varied with his order, his reputation, and his grade, a Superior costing much more than a plain monk.

If they had had a preacher of mark one year, for the next they generally fell back on the Abbé Tourasse. But if they had a renowned orator coming they would talk of it for months beforehand.

"I think you will be very pleased with the Father who is coming this year," Aunt Aurore would remark mysteriously, "Monsieur l'Abbé speaks most highly of him."

It was he, indeed, who put the preacher up for the whole period of the retreat. And sometime during the week Mademoiselle de Polyso was sure to receive a visit from Madame Tourasse, the Abbé's mother, a good old body in a black bonnet, who bore herself humbly, as became her condition, and proudly, as became her position of mother of one of the cathedral vicars. She would always begin—for it was she who ran her son's household—by bemoaning current high prices and the difficulty of existing at all, complaining that they were quite unable to entertain their guest in a fitting way. And Mademoiselle de Polyso, who knew very well what Madame Tourasse would be at, would listen shrewdly, amusedly, and pityingly, without saying a word to help her out.

"What can you expect?" Madame Tourasse would

sigh. "Poor man, he is so exhausted after preaching! Really, he needs something better than our poor fare! For we, you know, live simply on eggs and milk!"

So, Mademoiselle de Polyso understood. That very evening she would send round to the Abbé's with jars of the vegetables preserved so successfully by Jeannette every summer, to which she would add various dainties, such as four or five pots of jam, choice fruit from her store, and a bottle of old wine from her cellar, which she herself never touched.

On the Monday morning, when the retreat began, everybody would exchange comments as they came out of church. Mademoiselle de Polyso, importantly stationed in the porch, would catch her little flock as they went out.

"Well," she would demand, "and what do you think of the Father?"

And as they departed in twos and threes some of the elderly spinsters and old ladies of the Charity would agree that he was a success; others would recall the Fathers of past years—for they cherished their memories of preachers as others cherish memories of actors or opera singers. Mademoiselle Cazotte, for instance, preferred the Lazarite who had preached the year before, declaring that he had been more richly endowed with unction.

"Now this one," she said, "would drive us up to Heaven with a knife in our ribs!"

And they would make a little gentle fun of her and tease her.

"Oh, oh! Mademoiselle Cazotte always did like unction!"

If the Father was not a success Mademoiselle de Polyso would be in despair. And going home with a velvet bag containing the daily offertory, already counted in the sacristy, she would confide to Madame de Chappes that really these women were impossibly difficult to please.

"And I put myself to endless trouble," she would add, "to find somebody they will like."

The final sermon, given in the cathedral, always drew a crowd of people. In the vast spaces of the cathedral the Father seemed very unlike the Father they had known in their own little church; he looked smaller, and at the same time his voice seemed stronger and more vibrant. Dropping the intimate tone in which, up to now, he had exhorted them, he would speak out before this different, larger congregation in bold, oracular tones. They felt he was giving them now a carefully prepared and calculated bit of oratory.

Just before the end of Vespers they would hear the *Suisse's* halberd thumping somewhere down below, and then, almost before they could see how he had got there, the Father would appear kneeling in the pulpit high above them, barely visible in the light of the copper lamps ranged at intervals along the pillars. Only a small, round dark head above a white surplice could be seen as he covered his face with his hands, apparently lost in prayer. But when the canons and seminarists had conducted the bishop to the place he occupied during the sermon, directly facing the pulpit, the Father would rise and begin to speak. And if he was popular the congregation would gaze up at him with avidity, feasting their eyes on him as upon some fleeting comet, too soon to vanish and never more be seen.

As he entered on his peroration the four sideswomen would rise from their seats below the pulpit and march down to the main doors, preceded by four beadles, followed by their four cavaliers, and spaced out by the length of their respective trains. Seated in the arm-chairs and prie-dieu placed on either side of the doors, they would spread out the money already collected on their plates, and to this their cavaliers, bound to their sides while the ceremony lasted, would discreetly add a folded bank-note. Then two of the ladies would rise, and, still accompanied by their escorts, bring their own offerings to the other two; and these in turn would rise and reciprocate.

By now the congregation would be leaving. The bishop, in the process of being majestically escorted home by his clergy, would pause and deposit a substantial offering with each of the four ladies, extending his ring for them to kiss; the clergy merely contributed smiles. Behind them followed a crowd of the faithful, all trying to fight their way to the particular collector to whom they had promised their contribution: some, trying to get from one to another, could barely edge through the crowd of people pouring out. And the tinkle of coins falling in the plates grew duller and more muffled as the money piled up. Every now and then a respectably dressed servant with hat and black gloves would present a coin and a visiting-card both clutched together (or sometimes the coin would have been slipped into a nick in the card), murmuring: "From Madame . . . ," giving her mistress's name. The last of the faithful having departed, the beadle would come and close the great doors and the place would return to its emptiness. But for a long time even after that the carriages of the four collectors would be seen standing before the tall outer portal, and as night came on the coachmen lit the lamps.

One year the preacher was extraordinarily successful. Everyone talked about him. Even the gentlemen, over dinner in the evening, showed an interest in his daily exhortations, and many of them even proposed going to hear him. This was Father de Lister, a Jesuit who had not long been appointed Superior of the dozen or so members of the Saint-Loup community. His features were angular and fine-drawn, the nose prominent, and a startling pallor revealed the struggle between his nature and the rules that bound it. He spent himself in virulent attacks, in brutal apostrophes, hurled with undisguised contempt at all these pious ladies so used to being handled carefully.

"Do you really imagine," he cried one day, speaking of repentance, "that a confessor enjoys being shut up in a little box to listen to your disgusting sins and inhale your unpleasant smells?"

The good ladies were shocked and thrilled. When he touched on any questionable subject—and there were singularly many that year, a fact which attracted quite a crowd of young ladies—he would invariably invoke the Virgin Mary and the Holy Ghost first, in a voice that shook with passion and humility. Sometimes, again, he made jokes: and Aunt Aurore, hearing a ripple of discreet laughter run through the congregation, began to fear for her preacher's success. The Abbé Tourasse himself, seated in the first stall of the choir and half turned towards the pulpit, could not restrain a smile, but it was the slightly bitter smile of a man who knows such popularity to be beyond his reach and who can envy a brother's success while still despising the means by which it is achieved, condemning these as degrading and cheap.

One day the Father announced that he would receive confessions from the next day on, and well before the appointed hour there was a crowd round his confessional. Madame de Chappes, desirous of breaking the monotony of the Abbé Tourasse's rather uninspiring direction, determined to try the Father's. But instead of the dreaded censor she had been expecting she found an angel of gentleness, kindness, and pity; who called her not "My child" but, affectionately, "My sister."

And as a result she took him for her adviser, forsaking the Abbé Tourasse. Not long afterwards Marie-Armande's little brother, Bernard, although he had started his studies with the Oblates at Saint-Loup, was suddenly sent to Paris to continue them under the Jesuits.

5

ONE OF AUNT AURORE'S childhood friends, Mademoiselle Hortense Oguet, who lived in a little town not far away, lost her mother and was suddenly left alone and not very well off; so Mademoiselle de Polyso, pleading that to do what she asked would be an act of charity, persuaded her to come and live with her. They had the same habits and the same tastes, and led precisely the same life. Every morning they could be seen setting out for Mass, turning either to the right for the Franciscan Convent (and Aunt Aurore, as Superior of the Third Order, was very much at home there) or to the left for the cathedral; in either case they walked side by side, followed by Jeannette carrying the foot-warmers. All three wore voluminous cloaks, identical in pattern though differing in quality, and the two ladies kept theirs hugged round them against the chilly air. Mademoiselle de Polyso's was of a beautiful fine cloth lined with miniver; Mademoiselle Oguet's was of merino, wadded and trimmed simply with a modest strip of fur; while Jeannette's was of cinder-coloured molleton trimmed with the same material of which her bodice, petticoat, and skirt were made—a form of clothing which had never varied as long as anyone had known her, so that one was tempted to think that she herself was made of grey wool too.

When the two ladies returned they would find the dining-room table already laid (for Jeannette would have got back before them to do this and to change her black bonnet for a frilled white cap) with the great white porcelain coffee-pot with its broad gilt rings, the sugar-bowl to match, a plate of buttered rolls (the plaited sort), and two napkins of fine linen lying folded each beneath a silver ring. Mademoiselle Oguet poured out for Aunt Aurore, first the hot milk which Jeannette had just brought in, then the coffee; and Mademoiselle de Polyso, watching the mixture, would urge her to pour in more coffee:

"Go on, go on. It should be the colour of a Capuchin."

They both had a weakness for excessively sweetened coffee, and both were equally unwilling to confess the number of lumps they put in. So each would plunge her hand to the bottom of the sugar-bowl, swiftly drop most of the handful into her cup and then, as they went on talking together, with an air of sudden hesitation, of thinking—"Now did I put in three lumps, or was it two?" let the two or three last lumps in her hand drop deliberately into the cup.

Quite soon they would go out again, often to hear another Mass. Indeed, if they happened to be invited to a funeral or a wedding, they would sometimes thus attend several Masses in one day and be delighted at their good fortune. In the afternoon they were off to church again. There was always a pretext of one sort or another for some kind of religious exercise, if not in the cathedral, then in one of the neighbouring chapels —the multitudinous ceremonies of the various brother-hoods—retreats, novenas, triduum—all according to season—and then the customary May devotions and the prayers during the Octave of All Saints' or Advent or for the Feast of St. Joseph, which went rather unnoticed since this occurred during Easter. Nor did they ever fail in their daily celebration of Holy Communion, calling on God Himself in one or other of His numerous dwellings, now at the Franciscan convent, now at the cathedral, sometimes at the Chapel of the Good Shepherd where the Abbé Tourasse was confessor and thus always accessible if they had anything to say to him. It was there that they spent a part of every Saturday afternoon preparing for their weekly confession. And on their way to or from church they would often pay a brief call, do some little errand, or make a few trifling purchases.

The moment they got home from one of these excursions (and sometimes they would be at home for a quarter of an hour, sometimes for half an hour, sometimes for longer) they would take up their work at the point where they had laid it down, interrupting it on occasion to continue some pious reading begun that morning or the day before; either that, or they told their beads. Then, at the chiming of a little bell, up they would get again, put down their work and set off once more for church. And because otherwise they would have had to be constantly redoing their hair—for their false fronts, blue-black in the case of Mademoiselle de Polyso, red-gold in the case of Mademoiselle Oguet, were easily disarranged—they made a point of keeping their hats on all day long, from the moment they first put them on in the morning to go to early Mass to the moment they retired to bed for the night. Thus nobody who called was ever astonished to find the two ladies (in summer in the little drawing-room or the garden, in winter in Mademoiselle de Polyso's own room, hermetically sealed, with a wood fire damped down with tan) sitting facing one another over their needlework, their faces framed with identical black satin bonnets, the strings of which they would pin up behind only on the hottest days of summer.

On Thursdays Mademoiselle de Polyso scarcely went out at all, for Marie-Armande still came to spend the afternoons with her. And as always when she was at home no caller was ever refused. There would be various ecclesiastics, lady members of the Charity, relatives who called Aunt Aurore by her Christian name and were addressed in the same way by her, sellers of the work come to choose tapestries, embroideries, and laces. And in addition to these, always at the same time every year, the time of the retreat, the Abbé Tourasse would arrive with the preacher for the year—a Dominican in his great white habit, or a barefoot Capuchin. Sometimes, too, the parish priest would suddenly pay two or three visits in rapid succession, but this was only when he had a favour to ask. He invariably addressed Mademoiselle de Polyso with a flow of high-sounding compliments upon her virtues, her piety, her charity, following this up immediately with some little joke pretending to minimize—though actually it crowned—the praises which all the while she was doing her best to ward off, gently, with little murmurs of protestation.

"When the time comes for you to go to Heaven," he was fond of saying (and Mademoiselle Oguet, whom this opening would always plunge into delighted and admiring hilarity, would emit a succession of little sneezing cries), "I shall creep in under your hoops!"

And sometimes Jeannette would suddenly appear with a scowl on her face to announce the arrival of Mademoiselle Poire. Mademoiselle Poire was an old maid of forty or so, a member of every charity going and also of the Third Order, which allowed her to count herself a spiritual daughter of Aunt Aurore. Mademoiselle de Polyso would have her sent up, but not without Jeannette's trying to find some good reason why she should not be received: "You will only tire yourself, Mademoiselle," she would say, or "This is the third time she's been here this week!" The visitor would enter with a rapturous expression on her face, her hat inevitably half sliding off, black eyes blazing, arms outstretched. Throwing herself at Mademoiselle de Polyso's feet and kissing her hands (she would have

142

kissed her black cloth slippers had she dared), she would greet her as: "My Mother!" Marie-Armande would slip out at this, and as she shut the door she would hear some effusion of this kind:

"My Mother, I have fallen back into sin! The Tempter encircles me like a raging lion!"

But when it came to it the lapse would prove to be no more than a little quarrel, an acid retort, or an over-hasty judgement. And once there was a highly sinister affair of a lye-washing machine lent to a friend and there come unsoldered—all of which was not perhaps very evidently connected with the high spirituality of the Order to which they belonged. While Aunt Aurore played the affectionate, scolding mother, Mademoiselle Poire, still kneeling on the carpet, never ceased talking away with extreme volubility and in tones of utter despair. At other times—and with no less excitement than she displayed in her despondency —she would come simply to thank Aunt Aurore for some piece of advice.

Once a month Aunt Aurore would ask Marie-Armande to come and meet her at the seven o'clock Mass at the Franciscan Convent, a Mass said for the defunct members of the Tabernacle Charity.

The chapel, bare and clean, was remarkable only for a large grille which formed the far end behind the altar; in the centre of this, flanked with bunches of real flowers, was an opening for a monstrance, which was thus also visible from the interior of the private chapel of the nuns. The Order had, in fact, been founded for perpetual adoration, and thus the Host was always exposed to the gaze of the nuns.

There would never be more than a dozen or so worshippers at that early hour, yet one had a feeling that there were many more. Although absolute silence reigned one was conscious of invisible presences behind the grille. And indeed it sometimes happened (but very rarely, and only in wet weather, or at a change of season) that muffled coughs could be heard; and one year there were frequent sudden fits of hollow coughing, invariably from the same person. And Aunt Aurore explained:

"One of the poor little Sisters has consumption."

In winter it would be scarcely day when Marie-Armande set out to Mass, accompanied by one of the maids. The early morning air would be cold and misty; in the cathedral square the shops would just be opening. When she came to the house of her cousin, Olympe de Trannes, Marie-Armande would ring, having warned her the day before that she would be calling for her; and she would be ready and waiting, and would open the door at once and appear in her modest black dress and her fur toque, with her muff held up to her mouth to keep out the cold, foggy air. Then, quickening their pace, the two young girls would hurry off to the convent. Sometimes they arrived a little late.

And until they were safely there Mademoiselle de

Polyso would be in a fidget, wondering whether they were coming or not. But soon the two cousins would slip unobtrusively into their places in the row behind her, and Marie-Armande would lean forward, and whisper:

"Here we are at last!"

And Mademoiselle de Polyso would nod to show that she had heard and then silently pass them the foot-warmers.

After the Elevation, and for the Benediction, the congregation would join in the familiar tunes, their thin and feeble tones rising to the accompaniment of the harmonium. And as not one of them was sufficiently courageous to make a start it was invariably the organist, an old organist who played for them out of sheer kindness of heart, who started the hymn when the proper moment came, and if the volume of singing was too scanty he would join in himself, his loud masculine voice rising and drowning those four or five tentative feminine ones.

At the end of Mass practically all the congregation would take Communion. And since he was the only man in the place, and since in church men come before women, the organist would lead the way. Arms folded, his handsome and consciously artistic head held well up, he would stride forward, a solitary figure, preceding by some paces Mademoiselle de Polyso, stately and unhurried, who in turn was followed by Mademoiselle Oguet like a little shadow; and behind her in no particular order straggled the rest of that meagre flock of the faithful.

During the course of the service the lay-sister sacristan never ceased moving about the chapel; she put out the Communion-cloth, she took the collection, and then, a little before the Benediction, she might be seen emerging from the sacristy with an object like the parasol of some Oriental princess, a sumptuous white silk umbrella with gold tassels. This she would hand to the lay-brother, who was none other than the convent gardener, a little fat old man with a kind face and very well-scrubbed hands. In the shelter of this parasol-canopy the officiating priest passed behind the altar, painfully clambered up on to a stool, and took down the monstrance, which he placed at the foot of the ciborium.

And now the lay-sister emerged from the sacristy once more, this time carrying a heavy branched candlestick with glittering, tinkling crystal lustres, and all its candles lit. She moved quickly and silently forward, cupping her hand to screen the half-dozen flames all wavering backwards as she moved and shedding a rosy light on her face framed in the black ruches of her hood. She bowed to the altar, set down the candlestick, bowed again, went and fetched a second candlestick precisely like the first, and then took up her position for the Benediction with the ladies in the front row. At this moment the old organist would suddenly start swaying backwards and forwards on his stool as he worked the harmonium pedals. With eyes half-closed and fingers wandering over the keyboard, and with every appearance of improvising, he would begin to play the first of the three motets he had played at every Benediction for the past forty years.

After the priest at the altar had said the prayer for the Pope the Tantum Ergo came at last. This, according to the tune it was sung to, had various appellations which everybody knew. Thus there was the Seminary Tantum Ergo, the Cathedral Tantum Ergo, and the Abbé Prunier Tantum Ergo. And as the congregation chanted the final words of the responses to the prayer for the Pope, the organist would turn half round first to one side then to the other, and mutter forcibly and malodorously to the ladies round the harmonium (and although he purposely lowered his voice it echoed loudly in the profound stillness of the chapel):

"Cathedral Tantum Ergo!"

6

WHEN MARIE-ARMANDE knew the four rules of arithmetic, had learnt to spell after a fashion, and had recited for the second time the whole of her Manual of Holy History, her Manual of French History, and her Manual of Geography, Mademoiselle Cazotte announced that her pupil's education was complete. At Madame de Chappes' request, however, she continued her visits as before (or at least as far as her engagements permitted, and these were few enough), acting still as Marie-Armande's governess or kind of lady companion. She it was who accompanied the young girl on her walks, or took her to Mass or Communion or to a party of young people, returning to fetch her in the evening. And sometimes in the afternoons, when Marie-Armande had nothing to do, Mademoiselle Cazotte would ask Madame de Chappes' permission to take her to see one of her own friends, some old woman devoted to one of those obscure little charities known only to the dozen or so persons who belonged to it, and for whom Mademoiselle Cazotte recruited helpers. There was, for instance, a charity organized by a Madame Corpelet, whose son was a missionary, exclusively to provide woollen socks for priests departing

148

for abroad. But more often they would go to a work-room run by an old maid of sixty or so, Mademoiselle de Linfernat, a pensioner at the Redemptionist Convent.

She was president of the Clothing Charity, which made clothes for the savage tribes that the missionaries went out to convert, savages of unspecified nationality, living nobody quite knew where, and visualized by all these old ladies (with an innocent memory, perhaps, of the fake savages seen at fairs who eat live rats behind the bars of their cages) as having rings in their ears and noses, arrows in their hands, and no clothes on at all apart from a feathered headdress.

Identical in cut and varying only in size (there were three stock sizes: one for men, one for women, and one for children), these garments were strongly reminiscent of a herald's surcoat or a chasuble joined down the sides and with short sleeves added. Little odds and ends of every conceivable kind of material were arranged on the paper pattern until it was filled up, and the ladies vied with one another to produce the most variegated compositions. The results were mosaics of samples, odd lengths of old braid, remnants of dresses, scraps of chintz, and sometimes even bits of worn-out carpet. These scraps were arranged in a chequer-board pattern if they were small, or, if they were larger, quartered like a shield: the dress, that is to say, would be composed of four squares, one red, one yellow, one green, one black. Others would consist of only two colours, and even then as often as not one sleeve would be one colour and the other another; while to gratify feminine coquetry the women's dresses would have little posies of artificial flowers pinned on. But every single garment had, just above the heart, a little rosette of silver wire with a medallion hanging from it.

If anyone had been unusually successful in producing a confection even richer or more flamboyant than usual, it would be passed round to the accompaniment of delighted laughter and exclamations of:

"Well, just look at this! This must be for a chief at least!"

At the end of the meeting, when only three or four ladies remained, Mademoiselle de Linfernat would invite you to come and see her collection and conduct you to a dim little closet off her room where all these dresses were hanging. The visitors' cries of admiration would be as amused as they were genuinely admiring, and the little closet would resound with exclamations and praises.

"What a lovely dress!"

And sometimes, pulling one of the dresses out to show it better, Mademoiselle de Linfernat would remark:

"And this!—Look at this! I tell you, it's priceless!"

The first arrivals at these meetings were received quite like callers, with an interchange of compliments and polite inquiries. Then others would appear, and they would all settle down round a great round mahogany table and open their work-boxes and get ready to work; some brought theirs in their reticules, others in cloth bags. Those who had brought nothing with them would beg a needle and thimble. Then Mademoiselle de Linfernat would fetch her own work-box from a drawer, a little leather case lined with green silk, containing a thimble, a needle-case, and a pair of enamelled scissors. Spectacles or pince-nez would then be adjusted, and those who wore neither would lean far back and hold the needle at arm's length to keep it as far as possible from their eyes while they threaded it. Nor would they ever fail to congratulate Marie-Armande on her splendid sight, declaring they only hoped she would keep her young girl's eyes for many years to come.

Later-comers set to work at once, some even before they greeted Mademoiselle de Linfernat, who might be busy in the next room. She would reappear in due course with what looked like a scarecrow over each arm—dresses brought to show the non-initiate, or because one of the ladies had forgotten to finish something off, or simply to pack up and send off. And at once she would dole out bits of stuff for the newcomers to sew, and the momentarily interrupted conversation would gather way again.

Most of these ladies lived as pensioners with the Community; thus their gossip was principally confined to little incidents within the convent itself—the slamming of a door in the night, the howling of a dog.

If there had been a fire in the neighbourhood they would discuss it at length, each enlarging on her own impressions and how she had been startled out of her sleep. What went on in the town outside, chiefly among the clergy, they learnt from the ladies who were not pensioners like themselves.

Health, too, played an enormous part in their conversation, and remedies were freely exchanged.

At four o'clock a nun would arrive with two plates of insipid little cakes purchased at a neighbouring confectioner's. And before Mademoiselle de Linfernat was placed a saucer with two chocolates on it; that was the only nourishment the old lady would take until next morning.

Often during these afternoons one of the ladies sitting nearest the window would utter a faint cry and exclaim:

"Here comes the Father!"

And at once four or five of them would crowd round the window, quietly jostling, to catch a glimpse of the priest as he approached. He was the director of their charity, Father Polydoro, a fat Jesuit with a rubicund countenance and white hair; hat in hand, jovial and yet contemplative, he crossed the courtyard with his long strides.

From behind the curtain the ladies would anxiously speculate as to his destination. Would he come in to them? Or wasn't he going to Madame Perrot's perhaps —a neighbour who was unwell and unable to be with them to-day. No, he was turning to the right, making in their direction. At once they all went back to their places and sat quiet, listening: a heavy footfall echoed on the carpetless stairs. Their caller knocked; the youngest of the workers got up to open the door for him.

And as he crossed the threshold into the hall they could hear his powerful voice with its exaggerated stresses; he entered to accompaniment of little cries of joyous surprise.

Father Polydoro was greatly loved for his amusing ways and his affability and cheerfulness. He took part in all their little doings, was interested in everything everybody said and in every name that cropped up, whether it was known to him or not. In return he would relate a variety of anecdotes, usually of a humorous kind, recalling incidents that had occurred in other places, although he never specified these by name. He would always start off with a "Once when I was travelling abroad. . . . When I was preaching a retreat in a small town in the North—or the West. . . . At a certain conference of workers . . ." or simply, "When I was in Rome . . . ."

And so many different people were involved in so many different places that if one had added together all the circumstances suggested by these tales and the multitudinous situations they involved, the total would have been sufficient to fill several ordinary lives. Sometimes in a chaffing mood he was not above propounding a riddle or a conundrum. And if anyone hit on the right answer straight away she would pretend to be racking her brains for some moments before replying. But sometimes the problems were obscure to the point of insolubility. For instance—"A certain apple-tree," he would begin insidiously, "usually bore many apples; but one year it did not bear apples at all. What did it bear?" Then, shyly, some suggestion would be put forward. Pears, perhaps? Plums? The Father shook his head. They went on puzzling; they finally gave it up. And then, with gravely contained amusement, as though delighted by his own roguishness and wit, the Father produced the key: "That year the apple-tree did not bear *apples*," he explained, "it bore *one* apple!"

Further, to amuse the ladies, he would affect the deepest ignorance in face of all the sewing materials littering the table. And what an intimate delight it was for her whose pin-cushion or needle-case he singled out as the object of his nonsense!

"And this," he would say, holding up some unusual pin-cushion—made perhaps of little bran-filled cones arranged in the form of a star—"Is this a hat for the savages?"

And he would balance the pin-cushion on his head, sending his audience into ecstasies.

Suddenly his expression would become grave, and everybody, realizing that the time for laughing was over, would assume a serious air. Faces lengthened, hands were folded: and, sighing heavily, he would begin to expatiate on the joy there is in the saving of souls for the Good God, and in coming to the aid of the poor missionaries who undergo so many perils. At this point everybody would secretly be hoping for some tragic story of a missionary tortured to death or eaten alive, with all the horror of circumstantial detail. But such hopes were always vain. The Father confined himself to the vaguest generalizations, and these he retailed in monotonous tones, all gaiety gone from his eyes. He would talk of schools, of churches in the building, of the difficulties experienced by the Fathers in making themselves understood to these unhappy savages, of all the horrible diseases which decimated the little Christian band. . . . And sometimes as he spoke he would extract from his pocket a large black handkerchief, crumpled up in a ball, instinctively run his left thumb round the hem to the corner, pinch the monogram as though to make sure of its existence, look at it, turn the handkerchief over as though it were inside out, and blow his nose with a resounding blast.

7

THE YEAR BEFORE her coming out Marie-Armande suffered a great grief: her cousin, Olympe de Trannes, entered the Carmelite Convent. For some time it had been rumoured that she wanted to become a nun; but she had not confided her intentions to anyone, and at the parties and balls which she seemed to love so much her great beauty and gentle and lively nature made her a general favourite. Then one day, with no warning at all—only a month before she had been a bridesmaid at a wedding—it was known in the town that that very morning, after going to Mass with her mother, she had left for the Carmelite Convent where her little novice's trunk had been sent the day before. For many months nobody saw her again. Marie-Armande occasionally had news of her from Madame de Trannes; and she, though doing her best to comfort herself by thinking of her daughter's happiness, speaking of her now with a sort of resigned satisfaction, grew sadder and sadder after each of her rare visits to the convent.

Her novitiate over, Olympe declared that her resolution was unchanged, and fixed the date for taking the veil. She chose October 15th, St. Theresa's day, St. Theresa being the patron saint of the Carmelites.

Some days before this Marie-Armande received a letter from her written on white paper embossed with a cross surrounded by lilies. It was written in measured phrases, affectionate still, but cold, and signed prematurely with the name which henceforth would be hers: Sister Marie-Elizabeth of the Infant Jesus. Marie-Armande had recognized Olympe's handwriting on the envelope, and was astonished to find the letter signed with another name.

At noon on the day before the ceremony there was a luncheon-party in a room outside the cloisters at the convent, a gathering of all the novice's relations from far and near and of various intimate friends of her family. The meal consisted solely of eggs, vegetables, and milk dishes; the spinach, for instance, was not cooked with butter, but it tasted delicious nevertheless, and the recipe was a secret of the Community.

Monsieur de Trannes, speciously gay and cordial, and worldly even in these precincts, did the honours as though he had quite forgotten the reason for the gathering. And if they could have ignored the wretched setting of the bare room, the printed texts on the walls, and the lay-sisters moving to and fro, they might have imagined themselves back again at one of those familiar dinner parties at which, only a year ago, the novice had been present with her family.

For the last time she was wearing her own clothes, a dress she had worn in the outside world. But now it seemed to embarrass her. Her figure had filled out.

Her face, too, was more settled, as though refined by a sort of tranquil lack of consciousness. It was not the face they had known. Broad dark rings encircled the eyes which were still fresh and blue, and the mouth, once so firmly chiselled, had now a sort of insipid suppleness, giving her that expression of resignation and premature contentment peculiar to nuns.

With a pride so deep that it could only express itself in the guise of humility, she went on now to speak with perfect equanimity of matters often of a very painful kind, perceiving all the while with perfect clarity the effect she was producing and the emotion she was arousing. She cited various details of the rules she had observed during the past year and which would now govern her whole life. No meat was eaten at the convent. A Carmelite must never walk quickly, much less run; even threatened by the greatest danger she must not hurry. The daughters of St. Theresa must never sit down but only squat on their heels. They must never speak except in the hour of recreation; and permission to talk at table was given only twice a year, at Easter and on St. Theresa's day—and, in addition, whenever a new nun might arrive. And every day in the tiny cemetery they must remove a little earth from the spot which would be their grave. Constantly, night and day, two nuns would be praying in the chapel. . . . And she explained all she said indirectly, by referring at every point to St. Theresa herself: "St. Theresa," she always began, "wishes this, wishes that. . . . St. Theresa recommends . . ." She insisted, moreover, that the Carmelites were far from miserable; on the contrary, they enjoyed the most trivial things, as children do. When she had first arrived at the convent they had been full of eagerness to hear what was going on in the world outside. They had questioned her about present customs and fashions, even wanting to know what were the fashionable dances of the moment. And one Thursday, under the eyes of the Mother Superior herself, she had demonstrated in the garden one of the latest dances she had learnt. And then an old nun had made a diagram in the sand of the steps of one of the dances popular in her time. But now that she had ordered her bridal dress they were more excited than ever, full of questions as to style and trimming.

She herself had given long thought to it; and the month before, in conference with her mother and the dressmaker, she had settled it all, down to the smallest trimming, with all the meticulous care she had once devoted to her first ball-dress. And now in airy tones, which rang, however, a little false, affecting irrepressible frivolity for the last time, she complacently described what she would wear: first she had thought of having sleeves of such and such a kind, but the dressmaker had assured her that the fashion had changed since last year. And after lunch, alone for a moment with Marie-Armande, she confessed that she had had to put on her corset again that morning in order to wear ordinary clothes once more, and how glad she was to think that soon she would be rid of such things for ever, and how she pitied the poor things outside who would have to go on wearing them. But the trivial nature of such a confidence, coming at a moment when Marie-Armande had hoped they might recover something of their old-time intimacy, served only to mark more sharply than ever the difference between nun and old friend; and she had the feeling that for Olympe nothing at all was left of the childhood experiences they had shared in common, that for her all memory of the past was gone already.

The ceremony of taking the veil was to be at two o'clock on the following afternoon. But well before the appointed time the arrivals had begun. Carriage followed carriage up to the narrow convent porch as for a wedding, while high in the tower the little bell jangled away incessantly with a sound of discreet exultation. Women and young girls in fashionable clothes alighted from their carriages, bowed to acquaintances, accosted one another and exchanged remarks and greetings, falling silent as they passed down the short vaulted passage which led to the chapel itself.

Once inside all eyes were immediately focussed on the double gateway of wrought-iron which took up a whole panel to the left of the altar as far as the Communion-table; behind it hung a dark curtain. The more distant connections of the family were given seats quite close to those of the immediate family. Almost at once the sacristy door opened, and the priests filed out in their vestments (among them Marie-Armande made out Olympe de Trannes' confessor), preceding the bishop himself in cope and mitre, his crozier in his hand.

With his back to the altar, where bunches of white dahlias and chrysanthemums stood between the tall candlesticks, he seated himself on his raised throne, and to right and to left of him the priests took up their positions on a semicircle of chairs. Facing them, and very conspicuous, were a gilded chair and a cushioned prie-dieu hung with sumptuous hangings. Suddenly there was a faint grating noise from behind the grille, and the curtain was drawn back. All heads were raised and craned forward. Marie-Armande, who was sitting almost in front of the grille, could see a large, dimly lit room; two lines of kneeling figures stretched away from her; and in the space separating the two lines garlands had been laid out on the shining floor in a strange and incomprehensible rectangle; and there the grey forms knelt, motionless, faceless, like little pyramids of ashes.

At this moment the great door of the chapel opened; an invisible harmonium broke shrilly into a religious march, and to this deliberate rhythm, intended to sound triumphal, the procession slowly advanced. At its head, on her father's arm, was Mademoiselle de Trannes, and the other members of the family followed her in pairs. Her eyes were lowered beneath her veil trimmed with priceless lace—hereditary lace worn at their weddings by five generations of de Trannes and now to become the property of the convent; the orange-blossom, roses and tuberoses of the bouquet in her left hand gave out as she passed a heady perfume that brought to mind the bridal processions and society functions and balls which would never know her again.

Her father escorted her to the chair reserved for her and returned to his own place; and she remained kneeling beneath the impassive gaze of priests and congregation, many of whom had come simply for the spectacle. Her knees were buried deep in the soft cushion, and the long train of her dress, completely covered by the brittle and vaporous cloud of her veil, was spread out on the carpet behind her. It was all very like a wedding. But one looked in spite of oneself for any sign of a companion for this lonely bride; there was no companion: at her right hand, close beside her, a taper burned in a slender candlestick of silver.

Then a priest ascended the pulpit. Like everybody else, she too sat now; and on the other side of the grille the nuns also changed their positions. The priest pronounced a eulogy of the de Trannes family, expatiated at length on the beauty of the monastic life, and ended by recommending himself and all the congregation to the prayers of this new daughter of St. Theresa. Once again Mademoiselle de Trannes knelt down. And this was to be the last time in her life that she sat on a chair or knelt at a prie-dieu.

Then the bishop questioned her. And the silence of the congregation was profound as she pronounced the three vows, of obedience, of poverty, of chastity. Then, one after the other, he blessed the various pieces of apparel presented to him in a basket by an attendant Sister: that is to say, the veil, the gimp, the wooden crucifix, the girdle, and the rosary.

And when the attendant Sister had taken these away the procession reformed and left the chapel. Through the crowd which pushed out after it there ran a sort of shudder. Once again they passed down the vaulted passage (it was so close to the street that the noise of the traffic outside was clearly audible), and then, through a gateway kept closed as a rule but now opened wide, they passed into a little sanded court flanked on one side by great wooden doors. There they stopped to listen in the silence. Presently a slow, far-off chanting could be heard. As it drew nearer the double doors swung open. Still in two files, still veiled, the same grey phantoms they had glimpsed in the inner chapel advanced towards them, but visible now as they stood in the open air; at their head the Superior and two assistants bore a large crucifix of wood.

In that doorway they stopped. Mademoiselle de Trannes knelt down in the sand and her long moiré train glittered in the sun. Then she rose: deep sobs broke from her; she approached her father, who held her for a moment tightly to his breast; then her mother, then all her relations, embracing them one by one. Then, without any hesitation, she crossed the threshold. The Abbess took her hand, and the procession of phantoms reformed, carrying the living away.

When she had quite gone they returned to the chapel in no particular order, but for a long time the Carmelites' hall beyond the chapel remained empty: at the heart of the convent Sister Marie-Elizabeth of the Infant Jesus was assuming her habit and having her hair shorn. An interminable half-hour went by. Gradually the congregation began to talk among themselves. And the subject of every conversation was the new Carmelite's beauty. She was remembered at this or that party or ball; and some recalled that on her last appearance in society she had worn a dress of blue tarlatan with silver ears of corn in her hair. But now the chanting was heard again. In single file the nuns returned to their private chapel again, leading in their new companion in her serge habit, unveiled, her face calm—the only face in all those faceless ones— and somehow looking suddenly a little sallow, and with a curious sheen against the harsh white of the coiffe.

Hand in hand with the Abbess she approached the grille. The bishop advanced towards her. He intoned some questions in Latin; and she replied in the sad, monotonous Carmelite chant, made all the more moving by the intonations of a voice so familiar to them all. Then she lay down, her arms outstretched as though crucified, between the garlands forming the oblong space which represented her tomb: phantom-like forms detached themselves, carrying by the four corners a black sheet, and this they spread over her. The funeral service began, sung by the Carmelites, whose chanting alternated with the solemn chorus of the priests.

Meanwhile the interest of the congregation had begun to wane. This part of the ceremony, which the well-informed had said was the most moving, seemed to be something of a fraud. Curiosity was satiated; they thought only of getting away.

After the Benediction the nuns withdrew with a faint clicking of rosaries. And just as at a wedding the guests all file into the vestry, so now they made their way to the parlour: relations stood on one side of the double grille with its bristling spikes, on the other stood the new Carmelite beside the veiled and motion-less Abbess. In a soft and even voice she replied to their farewells, promising a prayer to some young girl, thanking someone else for having come, already seeming to confuse in a kind of general indifference close rela-tives, mere acquaintances who passed on with a greeting, and her old friends, who must call her "Sister" now. Never again, of all the people there (apart from her father and her mother, and even they would only see her through the bars of the grille) would anyone see her face.

Lying in bed that night Marie-Armande thought of

her cousin. And deep in her pillows, deep in the feather-bed raised high above the floor, she imagined the hard mattress on which at that very moment Sister Marie-Elizabeth was lying, fallen perhaps into that short slumber of the Carmelite which must end before dawn and which even then is often broken by midnight vigils in the chapel.

8

IT WAS AT THIS TIME that the death of the Dowager
Marquise de Chappes occurred. For eighteen months,
as was customary, they wore mourning for her. Then,
when this period was over, Madame de Chappes
embarked on the business of introducing her daughter
to the seven or eight families of whom Marie-Armande
knew only the younger members, since they were not
related to the de Chappes. Nobody had regular at-
home days; if one was at home one received callers
as they came. But on New Year's Day the drawing-
room would be opened, the fire lighted, the lamps lit
at night. And this exclusive little world was now
always ready to be called upon.

Marie-Armande was welcomed with complimentary
phrases at every house she visited. She was cross-
examined as to her tastes and occupations, always
with an eye to possible matches. Old ladies would
bring out their memories of her as a little girl. Others
declared how lucky they were to have her in their
houses now she was grown up. And everywhere she
went she met with nothing but politeness—a politeness
no longer met with nowadays, but the principle of
which was like a hidden core sustaining all classes of

society at a time when these still had their limits clearly defined; nowadays it is only met with in the restricted circle of an aristocracy, since only an aristocracy can stand aside from the inordinate spirit of envy which has overturned the world and still preserve a clear perception of its rank . . . a profound politeness which is simply a gesture of assent to the natural order of life, so that he who accepts his place in the midst of life and retains it unrebellious yet unresigned receives from Nature, who assigned it him, something of Nature's own impassivity and the serene indifference of her laws.

Even before she was eighteen Marie-Armande had been the subject of several attempts to draft a marriage project. The method of procedure was in every case the same. Some kinsman would invite Monsieur and Madame and Mademoiselle de Chappes specially to dinner or an evening party. There they would find themselves among acquaintances and friends, until, unexpectedly, some young man, quite strange to the town, with his mother or elder sister, would be placed next to Marie-Armande at table. As often as not the meeting would have no results; but sometimes the two families would begin to negotiate between themselves. Third persons would enter into correspondence; but rarely would they go so far as to ask Marie-Armande herself what she thought of the young man. Until, one day, at the instance of Father de Lister, Madame de Chappes got to know the wife of an officer of the garrison, a Lieutenant de Laignes. And some weeks later, at a ball, Mademoiselle de Chappes was introduced to the lieutenant's elder brother, Comte Antoine de Laignes. At first he seemed to her very old; but she knew she had to marry; all her friends did; and since she had no desires of her own apart from her parents', and since, moreover, he was rich, she replied in the affirmative when asked if she would care to be his wife. Then the Comte's sister—his father and mother were dead—Madame de Villedieu, arrived to make the official offer; and after the betrothal dinner, which was given at Saint-Loup, Monsieur and Madame de Villedieu had Mademoiselle de Chappes and her parents to stay with them at Monthuis. And there it was that Marie-Armande made the acquaintance of her future family, who all came originally from that part of the country.

The great house had a terraced garden running up to the edge of the steep slope on the narrow ridge of which the town was situated. Here they would stroll after dinner. The plain spread out below them stretched away as far as the eye could see, monotonous and vast. Monsieur de Laignes would point in the darkness— over there was the village of Fontaines with the Château des Menuls, which had come down to them on their mother's side; and there, beyond the forest which could just be made out as a dark, blurred mass, lay the Château de Laignes itself.

Before they left Monthuis Monsieur and Madame de

F*

Chappes went to the convent to call on Monsieur de Laignes' sister, who was a nun. Then they returned to Saint-Loup, where, a month later, the wedding took place in the cathedral. Monsieur de Laignes had invited his old nurse; and when the bridal procession came filing two by two into the huge nave, there she was in her black dress and her white peasant's cap, walking all alone behind the family.

After the service the Comte de Laignes introduced to his wife the various farmers who had come to see him married; and these apologized for absences—some for a sick father, some for a sick wife, some for a son. Then a grey little man with spectacles, whom Monsieur de Laignes received with marked kindness, came up and complimented the bride, stressing his devotion to the family: it was Monsieur Hotte, the schoolmaster of Laignes.

The old nurse had to go back the same evening. When she came to say good-bye to Monsieur de Laignes they talked together for a few moments. And with tears in her eyes she said she was sure now he would never come back to Laignes. The château had been shut up for seven years, and in all those seven years no one had ever visited it again, not even Madame de Villedieu, who lived so near. Without answering her directly Monsieur de Laignes did his best to reassure and comfort her, promising that on the contrary he would now be coming often. . . . And finally, like all peasants who will lose themselves in a wilderness of detail over even the most trivial matter, she launched into a description of how she would be returning. She was going with Cottenceau, the old farmer from Fontaines, and Monsieur Hotte. At Monthuis Cottenceau would leave them, going on to Fontaines, and she and Monsieur Hotte would take a carriage they had arranged to have sent out from Laignes. And she mentioned the name of the coachman; it was a new name to Monsieur de Laignes, but long familiar in the village, it seemed.

And as she talked away he followed her in his mind's eye on her journey. He pictured the road, the first houses of the village, the avenue leading up to the château, the château itself, the present state of which he found it hard to imagine. And as if in the midst of the ruins of a past already vanishing the only place which still seemed alive in his memory was the resting-place of the dead, suddenly he saw again the family chapel on its mound, half-hidden by trees. Then, as the old nurse prepared to depart, he gave her various commissions. And if any of his brilliant guests had happened to come in at that moment, they would have been astonished to hear him asking this old woman to keep a particular eye on the chapel and see that the place was decently kept up, that Masses were still said at the proper times, and that his parents' graves were kept always fresh with flowers.

CATHERINE DE LAIGNES

1

AFTER TOURING ITALY for two months, the Comte and Comtesse de Laignes established themselves in the mansion they had rented in the Cathedral square. During their absence the Marquise de Chappes had been putting things to rights for them, and now relations of the closest kind were at once established between the new household and the old; daily communication was maintained, and on both sides there was a constant display of respectful attention and affectionate solicitude. And since the new establishment continued without a break the habits of the old there was, between these people of such different ages, none of that ceaseless, bickering hostility which is found where insufficiency of means, diversity of tastes and origin, and a sudden rupture with the past on the part of the young people, all combine to bring parents and children confined to the same narrow circle (rarely by choice, almost always by necessity) to regard this tightening of bonds as the worst of all evils—bonds which should preserve, but which end by paralysing.

Monsieur de Laignes left his wife and mother-in-law to episcopal works of charity and education, on the committees and councils of which their names figured in various capacities, though they themselves were never seen at work-parties; and he, in imitation of his father-in-law, fell into that way of life for long pursued by idle, leisured men whose existence is sufficiently filled by the study of their own well-being, by a certain participation in municipal affairs and the work of local societies, and by the fulfilment of social duties. In winter he hunted. In summer he took the waters. When they were first married he had taken his wife on a short visit to the de Laignes' château. But she could not bear the vast, half-empty place, while he himself had been stirred by too many melancholy memories. They never went again. Like his father before him, whose habits he had blamed in the past, Monsieur de Laignes gradually came to relegate to Monsieur Hotte all the cares of management he had assumed on his brother Philippe's departure.

It was Monsieur Hotte now who did all the letting and selling, who collected all moneys, who renewed leases, undertook repairs, gave orders to the wood-cutters: so much, indeed, did his importance and authority increase throughout the district that nobody ever said now, in making a complaint: "I must speak to Monsieur le Comte about this," but always "I must ask Monsieur Hotte." And under cover of his employer he began to gratify his own hatreds and antipathies and to work for his own private interests—so-and-so should be dismissed; he was disloyal. So-and-so had suffered hindrances and set-backs; but he would be sure to pay next year. . . . Yet when the time came round the debtor would frequently fail to meet his liability, Monsieur de Laignes made no demands, and year by year the debts accumulated. But just this negligence on the part of their landlord fostered in the minds of those whom he imagined he was helping the idea that they could deceive him with impunity; and soon all the little dishonesties committed at his expense came to be regarded almost as legitimate. Certain of immunity, they took to marauding in his woods; neighbours began to cut down his trees from their side of the woods; his fish-ponds were deplenished. And to avoid the necessity for rigorous action Monsieur de Laignes closed his eyes to all this, assuring himself that he had good reasons for an indulgence which was really only powerlessness to intervene, and for this he was blamed by the very people who were profiting by this pilfering.

Meanwhile, as respect for the de Laigneses dwindled, so did all memory of the family fade, and others assumed the position they had vacated—secondary landlords, retired small officials from the town, and a handful of farmers from other parts of the country, who introduced new customs and ideas with their new methods of cultivation, while the bigger wages they offered all added to that changing spirit now becoming manifest among the peasants, who began to compare past and present to the detriment of the past. Some, for instance, would recall that in the old days the château had only paid labourers twelve sous a day and daily women ten. But they preferred to forget that they had also been taken care of all their lives, that their masters had regarded wages as the least part of their obligations, had indeed assumed endless further obligations on their behalf and had never ceased to pour into this village, which in the course of centuries had been brought into such close, willing, and fertile association with the family, as much and more than they received, utilizing for the general benefit the forces of which they were the guardians. Thus will a great tree live upon the earth it nourishes, and, as it grows with wise slowness, it draws out the riches of the earth, transforms them, and spreads them far and wide; and in time, though not in so apparent and immediate a way as in the recurring abundance of harvests, these fulfil their part, building up those lofty domes which have always aroused the envy of man in his littleness, his greed, and his impatience.

However, when it was a question of getting help or of obtaining a favour or a reference, Monsieur de Laignes still sprang to mind, and was never known to fail. And so from time to time letters would arrive at Saint-Loup with the Laignes postmark on their large yellow envelopes, the squared sheets of paper within expressing a persistent confidence in their master on the part of those to whom he meant nothing now but a vague sort of omnipotence, safely to be relied on and no more than was their due. Thus for the fiddler's son he obtained a position with the railway. To a nephew of the old nurse he lent money to buy a grocer's business at Monthuis. If his attention was called to any case of want he sent relief; he continued to pay his dues to the church. He paid for his pew and for the consecrated bread when it was his turn to provide it; and he regularly sent his ten francs for Palm Sunday, for all the world as though he still received the laurel branch —that symbol which in bygone days the sacristan had brought to the château, where it hung the whole year round above the great kitchen hearth. Since their father's death, moreover, the children had settled on their nurse, now helpless and returned to her parents' house in the village, an income which made her quite independent. For many years she had written every year to Monsieur de Laignes; but now it was her son, the priest of a neighbouring village, who gave him all her news.

She died one winter some time before the birth of the Comte and Comtesse de Laignes' first child. Not daring to show his grief to the world, a grief nobody could have shared with him, Monsieur de Laignes withdrew into himself and nursed his melancholy: for several days he thought of nothing but his nurse, her devotion to him, the grief she had doubtless felt at dying without seeing him again, she who had been so happy when in his student days he had returned to Laignes after long absence. And he heard again those

179

words he had so often heard before, which had flattered him then, which filled him now with emotion and regret:

"The Good God will punish me for it, but I love Monsieur better than my own son!"

When Catherine was born they sent for a sister of Jeannette's, Mademoiselle de Polyso's maid, to come and look after her; a good woman of fifty or so, who had just lost her husband and was left without means. And since she soon came to have far more to do with the little girl than did Madame de Laignes herself, it was Savine, her old nurse, whom Catherine in later years was to see in memory beside her mother. She came from a little township not far from Saint-Loup, and brought with her a whole store of stories, songs, and country proverbs; and so, indirectly, this rustic, peasant soul brought this little town-bred girl into contact with nature. It was through the sayings of her nurse that Catherine learned to recognize the progress of the seasons, to foretell the weather. Every year at the same time the same circumstances brought forth the same maxims. On December 13th, for instance, as evening fell, Savine never failed to observe:

"St. Luce's day; each day is a flea-hop longer now."

And later, on St. Anthony's day, she would declare:
"Now the days expand like a monk at dinner."

On Palm Sunday she would carefully fix the direction

of the wind during High Mass, for she was sure that the wind blowing then would dominate the rest of the year. In Holy Week a red moon was an object of dread: "It freezes, it drowns, or it roasts." And if it had been cold, and Easter itself was wet, she would declare:

"It's often like this; flowers at Christmas, fires at Easter."

She was utterly miserable if it rained on St. George's day, "because there'll be no cherries," or on Trinity Sunday, "because now it will rain for the next thirteen Sundays," or on St. Médard's day, "because now it will rain for forty days, unless St. Barnabas intervenes." She said too that Saturdays were never entirely bad:

"Because," she declared, "there is no Saturday in all France when the sun doesn't make his bow and depart."

When summer came her sayings all referred to the crops or the provisions to be made for winter.

"On St. Madeleine's day the nuts are ripe," or, "The best eggs for preserving are laid between the two Notre-Dames."

In summer, when they never went out until late in the afternoon, Jeannette, who often came to see her sister after her own day's work was done, would go with them part of the way.

At the back of the old quarter of the town, all along the river, there was an old deserted walk, planted with four rows of elms and built up like an embankment;

here they would walk, and from this elevation they would look out over the convents nearby with their symmetrical windows and large encircling gardens. Between the walls of these there were roads which wound away in different directions, the scattered houses on them gradually growing thicker until they were lost in the heart of the old city, where they could still be divined by the slope of roofs all turned in one direction. Further away still the new quarter of the town could be made out, wide-spread and comfortable, and the towers or spires of its eight churches.

Sometimes, about six o'clock, after the angelus, they would hear the passing bell being tolled in one or other of the parishes—that disillusioned, melancholy tolling to which popular imagination has fitted words expressive of doubt, resignation, and irony: "Your body is dead, your soul is gone, your wealth remains." Jeannette, always full of information, would remark:

"There! They're ringing for Monsieur this or Madame that."

And sometimes she would add:

"So he's dead at last!"

As the year wore on these walks would be taken earlier and earlier every day until the time came when they had to set out immediately after lunch. The trees shed their leaves, it was autumn, the avenue was deserted, the river ran turbulent and swollen. And the day would come, after a night of high wind or a week of rain which left the ground sodden, when they would see that not a single leaf remained on the branches; the elm walk had taken on its winter aspect. In this fall of the year a mournful gloom seems to spread suddenly over the face of earth: the old nurse merely noticed that the weather had changed and put on her winter dress, a dress of black and white molleton which Catherine called her "soft dress."

When it was wet they stayed indoors all day; Savine would sit and knit or darn. And according to the weather, as it was windy, stormy, snowy, or rainy, so she would think aloud to herself about what was happening in her own part of the country; and what she expressed thus for herself made stories for the little girl. In this way Catherine knew all the members of Savine's family: Lisa, Cendrise (every year at vintage-time she sent them an enormous grape tart), and Sublot, who got his nickname from his incessant whistling. Sublot, unlucky in the conscript's draw, was now a sailor, and Savine and her mother both thought him as good as dead.

In the evening, when the little girl was in bed, Savine sang songs to her, her low voice sinking a little at the end of every verse. And seated by the oil lamp on the table, sitting very upright, her face expression-less and white between the ruches of her bonnet, she would sing one verse after another while the point of her knitting-needle jerked in and out, in and out of the stocking she was knitting.

There was the song of Maumariée, about a girl who

refused to obey her father and was flung into prison; sadly she bewailed her lot:

> My sides are devoured by worms
> And my feet are rotted in irons.

The song of King Renaud was still more gloomy. It was all about the nailing down of coffins and the tolling of passing bells:

> For whom are they tolling, mother mine?
> They are tolling for King Renaud.

Catherine on the verge of sleep only heard the voice at intervals; now she dozed, now she half woke again, and now she dozed off for rather a longer time; and for her the romance ended with what she had last heard before finally falling asleep.

Savine, when she considered her sufficiently asleep, would light the night-light and go to bed herself in her big bed. But the sleep of this child, apparently so untroubled, had come upon her when her mind was full of these old tales of terror; every evening, moreover, she fell asleep in the fear of being awakened by the tocsin bell; for in this town of wooden buildings scarcely a week went by, especially in winter, without an outbreak of fire somewhere, and sometimes more than one house would be burned down. In the depths of her sleep she would suddenly be aware of a rapid, continuous humming which gradually became clearer and clearer and was still there when she opened her eyes. And, with her mind hovering between reality and dream, she would only become conscious of herself at the sound of her own voice calling for Savine. The old nurse, suddenly awakened, would clamber out of bed, slip on a petticoat, and run to open the window, followed by Catherine, who by now had got up too.

Down below in the dim square shadows could be made out moving about. On every side they heard windows being flung open, voices calling eagerly from above, and others answering from below. Suddenly, in the heart of the great black mass of the cathedral, in the fleur de lys gallery half-way up the tower, called the Gloria gallery, a tiny, moving spark of light appeared. It was the watchman with his lantern. In a few moments he could be made out on top of the tower, all shaken by the crashing of the tocsin, which abruptly ceased. Then, in the silence, a series of deliberate strokes boomed mournfully, indicating by their number the parish where the fire had broken out: one stroke for this parish, two for that, or three, or four, or sometimes as many as eight if the fire was in an outlying part of the town. But if in the intervals between the ringing of the tocsin no bell was tolled it meant that the fire was somewhere outside the town.

Then, before the tocsin came crashing out again, from the top of the tower a voice would call out into the night:

"The fire is in . . ." proclaiming such and such a street or suburb.

185

And four times, from each corner of the tower, the cry would be repeated. Then the tocsin would ring out again; and for all the world as if the great cathedral bell had awakened the bells of all the other churches it spread now from parish to parish, from belfry to belfry, in every variety of pitch, solemn or shrill. And soon all the bells in the town were ringing out, now together, now one after another; and in the general clamour the bells of the parish in question jangled breathlessly away, as though in celebration (people cried: "There! Listen to Sainte Madeleine"—or Saint Benoît, or Saint Martin—"ringing away like mad!"), and all these together formed a strange, dramatic, terrifying concert. Everybody was up now, gazing from windows and every possible vantage point; and in the distance a great glare would be seen, or, closer at hand, from the middle of some block of houses, there would be a sudden upward rush of sparks. Next day, if the house that had been burned down was not too far away, they would go and have a look at it on their walk.

Every year at fair-time or vintage-time Savine's family would come in from the country to see her and Jeannette. Savine would be told to give them lunch, and they might even stay the night. They were all vintners or small-holders, and even in their Sunday-best they smelt like peasants—that mingled odour of new bread, flour, and the slightly dank atmosphere of cottages never opened up except on holidays. They would bring with them their local flat cakes, or black

186

puddings, or roast pork, or perhaps baskets of mixed black and white grapes, fermenting already and smelling of muscadel.

In the course of the week Madame de Laignes often took Catherine to see Mademoiselle de Polyso or her grandparents. But these took very little notice of her; and once she was installed at a little table with two large picture-books in front of her—always the same two: the *Life of Jesus Christ* and the *Life of the Holy Virgin*—it was assumed that she could amuse herself with them for as long as the visit lasted, which might be several hours. On one such occasion at the de Chappes' Catherine met her Uncle Bernard, of whom she had often heard her mother speak but whom she had never seen. Some years before, indeed, at the time of her mother's marriage, Bernard had asked his parents' permission to take the final vows of the Society of Jesus, and since then he had never left Rome, where he had gone to study. He was an Abbé now, a tall, mysterious, and terrifying person to Catherine as, instead of kissing her, he traced a sign of the cross on her forehead. He only stayed a short time in St. Loup. He came again next year; but after taking his final vows he was never seen again. And although they still often talked of him, from thenceforth he practically disappeared from the family life.

At about this time Monsieur de Chappes, whose health had been steadily declining, had a seizure on the steps of the cathedral. This was the first of a succession of slight strokes, each of which left his faculties further reduced without, however, imperilling his life.

Sunday dinner at the de Chappes' no longer had its one-time animation. Monsieur de Chappes, become an old man in the course of only a few months, sat mostly silent, as much because of the difficulty he now experienced in expressing himself at all as because of an almost complete deafness which prevented him from taking part in the conversation. All through the meal he would sit there gently chewing, his still handsome features relaxed now into a fixed expression of bewildered stupor. Every now and then, to attract his attention, his wife would raise her voice and shout out his Christian name. He would start, gaze at her meekly, and answer: "Yes." When guests were present he made a visible attempt to assume the old attitude and tone, only so recently lost. Once he even ventured to embark upon an anecdote for the benefit of his neighbour at table: and he told it as he had often told it before, contriving the same effects at the same places, but a little slowly and hesitantly. Then suddenly, in the middle of a sentence, and without the least embarrassment or any sign of noticing anything wrong, he stopped and turned again to his plate; his neighbour, who knew the story, finished it for him, and he listened to her with polite attention, forgetting that it was he himself who had begun it.

A further stroke left him paralysed all down one

side. One of his eyes, those eyes that had once twinkled with such good-natured malice when he smiled, was now half-closed and almost blind. His mouth on the contrary, all pulled down to one side, hung open, and when he spoke now it was as though his flabby lips could no longer control the words that jumbled out with consonants all blurred. And now this man who had always been so untroubled by uncertainties was suddenly, on the very threshold of death, seized with terrors against which he strove in vain. He called upon the saints, recited prayers, never pausing save to babble little frightened phrases; it seemed as though his easy-going life, which had flowed over him without leaving a trace, had suddenly become in the very moment of leaving it a burden too heavy to be borne, overwhelming him now beneath its weight.

2

WHEN SHE WAS ABOUT to have her second child (a girl, christened Françoise) Madame de Laignes resolved to send her elder daughter to a convent. Catherine had now reached her seventh year. In spite of the discreet but none the less lively opposition of Aunt Aurore, who, knowing the Mother Superior of the convent in question, regarded her as a mere country-woman, greedy for gain, vulgar-minded, and coarse of manner (all of which in fact she was), Madame de Laignes settled on a certain religious establishment recently founded at Saint-Loup and directed by the nuns of an obscure Order, her choice being influenced by the fact that they took day-girls.

The convent was situated at the far end of the new part of the town, overlooking the avenue and next to the church of St. Benoît, which for long had been called St. Benoît Without. It was a large new building, built to the order of the nuns, who were very proud of it and always eager to show it off down to the least detail; besides class-rooms and dormitories it contained a sanatorium, a chapel, and a magnificent recreation-room which could also be used as a theatre, since there was a stage at one end. The neighbouring houses, too, for the most part ancient, ramshackle, tumble-down affairs, also belonged to the Sisters. Whenever one was put up for sale they bought it in. And this created round the tall white building a mysterious jumble of buildings of every shape and size and facing in every direction, the various parts intercommunicating in all sorts of fantastic and far-fetched ways. Thus, a door would unexpectedly open out of a cupboard; a little staircase would take one down to a courtyard where one found oneself faced with another little staircase. But the front rooms, cut off from the convent proper by blocked-up doors, were let out to peaceable individuals connected in some way, directly or indirectly, with the church—sacristans, undertakers, bell-ringers. And on the ground-floors, giving on to a dark and narrow street which widened to form a small irregular square in front of the convent-entrance, there were a few humble shops, run by their owners without assistance—a locksmith with a fringe of grey beard, a cobbler, a joiner—artisans of a vanished day who still appeared in frock-coats on Sundays at High Mass in St. Benoît's.

Catherine would arrive at the convent early in the afternoon—she often spent the morning at home. When all the little girls had assembled at two o'clock Sister Chantal, who taught the smallest children, would button up the gaiters which she had taken off only an hour before, put on their berets and hats, first examining the linings to make sure no mistakes were made, and inspect their hands, making them spread their fingers

191

out as she pulled on their gloves. All this was a very long and complicated business, but at last the little troop would be ready and then Sister Zoé would arrive to take them for their afternoon walk—a tall, thin, hollow-chested nun, with big feet, a long neck, red inflamed eyelids behind the bluish lenses of her spectacles, and only one tooth in a mouth perpetually twisted into a curl of disgust. The rest of her face seemed to be a matter of straight lines—the furrows in her forehead, her eyebrows, even the lines of her black woollen veil were all straight, and the folds of the white linen head-band below were sharply creased, as if her head were square, or as if there were little protuberances either side like budding horns.

They would go out by the door into the avenue, and their walk would often take them to the mother-house of the Order of St. Benoît in the suburb of Belle-Épine. There, beneath the wing of the Mother General (a poor, down-trodden woman whose title was more honourable than effectual—for the Community, depending for its material support on the boarding-school, was for all practical purposes under the thumb of Mother Appoline, the school's director) dwelt the postulates, the novices, and all the supernumeraries of the Order; the infirm, the superannuated, the sick, the illiterate, and those with no aptitude for anything whatever. As much, nevertheless, was got out of these poor wretches as was humanly possible, and those who had any capabilities at all were made good use of. Such Sisters as could give piano lessons gave them at the school at greatly reduced rates; one nun, Sister Sylvestre, gave extra drawing lessons, and as she still had plenty of leisure left over, spent it painting dinner-services, flower-pot covers, flower-stands, vases, and dishes, all of which she herself baked in a kiln; and this kiln itself became a source of profit to the Sisters, for there, for a small fee, they were ready to bake the handiwork of all the young and old ladies of the town. The majority, however, mended clothes, made dresses, or worked in the garden. Then there were the nuns who travelled. These could be seen setting forth with their big leather bags and their well-nourished peasant faces (for more often than not they took their meals out) with nothing of the usual timidity and distress of the nun faced with the practicalities of travel: tickets, luggage, time-tables. Each would go to her own part of the department, where she had connections, and there call on the priests in the important towns and the nuns of the various schools, working always for the next year's returns. And sometimes one or other of these wandering nuns would be appointed Superior of a new school set up in a large village or little township and designed to serve as a nursery for the convent at Saint-Loup.

As soon as Sister Zoé, clasping the youngest of her fifteen little charges by the hand, had entered the outer gates of the Mother-house, which were always open, she would stop to chat with the door-keeper, telling her the latest news from school, or leaving a little parcel with her from one of the nuns. If she had something peculiarly private to say she would take the fat concierge by the neck, bring her lips close to the black veil, and mutter away rapidly—apparently into the back of her head. And according to the nature of the confidence, the only visible countenance in this tableau, the concierge's, would lengthen, broaden, register astonishment, pity, indignation, or slightly shocked amusement. At length they would all proceed to the garden; and there Sister Zoé let the children amuse themselves, watching them from a distance.

It was a large garden with sanded paths flanked by thickets of close-clipped shrubs; and at the end of every path one would be suddenly confronted with a Virgin and Infant Jesus holding a bunch of grapes, or a St. Joseph with a lily, or an angel with a gilded spear conquering a dragon. In the middle of the garden a group of symmetrically planted hornbeams enclosed a gloomy spot called the "hall of verdure," provided with stone benches and reached by four archways cut through the foliage. A little to one side, shut off by low trellises, was the private garden of the Mother General, who would sometimes walk there with another nun as insignificant as herself, or with the Mistress of the Novices, or a canon, or the convent chaplain.

About three o'clock they would all return to school again; there was still an hour's work to be done. Under the eye of Sister Chantal, the little girls would find their places; the biggest on the front bench, the middle ones on the bench behind, and the smallest of all on a little bench in front of a tiny table fitted with slates. Four by four the little girls were called up to Sister Chantal's desk to read their alphabet. The Sister followed the lines with a long knitting-needle or paper-knife, so that nobody should lose the place; and led by her the sing-song voices rose in chorus above the murmuring of the others.

"Cross of Jesus, A, B, C. . . ."

The big girls, however, who were already on to pot-hooks or letters, were made to recite little pieces of poetry chosen from a book entitled *The Casket of Childhood*. And at Christmas and the New Year the whole class would learn to sing "When Christmas comes, Oh happy day" or "I am Father New Year's Day, the friend of all good children."

Sometimes a child on the smallest form would suddenly burst into sobs. The contingency would have been foreseen. Sister Chantal would calmly make her way to the scene of action, take in the extent of the disaster, and, scolding as a matter of principle, remove the tiny knickers and set them to dry—the two legs swollen with air standing quite upright—on her earthenware footwarmer. When an accident of a more serious nature had affected the air of the class-room and it was too cold to open the windows she would announce that she was now going to change the air. Whereupon she would peel the apple provided for her tea, stir the cinders of her footwarmer with the key of her cupboard until the little red embers glowed and waned, and drop the long, flexible spiral of peel into their midst: immediately it would begin to smoke and give off a strong smell of toffee.

After tea the day-pupils began to go home. Some were fetched, others taken home by nuns; pupils living in outlying districts went home all together in the convent omnibus. Passers-by would see it emerge into the Place Saint-Benoît with its load of little girls of all sizes, their hats appearing at various levels through the windows, while, near the door, a lay-sister sat reading from a little prayer-book, her black veil thrown back to reveal a placid face framed by the ruches of the frilled bonnet.

At the beginning of her second year at school Catherine began to attend morning classes regularly. Every day at eight o'clock she would set off to the convent hand in hand with Savine. They took the rue de la Cité, crossed the bridge, and walked the length of the rue Notre-Dame. The shops had long been open and the daily cleaning would be coming to an end. Every few yards along the street the little shop-girls— who would have been up since five, whatever the season, washing down the tiled floors by lamplight and lighting the stoves—would now be busily polishing the brass-work or sweeping the pavement or standing on step-ladders and wiping down the windows, behind which the older shop-assistants (their superiors now by reason

196

of their age, though they too had once been mere apprentices) were arranging the window displays, carrying in their arms some headless female figure in a long-trained dress, as rigid as a woman in a cataleptic fit.

Sometimes one of the big windows would be cleared for the day of its usual display, and two or three of the young ladies, under the supervision of the proprietress herself, would carefully set out the dresses for a wedding to take place next day. In the middle the wedding-dress itself would be displayed, and a little behind it, on another dummy, the going-away dress, as it was called. Then there would be the dresses of the bride's mother and the bridesmaids. And the townspeople who at one time or another paused to admire these lovely clothes would all know for whom they were intended.

3

THURSDAY AFTERNOONS Catherine spent with Aunt Aurore. Every two or three years Mademoiselle de Polyso would beg the ladies of the committee to find another president ("Just think," she would say, "it's eighteen years now—or twenty—I've been bearing this burden!") but it was still she who directed the Tabernacle Charity. And since the days when Madame de Laignes had been a child and come to the rue du Cloître-Saint-Pierre Mademoiselle de Polyso's life had changed so little that often, sitting at her table with her fine scissors, trimming the edges of the petals of some artificial flower (or ensconced in her armchair applying little lace or braid motifs to the muslin of the alb or rochet unrolled across her knees), and seeing Catherine wandering about the room, she would find herself calling the little girl by her mother's name. By this time, however, Mademoiselle Oguet had been dead some years. People had expected this to make such a change in Mademoiselle de Polyso's own life that they had asked each other how she would support it. But contrary to all expectations she very quickly reconciled herself to her friend's death, and now spoke of her only rarely and then without regret, showing that unacknow-

ledged satisfaction of the old who see in the disappearance of their contemporaries less a menace to themselves
than a guarantee of their own longer life.

Catherine, according to the season, would find her
aunt working by her fireside, in her own room, in the
little drawing-room, or out in the open by the garden
door. It was Jeanette for the most part who kept her
entertained. Once she had finished arranging her china
in the two big closets in the dining-room she would set
to work in the garden. One might see her removing
green-fly from the rose-trees, weeding a path, watering
the flowers, or moving up and down the hedge of
raspberry canes which screened the outbuildings. And
from time to time, without a word, she would bring
Catherine five or six huge raspberries on a saucer,
bursting ripe. When it was very hot she would fetch
a chair from the kitchen and take her knitting and sit
outside against the white walls of the house with their
pots of flowers on semicircular stands between the
open shutters of the windows.

Catherine, sitting with her aunt and practising
embroidery stitches on a piece of coarse canvas, would
soon grow tired of working and ask permission to play.

"Auntie, may I rummage?"

Whereupon they would open the cupboards in the
little drawing-room for her, and she would proceed to
muddle together all the artificial flowers so carefully
arranged there, putting them in her hair, making posies
of them, or laying them out on a piece of cardboard

or the lid of a box which she slung round her neck on a ribbon like a flower-girl's basket, to go and sell them to Aunt Aurore or Jeannette. Or, seated on the floor in a muddle of books taken down from the lower cupboards—books of every kind, including the Confessions of Rousseau and St. Augustine—she would pore over the illustrations in old bound volumes of fashion magazines dating from the First Empire, *Le Follet* and *Le Conseiller des Dames*. The miniature figures, high-waisted, long-legged, all had the most complicated coiffures; some had small, short braids, others little curls all over the forehead and ringlets falling on to the neck behind; some had their hair bound with ribbons; and occasionally there was a lady wearing a half-diadem, high in front, tapering away at either side.

After a few moments, though, Catherine would leave her books where they lay and run out of the little drawing-room to go and look at Aunt Aurore's dresses in the room where they were kept, a room reached preferably by a mysterious door out of the alcove in Aunt Aurore's bedroom, which always opened with a faint rustling of paper; otherwise one had to go down a long corridor and through a dark place where the wood was kept.

Here was stored all the furniture that had been damaged or was no longer used: chests of drawers, tables, little round pedestal tables, and great carved wardrobes in oak or walnut full of old dresses once worn on ceremonial occasions, some by Mademoiselle de Polyso herself, others belonging to her mother and her grandmother—these last contemporary with *Le Follet* and *Le Conseiller des Dames*, sometimes even cut from the patterns in those very books. There was one, for instance, of green moiré, garlanded with little mother-of-pearl buttons—and one day Aunt Aurore and Catherine counted two hundred and seventy of them. Another was a narrow sheath of mauve and white striped silk with a low-cut bodice half veiled by a fichu of loosely draped muslin caught at the breast with a large silver-gilt brooch; this had belonged to Mademoiselle de Polyso's grandmother: it had been her going-away dress.

Catherine would go over the dresses, stroking the silks, and always hoping to discover one she had overlooked before; or she would pull open the drawers of the chests of drawers, filled to the brim with things of no possible apparent use: old scraps of ribbon, bits of material, laces, muslins, braid, fringes, buttons. On one of the tables, too, there was a pile of flat boxes each with a label in the lid to indicate its contents; and these the little girl would bring down, leaving Jeannette to tidy them up and put them back in the evening.

When October came, and for all the world like rows of little lanterns ranged along the cornices of monuments on feast-days, rows of apples and pears would appear along the edges of chests of drawers or encircling the tops of little occasional tables; apples and pears, with here and there an occasional fat yellow quince with the bloom still on it. Bunches of black and white grapes of all sizes hung from the ceiling on a sort of machine consisting of three barrel-hoops linked together and looking like an enormous crinoline. As winter advanced the grapes would begin to wither, so two or three times a week Jeannette would come up armed with a pair of scissors and a plate to remove any that were spoilt. Climbing on to a chair, scissors in hand, and looking as suspicious as ever, she would inspect the bunches carefully, one at a time, slowly revolving the apparatus from which they hung.

Sometimes Catherine would stay out in the garden. There she hunted for little shells in the sanded paths or amused herself by making sets of "jewellery" from flowers: two little flowers, properly matched, made a pair of ear-rings, a third was a brooch. There were a few fruit trees in the beds, with old clumps of poppies, delphiniums, or phloxes in between, and she would wander slowly down the paths, stopping now and then to pick and compare with another some little bell of clearest blue or bright red star. Then she would go and sit by the well at the foot of a rocky mound sheltered by two low-growing trees; and there she spread out her trinkets on the leaves, disappointed because already they were limp and faded.

But her imagination would soon dart away on a new tack. She liked to imagine to herself that the rockery by the well with its fantastic outlines was the home of a whole tiny race of fairy people, redoubtable, energetic, and mysterious, whose society she shared without anyone

202

suspecting it. Often in class, however, she unconsciously betrayed the direction of her thoughts. It was not an uncommon thing to find in an exercise where, for instance, a list of feminine nouns had been asked for, a series of words very different from those chosen by other little girls; and the Sister, slightly surprised, would note their singularity, attributing it in her own mind to a desire on Catherine's part to show off. Thus there might be: "the fairy, the princess, the sorceress, the cavern, the tamer"—this last, in its feminine form, a memory of a certain menagerie to which she had been taken and which had led her to endow one of her fairies with the power of subduing ferocious animals. And the masculine nouns would betray the same run of ideas: "the prince, the knight, the genius, the enchanter, the talisman, the diadem, the page."

Once this little world had been invented it became perfectly familiar to her. She would often think of it, endowing the various personages, whose lives continued even when she was not there to evoke them, with different habits, likes, and dislikes. Sometimes there would be a wedding among them; or the princess would have a son. And for the baptism or the wedding itself there would be a grand banquet in the finest hall in the palace with nobody present but kings and queens, all sitting alternately round a long, narrow table, kings with white beards and queens with veils beneath their crowns, all looking just as if they had stepped from a pack of cards. But among the rocks at the bottom, buried deep in the earth, lived evil creatures, wicked sorcerers and genii. Here there were dungeons. And down at the bottom of that rock full of irregular and fantastic holes wasn't there a subterranean chamber where the old king had shut up his persecuted youngest daughter? At other times, with Aunt Aurore's permission, Catherine would take down the little statue of the Virgin from its usual place on the drawing-room mantelpiece in front of the clock with the glass shade and place it in a cleft in the rocks which she decorated with garlands and bunches of flowers; and for one day the fairy castle would be transformed into the Grotto of Notre-Dame de Lourdes.

At the end of the day the same stories which had amused her mother in days gone by would now amuse Catherine, and the same songs; so that Madame de Laignes, coming to fetch her daughter, would at once recognize as she entered the verse Aunt Aurore was singing in that little fluting voice of hers that had not changed at all. It might be "Do you know Maître Olivier?"—he being the curé's friend, a friend indeed, ready at a pinch to be his substitute, and the victim of all kinds of misadventures. In the final verse he fell from the belfry. "He fell," said the song, "on to his poor behind." And at this point Aunt Aurore would assume a mysterious air, lower her voice, and almost whisper:

So now there were five or six holes
As well as the one that was there before—
Oui-da!

Before taking Catherine home at night, Madame de Laignes would stay a long time talking with her aunt, for whom these visits were nevertheless always far too short. They were both interested in every circumstance of one another's lives. They would begin by enumerating in meticulous detail all the things they had done in the short time since they had last met. Then they would exchange plans for the next day and run over the forthcoming events of the week. One day there would be a wedding to attend, another day a funeral; or it might be an Ember Day, or the eve of a fast; and on Easter-eve they would both express their relief that Lent was over at last.

"To-morrow," Aunt Aurore would say, "we shall make up for Lent a bit by having turkey!"

4

Soon after moving up from Sister Chantal's class, where only a few years later her younger sister, Françoise, was to occupy her place, Catherine was for the first time allotted a part in the big play performed every winter on St. Apolline's Day in honour of the Mother Superior. On these occasions, indeed, a whole series of merry-makings was organized at the school. There would generally be two plays performed by the pupils, with songs and recitations in the intervals between the acts; and for about a month beforehand those who were taking part started preparing for the great day, forming a group apart, mysterious and important, and no longer subject to ordinary rules.

The last week before the actual day was devoted entirely to rehearsals and last minute preparations. All over the convent, which was filled with unusual activity, there was an incessant coming and going and chattering of voices. Up on the second floor costumes were tried on. Sister Calixte, who never for a minute left the recreation-room or theatre, spent whole hours in conference with the carpenter, who would later be encountered stumbling down corridors with planks and tools. Or it would be Monsieur Jules, the organist, with the operetta company in train; or Mademoiselle Chérie, the infants' music-mistress, hurrying along distractedly with half a dozen small children in tow, puffing, perspiring, and invariably good humoured—a big woman with a soft, plump face, dressed always in flounced skirt, a black knitted bodice stretched tightly over an enormous semicircular bosom, and a little black satin bonnet with a bow at the back which revealed an enormous coil of plaits in a net, fixed, impossible to say how, to a head of hair so sparse that the skin showed rosy and polished through the scanty grey locks. She it was who rehearsed the part-songs as well as the ballads and solos. With her little flock of pupils she would roam from top to bottom of the building in search of a disengaged piano, beginning with the parlours, then trying the art class-room (for the pianos were kept in the most varied and incongruous places) or the sewing-room; finally, finding nothing but pupils at work or mistresses giving lessons, she would end by retiring to what were known as the "pigeon-holes"— mansard attics used as emergency bedrooms, empty as a rule, but occasionally occupied by one of the nuns or the senior pupils.

These were situated on the topmost floor of the new building on either side of the infants' dormitory, a long room lighted at one end by three tall windows, which would have extended the whole width of the building but for these tiny rooms to the right and left of it under the pent of the roof; the doors to these little rooms might be seen alternating with the narrow cupboard doors between the beds. And it was to these rooms that the old pianos were relegated—instruments of every kind, mostly all but unplayable, uprights with ornamental festoons, others square as a table, with yellowed keys, missing ivories, and broken strings. And at certain hours of the day anyone in the neighbourhood of the dormitory would have heard an astonishing din as all these ill-tuned pianos were pounded by unskilful fingers attempting tunes which the absence of a note here and there punctuated with abrupt silences.

Preceding her pupils, who carried her music-rolls and albums bristling with markers, Mademoiselle Chérie opened the doors one after the other; in one room a lesson was in progress; in another a little girl was at work on her own; but a third proved empty. As they entered they were greeted by a smell of soap and drying towels emanating from the far side of the little compartment, a smell emphasized by the chilliness peculiar to unheated rooms. Behind the "pigeon-holes," in fact, the architect, instructed by Mother Apolline, had contrived a long passageway entered by a single door from one end of the dormitory, and here was installed the washing-place with its zinc trough divided off into separate compartments, each with its little tap.

Silently contemplating the piano which had fallen to her lot—the worst in the whole building, of course —Mademoiselle Chérie would toss her head and sigh deeply; then before she sat down she would lift up her skirts to reveal enormous cloth slippers, grey woollen stockings, and a black and white petticoat which scarcely covered her knees; plunging her hand into the pocket at the bottom of her petticoat with a movement that seemed to reach right down to her slippers, she would produce one by one her spectacles, her handkerchief, her pencil, and a large watch which she held to her ear before placing it on the lampstand. Then she sat down at the open piano and ran her fat red fingers rapidly up and down in a scale of extraordinary brilliancy. At length she would take up an album, look at the name inscribed on one of the markers, and call out a pupil; and in that icy atmosphere a feeble, childish voice would be raised to the metallic tinkling of the piano.

From time to time Mademoiselle Chérie would stop playing in the middle of one of the pieces and turn half round in her chair to speak to the child at her side, humming a passage over for her; or she would suddenly come out with some unexpected question about the great day itself, asking about the dresses they would wear, the play itself, and who was to act in it. And invariably, when she had come to the end of her questions she would tap you on the chest with her index finger as though to conclude the matter and call you her "good puss."

The festivities began on St. Apolline's Eve. They were continued throughout the next day, when the play itself and the operetta were both performed; and the performances were repeated on the third day after dinner, for the benefit of friends and relations. But for the children themselves it was a thing of the past by then, for everybody, with the exception of the actual performers, went to bed at seven o'clock that night.

Early in the afternoon of the first day pupils and mistresses assembled in the recreation-room, transformed overnight into a theatre. All the chairs and benches on the premises had been collected together—garden seats with legs and backs of iron, forms taken from class-rooms, while on either side of the big room smaller benches were perched on tables. The stage was screened off by a curtain of dazzling whiteness surmounted by a shield with the inscription "Vive Sainte-Apolline!" and the three sides of the stage were decorated with plants and pots of flowers brought by day-girls and old pupils—hyacinths, primroses, laurustinus, heather, and pink and white azaleas—a confused mass of flowers and foliage exhaling a spring-like perfume, mingled with a moist smell of moss and the pungent smell of the fir-branches on the other side of the curtain, where these were used as the background for one scene.

After a brilliant piano solo (which nobody listened to) executed in the wings by Mademoiselle Chérie, there came the recitation of compliments to the Mother Superior. She received these in her place in the front row, her enormous person installed in a broad armchair between the Mother General and the Mistress of the

Novices, with the nuns' chaplain to the right and the pupils' chaplain to the left of them, and beyond these the handful of ecclesiastics come to pay her tribute. Behind them sat the rows of pupils on their benches. And the incessant moving of their heads as they bobbed restlessly up and down now hid and now revealed the calm line of nuns sitting farther back in the last row of all, their faces relaxed and smiling beneath the black veils which they had thrown back. And right at the back of the room, on flower-stands placed against the walls, crowded the lay-sisters from the kitchens and the day-school.

The tiny children appeared first to sing or recite their compliments. They were followed by the older children, and finally it was the big girls' turn. One of these, the eldest, read the customary speech (and every time she came to the words "My Mother" or "Our Mother" she made a curtsey while her companions grouped around her bowed)—a veritable gem of eloquence, a copy of which, hand-written on a large sheet of white paper, was presented to the Mother Superior at the end of the ceremony and in the course of which she was begged to accept the pupils' gift—usually something useful, such as a holy statue or an artificial rock, which would be already installed in the chapel or garden in a place decided on by Mother Apolline herself.

Most of the children then returned to their classrooms, but those who were acting next day trooped

off and ran upstairs to the annex to have their hair
waved and curled. This was on the second floor at the
end of a long passage and consisted of a series of low,
well-heated rooms where the linen was stored and the
ironing done. In one of them would be Monsieur
Gelinet, the hairdresser, a little man with frizzled hair
brushed up on one side into a squiff which seemed
expressly designed to hold the comb he was continually
sticking in it. Then, with hair unplaited and each
clasping her own brush and comb, they waited their
turn, gossiping with Monsieur Gelinet about the latest
hairdressing styles while he, informed as to the character each was playing so that he could dress her hair
suitably, waved, put hair into pins, or rolled it up into
specially fine curl-papers. And at length the little girls
with their screwed-up hair and their heads that rustled
with the slightest movement, rejoined their classes,
objects of admiration, envy, and curiosity to their
companions, who asked each other—for the programme
was kept a secret to the very last moment:

"What parts can they be playing?"

Next day, immediately after tea, the actresses disappeared, not to be seen again until they appeared behind
the footlights. Up in the second floor of the annex they
had their hair dressed (and the older girls besought
Monsieur Gelinet to put a little gold dust in their hair
or—what was strictly forbidden—let them have a little
stick of rouge or some rice powder); in the two or

three rooms given over to dressing, Madame Oudin, the eminent dressmaker, and the nuns worked away in a deafening uproar, in the midst of which reigned an extraordinary fever and agitation. From the room used as the principals' dressing-room there would suddenly emerge a figure in a sugar-loaf hat, a soubrette, a coal-heaver, a nigger with face and hands completely blackened with blacklead, a marquise, a Druidess with her mistletoe and sickle, or a sailor. Since it had come to the knowledge of the nuns that certain people in the town considered the wearing of trousers indecorous for little girls, a form of dressing-up which had long seemed innocent enough, arrangements had been made to overcome the difficulty. The actresses still wore trousers when necessary; but now, attached to these, they wore either a short skirt in the same material, or else, like an altar-cloth, a sort of exiguous apron ending in a flounce.

No play was ever known to end without angelic intervention. Although the parts were generally very small and never entailed speaking more than a few words, to be chosen to play an angel was always a matter for great pride. The dress was invariably a trailing robe of white tarlatan over a blue tarlatan foundation, caught in at the waist by a golden girdle. Their foreheads were encircled by fillets of gold wire; their hair, divided into two great curly masses, fell forward over each shoulder; they would make their way cautiously along the narrow corridor from the dressing-rooms and staidly descend the little staircase, with everybody making way for them so that their wings should not be crumpled, golden wings, or silver, or pure white, made of feathers cut out of paper and mounted on a large cardboard foundation. For many years they had been worn short, stopping at the waist; but fashion had changed, and they were now very long, their pointed ends reaching right down to the heels. And with all this increased weight, the cord attaching them to your neck half strangled you, so that it was difficult to sing, and sometimes even to speak.

They made their appearance in the plays according to an unvarying ritual, appearing symmetrically in pairs, one from either side of the stage, face to face, advancing one step and then coming to a halt. Then one of them (the other was a mere supernumerary and said nothing) would sing the words allotted her, one finger upraised and pointing to heaven; after this they would perform whatever act they had come to do— place a loaf on the unfortunate children's table, or a sack of guineas by the poor old invalid woman's side, or comfort Clovis's daughter asleep in prison on her bundle of straw. Then, as slowly as they had entered, they would withdraw — backwards, because they couldn't show their backs; the whole effect of their costumes depending upon being seen from the front only, the back view had been sacrificed accordingly. With the passing of time and on the advice of the physics mistress, these apparitions came to be signalized by the lighting of magnesium flares.

In the poorly lit corridors the performers would wait with beating hearts for the moment when the curtain should rise and disclose the hall, from which they could hear an ever-increasing buzzing. The Sisters would all be busy at their appointed tasks. Sister Lucien, who presided over the songs, would go about soothing the throats of her singers with spoonfuls of syrup of erysimum or sips of highly sweetened syrup of gum. Sometimes a disordered stomach would be comforted with a little glass of Malaga and a biscuit —some little girl whom excitement had prevented from eating any lunch. Suddenly a princess or a bishop or a Roman consul would burst into tears—at the very last moment unable to face the stage. Or a singer would suddenly lose her voice. Those who were really devout, who would never appear on the stage without crossing themselves and muttering a hasty prayer to Jesus, Mary, and Joseph, begged the prayers of the nuns standing by.

"Oh, Sister—pray that I don't make a mistake!— Pray that I'll act well!"

At last Sister Calixte with her printed booklet in one hand and the curtain cord in the other would take a final glance round with a curt "All here?" and sharply pull the cord. The white calico curtain would part with a sound like the tearing of cloth and a swiftness which horrified the performers.

The big play was done first, invariably a drama which reduced the audience to tears: *The Crusader's Return*, *Thomas Moore's Daughter* (an innocent girl, persecuted by Cromwell, whose cruelty and hypocrisy were anathematized throughout three acts), or *Fabiola*. Catherine's own début was made in *The Miracle of Saint Geneviève*, where she played the little girl who was the object of the miracle. Unable to speak or to walk she was carried to the Saint wrapped up in a great cloak. The Saint touched her. She threw the cloak aside and got up, exclaiming: "Mama!"

During the interval the scenes were changed, and the scenery for the second act brought up from a cellar beneath the stage. Assisted sometimes by Monsieur Gelinet, who when his own job was finished would come to listen to the piece from the wings and on occasion obligingly lend a hand, the nuns who acted as scene-shifters laboriously hoisted, shifted, pushed, and hung, working with blind eagerness, unsmiling, like piece-workers. There would be Sister Edmond tugging at an upright, or perched on a ladder busy unrolling the blackcloth. And meanwhile there would be revived scenes of despair among the members of the cast. One of the older little girls was brought to the point of desperation by the idea that she could not have said her words, "My Mother cursed me!" with sufficient feeling, since no one had burst into tears. Between two others, standing a little apart, a quarrel was raging. One had left out a sentence and caused

216

the other to miss her cue, and now this other was bitterly reproaching the first—until finally a nun stepped in and negro and princess both bowed their heads to her rebuke. Broken phrases of it came to the attentive ears of their companions:

"Vainglory . . . take it upon yourself . . . ill temper. . . ."

At the end of this last evening a collection was always taken for the chapel by the heroines of the stage, who were swiftly dispatched by the nuns to the door of the recreation-room.

At once, at the head of the flood of guests, the noisy band of lay-sisters came hurrying out, their faces still glistening with tears and lighted up by the smiles with which, if the piece had ended in tragedy, they expressed their delight at seeing the heroine thus restored to life, and also their respect for the princess, king's daughter, or saint, and their pleasure at knowing the pupil. The leading players themselves, indeed, benefited from the sympathy their parts aroused, often winning an admiration (especially on the part of the little ones) which might develop into an enduring if unavowed passion.

The year after the performance of *The Miracle of St. Geneviève* they did *The Little Princes in the Tower*, and there was not a dry eye in the hall when the gaoler, Tyrrel, threw himself on the little princes whose dismal cries came ringing through the swiftly lowered curtain. And afterwards, when the two little girls, bag in hand, took up their stations in the corridor, everyone stared

217

eagerly as they filed by at the two small figures standing on two chairs to take the collection, one in blue, the other in crimson, both with plumed caps and puffed breeches beneath their prudish little aprons, both wearing the Garter and the Collar of the Golden Fleece —made of the massive bronze chain of a sanctuary lamp studded with bits of coloured glass for jewels.

The day after the festival (though even on the last day itself change was already in the air; a Sister, for instance, might remark: "To-morrow. Ah! No more amusement then! Benediction to-morrow!") was the first day of the convent's annual retreat. The moment Sister Amédée opened the door to you in the morning you were struck by a change so drastic that you wondered how it could have happened since the day before. Facing you, pinned to the top of the stairs on the first landing, was a large strip of paper with "Silence!" printed on it in large black letters. And this admonition was repeated everywhere—in all the corridors, on the way to the chapel, in the refectory, in all the class-rooms. The ordinary life of the convent was for the time being at a complete standstill. The days were exclusively devoted to instructions in the chapel, to preparing for confession, to the analysis of sermons. Permission to speak was given only during the short midday break. Tea was eaten in silence.

Some traces of the recent waving would still be visible on the little girls' smooth hair. In the recreation-room, through which one passed on the way to chapel,

218

the fir-branches were still in place on the stage, while at the back a Sister would be busy stowing away properties in the cupboards behind the scenes, shutting them quickly at the approach of pupils lest their minds should be distracted. But you might get an accidental glimpse of some gorgeous queen's dress.

The retreat was always preached by a Jesuit Father. The instructions of which it consisted were diluted with many anecdotes; but regularly on the last two days, and invariably in the evenings, there would be sermons on death, hell, and repentance, designed to induce a radical confession. The preacher would dwell at great length on the holidays, representing these as being full of perils, letting fall all kinds of allusions (quite incomprehensible to Catherine), and ending up with these words, uttered with an air of great severity and in a way that seemed to lend many things a hidden meaning:

"The older girls will understand me!"

And the little girls would listen, some impassive, others vaguely stirred, while the nuns at the end of every row watched quietly from beneath their lowered veils the effect of these allusions on those childish faces.

5

IN THE YEAR of her daughter's confirmation, Madame de Laignes, at Mother Apolline's suggestion, sent her to school as a boarder. Throughout the holidays they were busy preparing her outfit. Then, one evening after dinner, she went off to the convent. She arrived just as the pupils were lining up to go to their dormitories. The older girls stopped at the second floor, the little ones went up to the dormitory on the floor above —the attics—where Sister Chantal, who had come up in advance of her little flock, met them at the door. She showed each of them which was to be her bed; then they said prayers and began to undress in a silence only broken by Sister Chantal who, as she showed the new girls how to fold their clothes, hushed the occasional sounds or whisperings which rose from between the beds.

"Be quiet!" she said. "Sleep is the image of death. A dormitory should be as silent as a graveyard."

Catherine took off the garments she had put on that morning in her own home; but in this strange new bed she could not sleep. Between the half-drawn curtains, from behind which came the sound of regular breathing, she gazed at the double row of beds, each with its little figure stretched out, crowned with a nightcap; suddenly she could not help smiling a little, heavy-hearted as she was, they were so like an illustration she remembered to the fairy-story of the Ogre's seven daughters.

For a long time Sister Chantal continued to move to and fro. Catherine saw her come out of her attic, return to it again; then she began to say her office as she paced ceaselessly up and down the narrow strip between the rows of beds, with quiet, unhurrying footsteps. Occasionally a faint sound or a cough would make her turn her head, the end of her head-dress rasping on her starched veil. At ten o'clock a little bell rang downstairs, signal for the nuns to go to bed, and Sister Chantal lit the night-light, took the lamp which shone at one end of the dormitory, and retired to her attic.

They rose every morning at a quarter to six. Catherine often woke up before then, when it was still pitch-dark. The clock would strike from the neighbouring parish church.

Two hours more, she would think; one hour more.

And between sleeping and waking she would hear Sister Chantal opening the window of her room and lighting the fire. Then suddenly a bell on the ground floor would begin ringing hurriedly; and almost at once, cutting the icy air of the dormitory (while the same sound came up muffled from the lower floors), the vigorous jangling of a hand-bell would start, accompanied by Sister Chantal's loud voice pronouncing:

"*Benedicamus Domino!*"

With great upheavals from all the beds, for you had to sit up to answer, husky voices would sleepily respond:

"*Deo gratias!*"

The nun, having lighted the lamp, would go and hang it on a supporting beam in the middle of the dormitory near the stove and then walk briskly round, the pale light of her candle shining on her scrupulously clean and scrubbed face, the face of one who has for long been up and busy while all round her others are now only beginning their day. Meanwhile between the beds, now separated by one of their two curtains, the little girls were dressing. On Sundays, when they changed their underlinen, both these curtains were drawn, and to avoid being naked even for a second they stood on their beds, slipped head and arms into the clean chemise and held it up with their teeth while the old chemise was slipped off.

When everyone was ready they put on their hats; heavy lamps were burning at intervals against the walls of the corridors they passed through on their way to the chapel where the pupils' chaplain, Abbé Missotte, said Mass; the convent chaplain took the service for the nuns an hour earlier than this. The Abbé Missotte was a very old priest in a neat and well-brushed hat and soutane, very small and nearly blind, with thin white hair and a mouth so absolutely tooth-less that when he opened his lips it was as though, so to speak, they were coming unstuck.

Day would be breaking as the pupils entered the icy chapel, lit only by the candles on the altar. It was a large room with three windows and a polished floor, like an ordinary drawing-room, but to increase its size the upper part of the wall which separated the chapel from the passage leading to the sacristy had been pulled down; at early Mass the youngest children, and at other times the day-scholars, would occupy this sort of open gallery.

All at once, near the main entrance, another door would open—a door contrived in one of the corners of the chapel and leading to the Mother Superior's bed-room—and Mother Apolline herself would appear; her prie-dieu stood ready for her on the threshold, so that she had scarcely to move at all but could step straight from her bed to her prayers. She would give out the text of the fifteen minutes' meditation to be made before Mass, and in a haze of sleepiness the boarders would hear her voice murmuring on and on, with occasional intervals of silence.

"First point. . . . Second point. . . ."

The meditation finished, the priest would enter the chapel. Feeling with his foot for the first step up to the altar, he would laboriously mount the two remaining steps, often helped by his acolyte; and Mass would begin. A candlestick beside the missal enabled him to read his Mass; and at the Evangilium the acolyte removed it when he removed the book.

On chairs at the end of each row, or on their own forms which ran all down one side of the chapel beneath the three windows, the nuns with veils pulled low over their faces followed the Mass in their large, black, cloth-bound books. Every now and then one of them would blow gently to separate two pages, which came apart with a tiny rustling sound while the breath from her mouth hung for a moment in a little white cloud. Sometimes it was possible to get surreptitious glimpses of pictures betweeen the pages, pictures of the Crucifixion or the Virgin, veiled and standing beside a lily with half-opened arms, all surrounded with paper lace.

Catherine, from her seat, watched the Abbé Missotte's movements intently. Every time he had to kneel he rose again with difficulty, holding on to the edge of the altar. Then, at the moment of Communion, he took the broad, thin, shining wafer and broke it into two pieces according to rite, placing one upon the other, breaking off a portion which he placed in the chalice; and then, with his elbows on the altar and holding the broken Host in both hands, he opened his mouth very wide, introduced the wafer, and began to eat with what seemed to Catherine a greedy and even famished air; but perhaps that was because she was beginning to feel so hungry herself. For a moment, hands clasped beneath his chin, he munched away with great gulps and without opening his mouth, as if eating something very good: and at each movement of his jaws, nose and chin nearly met. While all this was happening, the pupils in the front row had taken their bench with its rail on which they knelt during Mass and which was used as a Communion-table, and moved it to the foot of the altar, returning to kneel on the floor. Sister Florentine, the sacristan, immediately covered the bench with a lace cloth fastened by three cords; and those of the nuns who had been unable to take Communion at the early Mass moved silently forward along the narrow aisles contrived on both sides of the chapel, their joined hands long and white and pointed, the ends of their sleeves between their palms. As they bent their heads to receive the Sacrament their veils all creased sharply at the nape of the neck.

As the service drew to a close the drawn faces of the little girls began to be distinguishable in the daylight which filtered now through the white curtains drawn tightly over the windows. From the refectory came a smell of coffee as they began to bring in the breakfast. But after Communion there was still a short Benediction, lasting some minutes, and while they sang the last hymn the Abbé Missotte returned to the sacristy. Once more Sister Florentine appeared. Mounting the altar steps she approached her face to each candle in turn as she lifted it down; but for the tapers in the candelabra set lower on the altar she stood on tip-toe, pursed her lips, and blew: her face, one moment brightly lit, retreated bit by bit into the shadow. With the last candle the artificial light was finally replaced by a daylight as yet still tentative. Before the end of the Benediction a nun in a blue apron would appear coming rapidly down the corridor and carefully holding at arm's length a napkin folded about a roll and a large bowl of steaming café-au-lait —Abbé Missotte's breakfast, which was brought to him in the sacristy.

After breakfast the pupils formed up into classes. Led by Sister Edmond, whose peculiarity it was always to walk backwards before them, the fifth form children went to their class-room on the ground-floor, the last at the end of the corridor, next the door into the garden. It was at once plain on entering this room that here was a class who set piety above science. Instead of the usual white plaster saint of modest size —a Holy Virgin under a glass shade, a St. Joseph, an Infant Jesus, or a Sacred Heart, each garlanded with white flowers—here, on one side of the room, was a large rock fastened to the wall, in one tortured crevice of which stood Our Lady of Lourdes, hands folded and eyes raised to heaven; at her feet, amidst branches of wild rose, knelt a little St. Bernadette, rosary in hand. On the opposite side of the room a small table bore a coloured statue of St. Joseph. Besides this, above the cupboard where the day-girls kept their hats and coats, was a beautiful niche in artificial white marble, empty, and awaiting the final touch of a new Sacred

Heart—the old one had become a little worn—which had not yet arrived.

After gabbling through their lessons they were set to reading aloud, often from the Psalms, that they might learn to pronounce Latin correctly at Vespers, or, to accustom them to reading difficult handwriting, from a book entitled *Manuscripts*, which contained the most extraordinary examples of illegible, weird, and contorted handwritings: from that they passed to exercises in preparation for their confirmation. They studied Bible history, church history, the catechism—a sort of higher catechism called the Improved Catechism—and the Gospels: all these the Sister expounded.

Speaking of Judas, Sister Edmond gave them the most precise and terrifying details of Hell, as if she herself had only just left it and were recounting her impressions of the journey and describing all she had seen.

"First of all, children," she said, "at the entrance to Hell is a great red gate; and behind this gate is a huge pendulum which swings to and fro, repeating through all Eternity, 'Never, for ever, never, for ever,' which means, 'Never escape, for ever in Hell.'"

It was, according to Sister Edmond, in the darkest deeps of this appalling place that for nearly two thousand years Judas had been falling in a bottomless abyss, fire above him, fire below him. And Catherine, terrified by God's power and dizzy at the thought of this eternal descent, yet could not help visualizing a

227

sort of improved footwarmer, with Judas between two layers of ever-glowing embers; and she remembered a cake, too, that they often made at Aunt Aurore's, cooked with live coals on the lid of the tin, and called "quickly made."

At about ten o'clock the door would open, and Sister Amédée would enter bearing a great tray of saucerless cups of all shapes and sizes, some of them very old. From the doorway she would call:

"Come along, those who've got colds!"

Half a dozen little girls—with shawls or fichus round their shoulders or over their heads, and mittens and knitted wristbands—would get up and drink their infusion—of lime-flowers, or borage, or other herbs good for the chest. From class to class went Sister Amédée, calculating the number of colds in each and the number of cups she must fetch from the kitchen. In one class there would be twelve with colds, in another seven, in another twenty. For those who had taken a purge in the morning (and at the least sign of ill health you were dosed with magnesia, drunk from a large, blue-ringed cup) there were bowls of lemonade or herb soup.

At a quarter to twelve it was the turn of the anaemic; but these had to leave their places. From all the class-rooms little girls emerged in threes and fours, all bound in the same direction, towards the cellar-door, a stately door behind the main staircase, opening into a corridor with shelves adorned with bottles in various stages of emptiness; gentian wine, quinine, strengthening Malaga, or Bordeaux, anti-scorbutic syrup, or syrup of iodized horse-radish: each little girl had her own particular bottle, and there they all stood, each with a glass inverted on it. Sister Amédée gave you your glass and you waited until your name was called out; then you stepped promptly forward, she poured out your dose, and you drank it off quickly, down to the last drop.

But some little girl was sure to be late and come running breathlessly down the corridor. And then— for he was always skulking somewhere round the refectory or the kitchen or the larder, wherever there was anything to eat, in fact—Pyramus would come bounding out from somewhere; Pyramus, Mother Apolline's second shadow, a pampered tyrant, a great, short, fat dog with minute and delicate paws, a mongrel head, and a tail cocked up like a corkscrew and glued down over his rump; his coat was whitish, half bare behind and very frizzy in front, and marked with large irregular blotches the colour of mould.

Like a sack of bran sent flying by a vigorous kick, he would come hurtling forward, mouth on a level with the floor, suffocated with rage, his barking subsiding for a moment to a growl at the back of his throat and then starting off again so convulsively that it looked as though he would spit out his tongue at any moment—snapping murderously as he went by with his old sugar-ruined teeth at the little boots that jumped about agitatedly within reach of his jaws. Sometimes he would hurl himself apoplectically at a foot. At the sound of his barking the nuns in the refectory would all come running in, and the Mother Superior, and all the lay-sisters from the kitchen in their blue aprons and blue sleeves. They would implore the dog to let go of the foot, they would try and reason with him, or distract his attention with some tit-bit. The Mother Superior would speak to him as to a spoilt child who is given way to even while he is being reproved. And the little girl would be reproached with having run on purpose to tempt poor Pyramus, although everybody knew perfectly well how it really was.

At midday the lunch-bell sounded, and the anaemic ones, now fortified, rejoined their companions in the refectory. This was a large three-windowed room, the same size as the chapel and above it, with long tables covered with yellow oilcloth and wooden benches; all dominated by an enormous engraving of the Last Supper on one wall. In front of the windows was the Mother Superior's armchair and her own special little table, touching that of the nuns'; besides her knife and fork a little shining new roll lay on the oilcloth, which in her case was white.

The dishes were not brought in until the Mother Superior arrived. The sound of the door opening produced an answering noise as all those who had sat down now rose to greet her. Pyramus came first, self-important and surly, growling, barking, or making a nuisance of himself in some other way, always annoyed about something; and he was followed by Mother Apolline and two or three Sisters, one carrying the footwarmer, another a thick cushion for the back of her armchair.

She would come trundling in on her little short legs, the girdle of her black apron tied like an odalisk's (the older girls called it "Oriental style") at the lowest point of her thick-set and inflexible torso; in she came, as though propelled forward by the weight of her stomach, in a sort of involuntary run which she did her best to render majestic.

She would go up to her chair and, standing behind it and leaning on the back, say grace. Then the lay-sisters came in with great steaming dishes piled high with brightly coloured mashes—a shining brown, or a sharp green studded with white and yellow, or reddish, according to whether they were full of lentils, spinach with quartered hard-boiled eggs, or red haricots: to and fro they went between the tables, and the meal began. But certain smaller plates found their way in Sister Amédée's hands to the little table with the white oilcloth; Mother Apolline, in fact, owing to the delicate state of her health, was accustomed to submit to various building-up diets, most of which—for she prided herself on her medical knowledge—she had prescribed for herself. A little sole might be set down before her, or a cutlet, or a small pigeon, or brains, or creamed veal, or a chicken wing; and to follow there would be a pastry, or fruit, or cream—all of which she accepted only after a great show of reluctance, and only then as if giving way solely because of the exigencies of her prescribed diet, of which Sister Amédée would firmly and respectfully remind her. Often she would offer some little delicacy from her own table to one of the nuns sitting near her.

Silence was obligatory during the meal, and only the Mother Superior spoke, outlining future projects, raising her voice so that everyone should hear as she gave her orders for the next day, the Sister addressed assenting in a murmur. Suddenly the front-door bell might be heard ringing, followed by the familiar sharp click of the door opening and shutting; it was a day-girl who had had to wait in the corridor and was only now being fetched. From Pyramus, ensconced beneath Mother Apolline's armchair, would immediately come a furious and surly growling (his peace of mind was disturbed by the smallest incident, such as anyone's passing him too closely or too quickly, or dropping a spoon); the Mother Superior would shake out her skirts, and from out of the folds of her black habit appeared his ugly, sullen head.

Occasionally—it might be a saint's day, or to celebrate some happy occasion, or simply of her own good will—Mother Apolline would ring the bell on her table and unexpectedly announce:

"Recreation!"

A chorus of sing-song voices immediately responded:
"Thank you, Mother!"

And without the slightest pause the silence, hitherto broken only by the continual clatter of spoons and forks on plates, would be succeeded by a terrific uproar: the Mother Superior would interrupt it by ringing her little bell again and crying:

"Quieter!"

As milk on the point of boiling will suddenly seethe up and boil over but quickly subside when the saucepan is removed, only to froth up again the moment it is replaced, so the hubbub began again, worse than ever.

On leaving the table they went out for a walk. Afternoon lessons began at two and did not end until the tea-time break. Games varied according to season. In spring there was skipping or knuckle-bones. But in autumn it was round games. In the deepening evening mists the little girls would dance round hand in hand, their clear voices reflecting the joy of dancing and getting quite out of breath in the choruses. They sang "Miller, are you asleep? Your wheels, your wheels go round too fast," or "Behind our house at home there is a little bird." Sometimes a young nun would break the ring to join in. At certain moments the rhythm became faster and faster: hair flew out, plaits bobbed up and down. The nun, stepping sidelong in the midst of all these bounding children, would lengthen her stride and her black veil would stream out like their flying tresses. Then the circle would be reformed to enclose a second, smaller one; and at a given signal heads bobbed under raised arms and the inner circle now enclosed the outer, forming a closely packed and suddenly motionless mass, a circular clump bristling with heads and woven of interlaced arms.

In winter it was impossible to go out of doors. Games were organized in the recreation-room in the light of three oil lamps fixed to the pillars, which left great shadows in the corners of the room. One group would be playing "Take care, La Tour," another "My fine castle!" Boarders back from the refectory where they had been to choose some dainty from their own private store of provisions would wander about among the rest munching raisins, or an apple, or a large juicy pear which they would eat with the skin on, throwing away the rapidly browning core into the cinders of the open tray beneath the great iron stove. The atmosphere would be thick with dust visibly swirling in the smoky light of the oil-lamps; the pungent odour of fruit mingled with a smell of caramel and burnt paper —for some of the little girls would kneel round a foot-warmer and melt the scrap of sugar or chocolate intended for their tea on a sheet of paper—seemed to be the very smell of winter play-time.

If they seemed to be talking together instead of playing, the nun in charge would set them to playing some game in which they must all join—they would sing the "Chevalier de la Marjorlaine," or "It's mid-night and the watchman's going by." And two by two, clapping loudly or gently according to the directions for each verse—"no noise, a little noise, a lot of noise"—the little girls marched round the room accompanied by a mute frieze of confused and gesticulating shadows all along the wall. Those with colds crowded round the stove, their feet on footwarmers, comparing symptoms in low voices as they waited to go up to the dormitory. About six o'clock they would rise to go, after fetching their little jugs of hot water from the kitchen, so hot they could scarcely manage to carry them even wrapped round with a fichu or the corner of an apron.

Sister Edmond's Sacred Heart for her class-room did not arrive until the beginning of December. It was unpacked in Mother Apolline's room, and Sister Edmond brought it down after tea, carrying it tenderly in her arms like a new-born babe.

Before they had even looked at it the little girls began to exclaim admiringly—partly to flatter the Sister and partly to conciliate the new arrival:

"Oh Sister, isn't it beautiful!"

But Sister Edmond seemed disappointed. She turned it this way and that, studied it, discovered faults in it for all that she held it in such respect: the body was too stocky, the head too small. And the attitude was absolutely wrong. She considered it had an air of indifference about it and that the hands were too tightly closed.

"It's not at all what I asked for," she said. "I meant something much grander. This is no good at all!"

When she had placed it in position the effect was still more distressing. The height of the niche made it look insignificant, and it stood out against the white background in a most unfortunate way.

Her face drawn with disappointment and vexation she stood frowning at it, shaking her head and reiterating:

"It's wretched. Wretched!"

Then, since it was still not quite set, she climbed up on to a stool and gingerly opened the fingers out a little: for many days afterwards she spent all her time in class cutting out gold paper stars which she proceeded to stick all over the interior of the niche, now painted by Sister Sylvestre, at her earnest entreaty, to look like grey marble.

6

ONE MORNING SISTER EDMOND—who for some time past had been in the habit of bemoaning the evil state of current affairs and prophesying at every opportunity, in hollow tones and the most enigmatic phrases, the most dire calamities and frightful catastrophes—faced her class with her pinched face even yellower than usual and announced that they were going to pray for the poor persecuted Jesuit Fathers. And indeed the Society of Jesus had once again been dissolved: only the day before their chapel in the rue du Palais-de-Justice had been closed, and the interdicted Fathers were leaving.

This news made all the deeper impression in that the Fathers were all well known in the convent, where they preached the retreat and ran the Sisterhood of the Children of Mary: it really felt as if they were all back again in the age of persecution under Nero or Diocletian. The day-scholars brought fresh news with them from day to day, each striving to outdo the others. One had seen a Father between two gendarmes; another announced that they were all sealed up in their chapel, and that if you walked past it now you could hear their groans. A lady was alleged to have endeavoured to get bread through to them and been put in prison for it. One pious young lady, Mademoiselle Poire, was known to have broken the seals—no one knew exactly what this meant, but it seemed on a par with the saints' action in tearing down idols. Some of the Sisters themselves quite expected to see their own chapel burnt down, their convent laid low, and themselves thrown to the flames. The lives of the saints took on a sort of reality. Every time the name of any saint came up who had been boiled in oil and tortured with pincers after having been sent to what the narrator called "those awful places" (irresistibly suggesting particularly dirty water-closets from which the saint, according to history, by special permission of God invariably emerged unsullied), Sister Edmond, filled with mingled terror and ardour at the thought of martyrdom, would think to herself that one day or another just such a fate would befall her, and that she too would be called upon to witness to her faith.

In the meantime Lent came round. Every evening now, about five o'clock, the whole school went to the church of St. Benoît for compline. They would set off down the avenue by the path that ran under the garden walls, a diminishing file of pupils flanked by seven or eight nuns clasping prayer-books; the head of the procession would be already at the church porch before the Sister who terminated it had pushed the little iron door to behind her and run a few steps to catch up with the vanishing tail.

Sometimes it would be raining, that March rain that can often be so cold, mixed with melting snow; and then as they entered the church their rubbers would shuffle and squeak as the soles stuck to the flag-stones. Besides the school attached to St. Benoît, a lay-school run by a Mademoiselle Vincelin, which had its place at the top of the nave, and the day-girls who could be seen on the opposite side of the aisle, five or six of them, heads and shoulders covered with tasselled capes— besides these, only about fifteen other persons ever came to evening service, familiar silhouettes who seemed almost a part of the church, and perhaps two or three mothers of day-girls come to take their daughters home at the end of the service.

Crowded close together on their benches, at the ends of which sat the nuns, the girls were soon chilled to the bone with the cold and dampness that floated about between the grey walls with their smell of damp and saltpetre. Gradually night came on. In the pulpit the curé knelt and prayed. His quiet voice echoed mournfully in the dim silence of the church, and down in the shadows a muffled and uniform murmur rose in response, hardly audible, and ceasing abruptly.

After the Litany at the close of the prayer there came the meditation on Death. And the sombre majesty of the words they heard awoke in these childish minds a sort of terror that haunted them till they

239

were safely back again in the warmth of the class-room, half an hour later, each in her own place. But in bed in the dormitory at night those words, like a solemn warning, echoed again in the depths of one's soul.

"Let us always remember that we may die to-night, let us see if we are ready to appear before God. . . . O God! O Moment! O Eternity! A God who is all, a moment that is nothing, an eternity that can deprive you of all or bestow all upon you for ever. A God whom you serve so ill, a moment that you turn to such little account, an eternity that you leave to chance. . . ."

Some of the little girls, afraid of dying in the night, recalled Sister Edmond's advice and traced the names of Jesus, Mary, and Joseph on their foreheads with their thumbs.

The Easter holidays arrived and Catherine, for the second time that year, went home. She had been given as an Easter present two religious books—*Fabiola* and *The Martyrs*. Her enthusiasm was kindled with the first pages of these homely and heroic tales, full of intimate details and supernatural revelations, which were only a glorified development of what she had been taught at the convent; she flung herself with passionate interest and no feeling of astonishment into this antique world, so different from everything she had known hitherto, but where at every step of the path she found souls to guide her filled with just such emotions as her own. Her imagination, so long con-

240

fined by the routine of school life, soared suddenly afresh. The strange and fabulous creatures who only a year ago had been the companions of her leisure hours now disappeared, and queens, princesses, and genii gave way to very different personages—beautiful blonde virgins in white robes, noble martyrs in tunics, or the Christian slave-girl brutalized by her idolatrous mistress whom eventually she converts. The first time she went to Aunt Aurore's and saw the garden again she discovered that these heroes lived in the depths of the rockery, where they occupied the ancient dwellings of the people they had overthrown. The fairy-palace was now Fabiola's house, and its sombre corridors, that once led to sorcerers' dens, now penetrated to the catacombs, in the depths of which the Apostle Peter preached, and where old, grey-headed, trembling bishops interred the bodies of young violated Christian martyrs by the light of torches and to the chanting of psalms.

All that she saw and heard around her added to the impression made by her reading. Everybody was talking about laws against religion and persecuted Christians. The priests in the pulpit were for ever announcing prayers for what they termed reparation for injuries done to Jesus Christ in the Holy Sacrament. One day Catherine heard that the Fathers, braving the edicts against them, were still living on in their house and secretly continuing to hold services and hear confession in their chapel.

241

This subterranean resistance, which was generally regarded as a stout blow to the power of those who were persecuting them, was the one subject of conversation in all the religious households of the town. People described how for the first time since what they called "it" had happened, they had gone to the Jesuit chapel again; those who had had the courage to do so were pointed out and admired; those who had hung back determined to follow this example. There was a great deal of mutual encouragement. Ladies held mysterious and low-voiced meetings, and arranged to go together to such and such a service, but never more than six or seven at once, so as not to attract attention. The little band would meet at the house of one of its members who lived near the Fathers' residence and walk silently down the rue du Palais-de-Justice and past the newly walled-up main door; with a conspiratorial sign to the porter they would advance trembling down a narrow passage between ivied walls, from which opened a little side door to the chapel. Gradually, as the weeks went by, they became quite used to these dangers, and took fewer precautions. The Fathers, too, on their side became bolder. The harmonium was heard again. Then the chapel bell. And twice a week at five o'clock neighbours and passers-by and the magistrates leaving court might hear behind that grey façade, in which the brand new bricks of the walled-up door made a conspicuously bright gash, the sound of the Fathers' choir, which seemed to say, "Here we are still!"

When Catherine returned to the convent after her fortnight's holiday spring had come. Leaves were bursting out on the trees, the seats had been put out again under the plane-trees in the courtyard, and evening playtime now was out in the garden. This extended from the courtyard, from which it was separated by a low wall, right up to the church of St. Benoît, which formed its furthest limit, and was divided into numerous narrow strips of beds, always gay with flowers; on a rock in the central path, dominating all, stood an old stone figure of the Virgin with a high sculptured crown.

Seated on the forms which they had dragged from the courtyard, the little girls played their quiet games. Here and there a nun stood talking in the midst of a group. And up and down the alleys paved with large white cobbles, as white as if each had been separately washed, the older girls walked arm in arm; sometimes one group would walk backwards before another, keeping its distance. All of a sudden two little girls who had been whispering together, after many hesitations and mutual encouragements, took their courage in their hands and butting into a group jumped up and clasped one of the older girls round the neck, wordlessly. Then they fled, at once delighted and terrified by their audacity, and pretending they were merely fulfilling an obligation, which the small daily sacrifices they were always being recommended to make allowed them to picture in this case as a voluntary

243

penance; under the cloak of this idea, and with innocent disingenuousness—divining perhaps in this delicious compulsion a completer submission, the pangs of which they already began to feel—they gave rein to a complicated mixture of emotions: shame, pleasure, pride, and bashfulness.

Each of the little girls had thus her own particular big girl, to be admired and made the object of a cult. But however constantly you might think of her and however frequently your allusions might reveal the object of your affections, never was she referred to by name; that remained hidden in the depths of your heart, like the sanctuary lamp whose flame burns only before its altar. You would have been content simply to be noticed, though you could have desired to walk hand in hand with her. Just as much did you long for her to distinguish herself and do something wonderful. However, as she was nearly always in her last year at school, one was saddened by the thought that there would not be much more time in which to see her, and that next year she would be gone. And one's feeling for her became coloured with a sense of transiency, of uncertainty, that rendered it more intense still.

Things that had belonged to the adored, or that she had given you, were jealously treasured: an old exercise, a picture, a flower or a frond of moss mounted on a card. Catherine kept a black ribbon in her desk in this way that one of the members of the first form,

Julie Chavanges, had lost one day during break. From then on the initiated never spoke of Julie Chavanges save as "the lost ribbon." And when the Virgin Mary was spoken of in class, in the catechism, or during a sermon, one or two girls would always remember how Julie had taken this part in the Christmas tableau vivant and exchange surreptitious and meaning glances with Catherine.

But now, high and low alternately, the four quarters chimed from St. Benoît: then, on a new and different note, eight o'clock struck. The nun in charge immediately clapped her hands, the girls lined up, and before they reached the passage door the girls in front would begin the evening hymn, which they sang as they went upstairs. Very often they would meet Mother Apolline on the landing of the first floor, motionless and smiling, with Pyramus at her feet, and a nun standing a little behind her with a hot-water bottle, however mild the weather might be, wrapped round with some blue stuff.

The ranks lost their precision a little as they left the landing; some, to get undressed as quickly as possible, bent down and, almost without stopping, unbuttoned their boots with a single tug at the top button. Once in the dormitory, they put on dressing-gowns, brushed their hair, and advancing between the two rows of beds, said good-night to Sister Chantal who would be lighting the night-light at her table.

"I wish you good-night, Sister."

And then each, turning to her companions, would add:

"Good-night, Mesdemoiselles."

Two or three might be in disgrace; in dressing-gowns and with plaits hanging down their backs, they stood near Sister Chantal, muttering over the Epistle of St. Paul, which they must repeat by heart before going to bed. But soon they too were in bed, and complete silence reigned. A glimmer of daylight entered through the white cotton curtains drawn across the open windows. There was a sound of footsteps outside in the street: tranquil voices, dogs barking; the soft air puffed at the curtains and they blew out from the window frames and settled slowly back. Sometimes a little girl would sob quietly in her bed, dreaming of home and her own little empty room. At ten o'clock the sound of bugles came from a barracks close by, ending on a long, dying note.

Some evenings there would be a sudden hurrying of the footsteps outside in the avenue; down below in the house windows would be shut; then, after a moment's utter silence, a soft rumbling of thunder and almost immediately the pattering of rain among leaves.

7

IN ORDER TO KEEP a more exact account of their progress along the path of Christian perfection, the communicants, for a month before their confirmation, made much use of what was called the rosary of mortifications, a kind of rosary with beads that could be easily moved from one side to the other. At each victory over self—if, for instance, the desire to eat chocolate at tea-time or to answer impatiently had been successfully resisted—a bead was slipped to one side. But if you yielded to bad temper, or took a sensual pleasure in your chocolate, another bead was slipped to the opposite side. In the evening victories and defeats were added up and the separate totals recorded in a sort of spiritual accounts-book, called the book of mortifications. The pages of this book were ruled into columns; one for mortifications, one for fasts, one for rosaries, one for victories, one for defeats. A balance was struck at the end of each week.

As confirmation day approached the "victories" column bristled with little ticks, while the "defeats" column remained white. By this time life would consist of nothing but prayers, pious readings, and visits to the Blessed Sacrament: everyone was feverishly pre-

paring for the examination in the catechism. From time
to time some little girl would be called up to the linen-
room: the dressmaker had brought her white muslin
dress to try on. But now everyone pretended to a
complete lack of interest in matters of dress—an
achievement which entitled you to slip still another
bead to the "victories" side.

On the last day, during evening recreation, the
prospective communicants finished distributing their
confirmation badges, begun some time before, but
interrupted by the three days of retreat.

With the rapidly diminishing little packets in their
hands they moved about among the other girls, who
stood in little groups gazing at them with fluttering
envy and respect; with lowered eyes, conscious of their
fleeting royalty, like a young fiancée who conceals her
bliss—so, swollen with vanity beneath their modest
looks, they went from friend to friend, until each had
got her badge. And you chose out the very prettiest for
your "big girl," who would say—and this filled you
with pride and joy:

"Don't forget to pray for me!"

Sister Calixte, indeed, was very clever in the way
she profited by the well-known fact that a little girl's
prayers are always granted on the day of her confirmation, for with an air of stern authority she would
recommend her eight to you—the eight girls of her
class, that is to say, who were preparing for their finals
that year. At length—but these must be black, with

no dedication—you would offer your badges to the nuns, who would thank you, put them carefully away in their prayer-books, and later in the evening turn them over to Sister Edmond, who would sell them all over again next year.

On the day of the ceremony Mass was celebrated at St. Benoît's, and afterwards the communicants all returned to school for lunch. And those who had set out anxious and faint with emotion now returned with minds at rest, happy to be delivered at last from the unknown fate which had been hanging over them so long, which had been, moreover, at the back of every-thing they had said and done for more than a year. In the afternoon they would all assemble in the recreation-room, where relatives were allowed between lunch and Rosary, and again a little before Vespers. And between these visits they would play little quiet games together or confide to one another their impres-sions of the day.

"When I saw the Curé coming out of the sacristy I thought I was going to be sick!" one would say; while another would complain of the way her companion had trod on her dress all the time. Or they would compare their books and rosaries: this one was the best—no, that one was!

Then, about half-past two, putting on the veils they had taken off that morning when they got back from church, they played at what they called "Jacob's Ladder"—that is to say, they knelt down face to face on the steps up to the stage, right up to the foot of the little altar which had been set up overnight, and stretched out their arms, holding their veils in their finger-tips, so that they seemed to make a long ladder up to the flower-decked altar, like a ladder of angels with wings outspread.

At the end of the afternoon Catherine was taken to see her grandmother, whose ill health had prevented her from attending the ceremony. She was out of danger now and already convalescent, but in that kind of drowsy oblivion from which those who end their days immobile in an armchair never seem to emerge, and to which she had now abandoned herself unresistingly; as she lay there the symptoms of final dissolution might have been discerned appearing one by one. Forgotten memories returned to her; little by little her thoughts went back over the course of her life, as if she would prolong it now. And it was above all of the one who was absent, of Bernard, of whom she thought. After years of resignation she now revolted against the idea that she herself in bygone days had, by her own inability to stand firm against his entreaties, contributed to her son's estrangement from her. If he had to be a priest, she would say again and again, he need not have chosen the one Order so strict that it destroys all human affection. In September she had a relapse, and never again left her bed. Her faint voice when she spoke now sounded far away, as though muffled by a

250

cloth. Three times the parish priest came to give her Extreme Unction. In the last hour of her life she repeated Bernard's name untiringly, over and over again. With every breath the sound grew less distinct, until at last speech and breathing ceased together.

Catherine was taken to see her grandmother for the last time. The thing that most struck her as they entered the room was the exaggerated smallness of her face, which seemed scarcely larger than the face of a child, and looked like an earthly stain amid the shining whiteness of the sheets. She might have been sleeping. But Catherine, for whom death until then had been no more than a word, suddenly had a sense of something dreadful between her and the body lying there, of something like an invisible barrier separating the living from the dead; perhaps it is the absence of those vital emanations which stream from one living being to another, and which are apprehended by other similar vibrations.

The holidays came to an end some days after the funeral, to which Catherine was taken by a nun, the mistress of the class she was about to join. All the companions of her own age who had left the convent only two months ago as little girls now returned greatly changed in build, behaviour, and dress. Their minds had changed as well. The religious perplexities of the last year had given place to all kinds of vague preoccupations; and these led to secret conversations which had later to be confessed as frivolous or immodest.

For instance, they worried a great deal as to how children were born. One evening during homework, Catherine extracted the long-desired information from Alice le Hombre, one of her friends and her senior by some years. Her friend refused to tell her anything at first, taking refuge in the promise she had given the girl who had told her. At length, to avoid saying what she had sworn never to repeat, she took her compasses and pointed to various words in her New Testament. And so Catherine learnt that children come out of one's breast. This opinion, moreover, was the one most widely favoured by other little girls of the same age. But the word—breast—represented in their eyes something hardly seemly, if not actually repugnant; in secret, however, each looked to see if her own chest was developing. And seeing the flat chests of the nuns, they wondered what the reason could be for such exceptions! Then one little girl announced that novices had their breasts planed away. Well, some of the nuns still possessed a few signs of having chests; but wouldn't it be possible to take every vestige away from those who were still too well developed? And the idea of such an operation seemed by no means too improbable, since it carried suggestions of penance, of a sacrifice pleasing in God's eyes, and even of martyrdom.

Among the older girls in the class there were some, in the throes of physical transformation, who lived in the expectancy of a mysterious event which would finally raise them to the category of "big" girls. They knew that when that moment came they would at last have a figure, and then you could wear real whalebone corsets and fitted bodices to your dresses! But up to then there was, somewhere round your middle, a sort of little pouch full of blood which was suddenly going to be expelled, leaving the place quite empty. Every now and then one or other of them would complain in class of feeling ill; the announcement would be received with understanding smiles. Sometimes a girl would be absent for one or two days and would return to the convent looking very mysterious and proud. But once it was all over and done with the pride generally disappeared.

Little by little there reappeared that sentimental fever inherent in boarding-school life, augmented by the long preparations for confirmation, and only temporarily ousted by these new and different pre-occupations. Now it made fresh demands and sought fresh outlets. Emotions nowadays demanded reciprocal emotions, and of course intimacy with one's chosen "big girl" was out of the question. Besides, one was becoming too big oneself now to have a big girl any more—the Sisters, on the other hand, were all either plain or elderly, by no means lending themselves to those fervent adorations which, in most convents, centre round particularly pretty or fascinating nuns. Such a confused emotion might have spent itself within the convent in passionate friendships between girls of the same age, had it not about this time suddenly found vent in an unexpected direction: the spark of this conflagration was introduced by a day-girl, and it spread to nearly every girl in the class, satisfying their imaginations, to a lesser degree their hearts, their dawning sensuality, and that irresistible need for intrigue which sleeps in every woman's heart and entraps her as much as love itself.

A little time back, in fact, the day-girl in question had got to know (outside the convent) an assistant mistress at the Vincelin school, who had started writing to her and to whom she wrote back. There arose between the girls of the convent and the girls of this other school, whom they called the Vincelines, an exchange of letters full of protestations of love and good advice, and containing a mixture of locks of hair, dried flowers, and symbolical badges; they swore eternal friendship and promised to pray for each other in exams. And on Sundays Claire Legay, the day-girl, would collect the convent letters and surreptitiously exchange them in the darkness of the church porch for another bundle of letters that Mademoiselle Louise, the assistant mistress, gave her.

One day there passed from hand to hand through the class a picture that Mademoiselle Louise herself had painted and sent to Claire Legay; it depicted a bunch of violets with a quatrain inscribed in letters of gold and ending: "Love has caught me." Alice le Hombre also showed Catherine a letter she had received from her particular friend. And Catherine, with secret resentment at having nothing like it herself to show, read: "I would swim the ocean for you, even though it were in flames!" Another girl swallowed some pins, defying her rival to give so striking a proof of love.

Meanwhile the retreat came round again. And the score or so of girls in the second form, as though recapturing the emotions of their first Communion, followed the exercises with extreme devotion, finding all the chief elements of their trouble touched on in the course of their instructions, implied as well as explicit, in the searching out of their sins, and in the interrogations of the confessional.

This year the retreat was preached by Father Cochet, one of the banned Jesuit Fathers, and thus something of an outlaw, which fact gave him with some of the girls an added prestige. He was a dirty-looking priest with a coarse and powerful nose, greasy hair, an oily skin blackened as to the lower half of the face and the cheeks by a vigorous growth of badly shaven beard which would grow again in a very few hours, and a chin which rested in a soft bulge on the top of his dirty soutane.

Apart from the traditional sermons on death, divine mercy, judgement, and hell, his instruction, whatever its ostensible subject, sooner or later invariably came round to a certain point which, it was felt, even more with him than with the Fathers who had preached retreat in the past, was the perpetual object of his thoughts. It had to do with intimate friendships, and the period of the holidays; and although he was talking to girls the heroes of his anecdotes were always boys. He told, for instance, how one of his pupils ("poor, unfortunate youth," he said) had hesitated long before going out to walk in the town one holiday. The Devil, one might say, was urging him to leave the paternal roof, while his good angel was holding him back. But the Devil conquered in the end; he went out; and when he came back to the college that evening he asked leave to confess to the Father Superior. When he had made his confession he went to bed; and in the morning they found him dead in his bed. But how lucky for him that he had received absolution, for that very day he had lost his innocence.

Leaning back against the altar, the Father talked on interminably. He did not gesture at all, but all the while his eyes went from face to face in his attentive audience, the lenses of his rimless glasses flashing as he turned. At times his voice would soften and melt and cease altogether; and when he stopped speaking his straight, thin lips would close with an effort over discoloured teeth which seemed completely rotted.

To squeeze the last drop from the curious mood of pleasurable apprehension produced in them by the thrice daily repetition of these exhortations, some of the girls took every opportunity of going to the chapel. There they would prepare themselves for confession, recite prayers, do the Stations of the Cross, and ponder their besetting sin in prolonged meditation. Back in the class-room they would write down their confessions on a sheet of paper, consulting their books of mortifications to do so. And then, in groups of ten, they would go back to the chapel, each with her list of sins clutched in her hand or folded in her missal; and always at the last minute some forgotten sin would be recalled and have to be added to the list in pencil.

Each entered the sacristy in turn, with a hurried whisper—"Is he very strict?"—to the girl who was just coming out, who would reply with a word or a reassuring wink. It was a long, dark, narrow little room, and the Father would be sitting in an armchair near the door beside a little compartment pierced with a grille, his face completely hidden in an enormous red-patterned handkerchief which he held to his eyes. Making the sign of the cross he asked you your name and referred to a list placed at hand; and through the handkerchief a low voice issued, questioning, gradually growing more animated, demanding details, forcing you to be specific. But if the greater part of the commandments were very quickly disposed of there were some, nevertheless, on which one dwelt at length. Many girls tried to clear up points which they still found obscure. Some, indeed, while their waiting companions exchanged smiles of mockery which yet contained a certain admiration, made their confessions last as long as three-quarters of an hour.

Next day there would always be some who suddenly discovered they had forgotten three or four sins; and these would at once ask leave to revisit the confessional. Or you might go again to clear up some scruple, some hesitation, or because you felt the need of direction or advice. And then, with a whispered, "I shan't be more than a moment!" you would beg the girl who should have gone in next to let you go in her place. You might even go as far as to borrow another girl's hat—"So that the Father won't recognize me," you would say.

At the beginning of June the convent made its annual pilgrimage to Notre-Dame du Chêne, a pious outing which Catherine had never yet made, since only girls who had been confirmed could go. As they had to start very early in the morning, Catherine, who since the previous October had been a day-girl once again, spent the night at the convent. Long before daybreak—indeed, it was barely two o'clock—she heard the bell which had awoken her so many times in the previous year, and murmuring *Deo gratias* with the others, she jumped to the foot of her bed. To-day, however, everyone dressed as quickly as she could, moving with a cheerful liveliness. As soon as they were ready they made their way down to the refectory where the picnic baskets had been put out on the tables; each found her own, the procession formed up; and with Sister Calixte at its head and the class-mistresses on the flanks, the column set off for the station, followed by the lay-sisters, one carrying a medicine chest, others the Sisters' picnic baskets and

Mother Apolline's own supplies—her folding arm-chair, her shawls, fichus, and special provisions—while she herself, a knitted shawl hugged over her chest, brought up the rear, leaning heavily on Sister Edmond's arm, Pyramus at her heels.

It was still pitch-dark. The avenue was dim and deserted beneath the stars. The houses were all shuttered, and the trees that ran parallel with them seemed to hold their boughs immensely high up over-head in the darkness full of night scents from the gardens.

Arrived at the station, brightly lit and quite deserted, they made their way over the tracks to their own train, which was waiting at a distant platform. Here and there the silhouette of a porter or a traveller was faintly visible. An incessant lowing came from distant cattle-trucks.

The train waited in the station for some time. Some of the girls fell asleep despite the incessant chattering of the others; and when they were awakened by some practical joke their bewildered return to consciousness was greeted with explosive laughter and delight. At last the train moved off. It was still night as the porters called out the names of the first few stations. At one stop the phrases of a familiar psalm were heard rising from one compartment; it was the older girls chanting. Pupils and Sisters all joined in and began to intone the Ave Maria, and as one party followed on another the confused burden spread from compartment to compartment, from coach to coach, until it was drowned by the noise of wheels again. Meanwhile day was beginning to break, and beyond the curves of the horizon, bounded now by the low wooded hills which had succeeded to the plain, they watched out for the sun to rise.

At the end of an hour's journey they alighted at a little country town; the station was still fast asleep, and an omnibus stood waiting in the yard, drawn by an aged horse. They drove right through the town, crossed a little river, and stopped at the foot of a high hill crowned with thick woods. The path they now took wound uphill through open country, skirting fields of ripening corn and clover, until it reached the higher pastures where cattle grazed or lay and chewed the cud. All had bells about their necks, and every time they raised their heads or tore at the grass with blunt muzzles the bells would clang. And in that fresh, pure air the whole grassy mountain-side was alive with crisp, clear janglings in many different tones, beneath the solid wall of woods that crowned the summit.

The path went up and up, and the little girls walking in the rear saw the older girls in front plunge beneath an arch of greenery, deep and sombre. It was now that the pilgrimage really began, and they started singing. They sang with spirit, but their voices were muffled by the early morning dampness which rose up from the great sleek cushions of moss at the foot of beech and oak and dripped back from the dew-sodden leaves above. Far off the chapel bell was ringing. Mother Apolline, still followed by the panting Pyramus, head low, tongue lolling out, interrupted the march for a moment to announce in tones made tragic by exhaustion:

"Listen! The Holy Mother is calling to us!"

Oaks gave way to pines; and there in the dry shade it suddenly seemed warmer. The path was widening now, and at last on the very summit of the mountain the chapel itself came into view in the heart of a large clearing of mown grass.

From the main doorway at the bottom of the light and narrow nave with its columns adorned with the banners of all the different towns that had come here on pilgrimage, the first thing to catch one's eye was a sort of column behind the altar, consisting of a tree-trunk enshrined in glass with the figure of the miraculous Virgin fixed in a crevice—a little black Virgin in a large white satin robe, sleeveless, triangular, shapeless, apparently unsupported by any body. From this dress there emerged—like a mushroom, so worn and blackened by time was it—a very small head carved in wood and surmounted by a high metal crown. Shepherds, it was said, had found it at this very spot three hundred years ago.

The first Mass was said by one of the two convent chaplains, who had come all the way by carriage; and breakfast was taken under the trees outside. And while they ate their bread and chocolate, Mother Apolline, comfortably settled in her folding chair and ministered to by her customary slaves, Sister Edmond and Sister Amédée, drank down a large white bowl of fresh milk which had been brought up from the village specially for her. Then, an hour later, they attended a second Mass, said this time by the second chaplain. This Mass was sung, and at the end there was a solemn distribution of scapulars. The communicants of the year received the scapular of Mount Carmel—two little squares of chestnut-coloured cloth, each sewn with an image of the Holy Virgin; the older girls got the blue scapular of the Immaculate Conception. There was also the red scapular, called the scapular of the Passion, and worn by the nuns; but few girls would venture to apply for this, since the wearing of it entailed certain obligations, one of which, it was believed, was never to appear with neck and shoulders uncovered; and this would have prevented them from going out into society.

Lunch-time at last arrived. Separated into little groups of friends, sitting on a heap of faggots or a fallen tree-trunk, they opened their baskets. In theirs the boarders found the modest provisions supplied the previous day by the convent cook; perhaps a piece of sausage, hard-boiled eggs, cheese, a handful of cherries, and a little bottle of wine and water. But the day-girls close by were plentifully provided with cold chicken, patties, cakes, fruit of every kind, flagons of burgundy, or even champagne. Some even had tiny bottles of liqueur. And, despite the admonitions of the Sisters, who suggested restraint and modesty, begging them to remember the scapulars they had just received, a noisy chattering began, interrupted only by the Rosary at one o'clock.

The hot afternoon hours were spent playing little games, playing hide-and-seek round the chapel, gathering flowers on the wooded slopes. Two or three of the older girls managed to lose themselves and did not return until the evening. Every now and then a little girl would piously go off to light a candle on the triangular candlestick which stood at the foot of the altar of the Virgin, or to drink at the miraculous spring —a spring full of frogs and weeds into which, before leaving in the evening, they would all dip a corner of their handkerchiefs or plunge a little bottle to keep the water against future injuries or illnesses.

Benediction at five o'clock brought everybody back into the chapel, and afterwards they settled down outside again for dinner. The noise they made was deafening by now. They finished up all the food, and tried to make the nuns tipsy with a mixture of all that was left of the various wines and liqueurs, but in vain, though one or two of them were a little gayer than usual.

Gradually night fell. Beneath the trees the shadows deepened and laughter was extinguished. A kind of melancholy fell upon them all. For the last time they returned to the chapel. One of the chaplains said the evening prayer and they made the responses in hushed voices, prey to a sort of fearful fervour engendered by oncoming night.

From minute to minute the little nave grew darker. Before the altar, in a halo of reddish light, many candles twinkled. And all around, at different heights from the ground, on the walls between the marble plaques or inside the shrine itself or hanging by blue ribbons from the Virgin's monstrous dress, brighter now in its glittering glass cage, little metal hearts shone like little golden flames. Now it was that vows were made and special mercies entreated. Piety grew sentimental. One would pray to become Mademoiselle Louise's favourite, another promised a dozen rosaries if she might meet her friend before the end of the week, or if their parents might only become acquainted through the intervention of the Holy Virgin. Some, when the prayer had been said and the farewell hymn sung, lit a last taper before the image of the Virgin, so that when they were gone something of themselves should still remain in the solitude of the chapel, back once more in its normal stillness.

Involuntarily they hurried through the woods, in which nocturnal life was beginning to stir. And it was only when the edge of the open country was reached and the last of the day rediscovered that they began to talk again. A need for confidences, for mutual trust, brought little groups together: two by two they walked arm in arm. And little by little they would reveal their secrets, and expose the very depths of their souls. They confessed the objects of their prayers, and why. The little ones, meanwhile, suddenly overcome by tiredness, were dragging behind; it was a painful effort to carry the baskets, that felt so heavy now, although they were empty.

Back in the town they filed through the church to salute the Host. Then, a few minutes later, they were safely back in the train, packed into the compartments where they huddled shoulder to shoulder, worn out, their heads buzzing, their eyes closing on visions of endless pines.

8

For a whole week Claire Legay did not come to school—they were in the First now, Sister Calixte's form, where one generally remained for three years—and all that time nobody knew the reason for her absence: they wondered if she were ill, or if her parents were leaving town. It was all rather mysterious. Then, at one of those meetings held three times a week by the Mother Superior and called "Reunion," Mother Apolline announced that from then on they were to put her out of their minds, as she would never be coming back. On her advice Claire's parents had entered her as a border at the Convent of the Annunciation, where the stricter discipline would be better for her. The girls greeted this news with expressions of pity and consternation, but many of them looked embarrassed. They knew what had happened—Claire had been writing to a boy and one of her letters had been intercepted—and they felt distinctly uneasy about themselves and what might happen to them.

For several months now—at least for many of the girls at the convent—the secret friendships they had formed with girls from the Vincelin school in the old clandestine days had become normal friendships as they got to know each other in the ordinary way. This in its turn had led to a series of tentative intrigues. Some, if they happened to meet in the street, were content to cast covert glances at the young man accredited them by their companions; others, bolder, wrote. But the intrigues were no more than the fruit of suddenly unoccupied imaginations; it was not love they sought, but a continuation of that artificial excitement which had left them exhausted in heart and senses with its sterile adventures; and now, when they might really have begun to feel something, they were as unmoved as though they had already run through all the emotions. They saw the whole thing merely as a fickle, fleeting game, the greatest charm of which was its secrecy, and this in itself narrowed down their field of interest and left them, despite the ardour of their words, astonishingly unmoved and unawakened. None the less, to make their game seem real, they thought and talked incessantly of marriage. And since they could not think of love apart from marriage they tried to relate these clandestine romances to what they believed was the proper end of all such things—which yet was something quite unknown to them, and visualized only in terms of a material establishment; and somehow they found this hard to reconcile with the idea of the young lover of the moment. Further, though constantly thinking of a certain young man and determining to marry him, they knew perfectly well that no such thing would ever come to pass. And when, to

kill time, they told their fortunes and found the pre-
dictions by no means living up to their expectations,
they would hardly worry at all about what should
rightly have been a bitter disappointment: if they did
affect a broken heart it was merely to win the sympathy
of friends and to be able to play an interesting part.

To tell the future they had recourse to all kinds of
trivial occultisms—practices handed down from one
generation of schoolgirls to another and believed in
with the blindest faith in spite of affected airs of
amused incredulity. To see your future husband all you
had to do was slip a mirror under your pillow on the
day of Epiphany and placing one naked foot on your
bed recite an incantation which began:

> On the feast of Three Kings it is said
> Put your foot on the rail of your bed.

There was also an incantation to the moon which
had to be recited at a certain point in the month:

> Oh lovely crescent moon
> In dreams I crave this boon
> To see my husband soon.

And there was a legend to the effect that a girl who
had dreamt of a hearse after saying these lines had
died within the year. A good way of discovering the
initials of your husband's name was to consult the peel
of an apple or a pear, or the rind of an orange. Or you
could pull the petals of a daisy one by one, which

would tell you "whether you would be loved, how you would love, and whether you would be spinster, wife, widow, or nun or Carmelite." The downy clocks of dandelions were also reliable oracles.

Meanwhile the idea that nuns, who alone among women could not marry, were excluded from a life of sentiment, now revealed their mistresses to them in a different light. And in a sort of mockery of this state of voluntary celibacy, which seemed to them both pitiable and slightly absurd, Catherine and her friends would make up malicious romances, sometimes illustrated pictorially by the fancy of some young artist among them. Thus one day a caricature of Sister Calixte and the Vicar at a romantic rendezvous was passed round the class: there they stood holding hands at arm's length, like those stiff and mystical couples in the centre of ancient stained-glass windows representing the nuptials of the Virgin.

And Catherine herself was more amused than shocked when one day she glimpsed through the open door of the store-room an unexpected fulfilment of their casual jokes: the new chaplain was in the act of embracing Sister Bonne-Marie. It was only on second thoughts that she found anything astonishing in it. She saw now that, contrary to all she had hitherto thought possible, this priest and this nun could in fact love although they could not marry; but she judged it an exceptional case and was more surprised by its unusualness than by the furtive kiss which had brought the fact home to her—seeing in this nothing but the outward manifestation of the thing which really shocked her.

Catherine, in fact, as well as all the rest of her little group of intimate friends, was completely oblivious of the law of the senses—a law which had been kept so closely guarded a secret from her that she did not even suspect its existence. The private preoccupations with their physical development which had at one time troubled them so much were now completely vanished, nor did they feel the least curiosity in face of men. Birth still seemed a somewhat strange occurrence to them—a sort of accident which occurred in married life but had no other connection with love. And as they drew near to the time when they in their turn would have children, the phenomena of childbirth, with which they were by no means well acquainted, seemed to them perfectly natural and they made no more attempts to penetrate its mysteries.

It was only a few months before her final examinations that Catherine met a young man whom she could talk about to her friends. He had been introduced to her at a wedding, and the moment she set eyes on him (he was in the uniform of a Paris religious college and had the monogram of his school stamped in relief on the buckle of his belt, which was drawn very tightly round his waist), she knew she had met her fate.

Next day, describing the wedding to her friends, a

certain Emmanuel was so often dragged into the picture that they soon realized the place he had in her heart. For the next few days she met him daily in the street, and he would bow. Then for six months she did not see him again. But her thoughts were constantly with him, and she discussed him to such an extent with her friends that soon this young student, whom most of them had never set eyes on, had become a figure closely bound up with their own lives, growing ever more familiar with the passing of time and the recession of the day when Catherine had first met him. Anything was a pretext for discussing him. The slightest happening was occasion for providing him with opinions, tastes, preferences. Now, separately and almost simultaneously, some masculine figure was similarly implanted in the minds of all the older girls, the constant object of their conversation and their thoughts. And thus, parallel with their placid schoolgirl lives, they led another life, mysterious and secretive—and, for some, adventurous—of which none of those around them had the least suspicion.

Now as in earlier days—as in the time of the passions for the older girls, and again during the episode of the Vincelines—a certain Christian name had only to be mentioned for a dozen pairs of eyes to look up furtively and exchange swift, conspiratorial glances before converging on the one among them whom this name implicitly singled out. In the course of the whole year —except during February, which was full of the

271

accession of the Valois to the throne of France—Alice le Hombre, who was embroiled with a certain Louis, was probably the most favoured in this way. But at Christmas, whenever they sang the hymn "O come, O come, Emmanuel," the eyes of all the initiated would converge on Catherine, who would bring out the words with ostentatious fervour to show the intensity of her feelings.

He, moreover, by his own constancy, deserved the love he had inspired in her, and Catherine knew that as long as she was faithful to him she would never be betrayed. He was interested in everything that went to make up her life; he made efforts to find out all that she was doing, and counted the days that stretched between him and the holidays, when at last they would meet again. Meanwhile the year was coming to an end, and as much for his sake as for her own Catherine was eager to succeed in her examinations.

Although her excellence in spelling and composition made her almost certain of passing, there was one test which she particularly dreaded. This was needlework. Away from class, while others repeated long lists from their notes on history and geography, she could be seen at almost any time of day with an odd piece of stuff and a needle in her hand. And at home, whenever she could, she practised darning, button-holing, or overcasting under the eyes of Rosine, the middle-aged spinster whom Madame de Laignes employed as needle-woman several days a week.

Rosine was a pensioner of the patronage founded some twenty years before by Father Jond-Nécan, Superior of the Oblates, on behalf of female employees. It was on the model of their Workers' Circle, and was run by the nuns of the Order. Thus no event seemed more important to Rosine than the little happenings in the bosom of the Community, nor did it ever occur to her that anyone else might be interested in other things. She was a perpetual fountain of trivial news— the Children of Mary had elected a new president, such-and-such a Father or such-and-such a nun were about to be transferred, one of the chaplains was ill in bed. . . . Or she would expatiate, thereby reminding Catherine of the plays she herself had acted in at the convent, on the drama or comedy to be played at the Community; for the Oblates had a magnificent theatre with a dramatic company recruited from members of the Circle. And if Rosine herself had been given a part she would regale Catherine with detailed and enthusiastic descriptions of the play and the costumes, hoping to lure her into coming to see it.

Settled in the bay of a window, so short and so slight that her round head with its reddish-brown bandeau scarcely overtopped the back of her chair, she would chatter away tirelessly in her piping, childish voice, never ceasing to ply her needle with quick, precise little movements. Every now and then she would take up her scissors or her pin-cushion; or she would empty her needle-case into her hand, turning over the shining

273

heap with one finger; then, having meticulously chosen a suitable needle and stuck it for the moment into her bodice, she would put the case back on the table of the sewing-machine in front of her, where there lay, unexpectedly rubbing shoulders with buttons, scissors, pins, and cotton-reels, a little shapeless lump of lead, like an ingot or a door-hinge, which on closer inspection turned out to be a statuette of St. Joseph holding a lily. And if as she was talking she accidentally knocked the little saint over, or if it fell down, or she had to move it, she would cover it with a whole succession of pious little kisses.

So convinced was she of the efficacy of her saint, whose power and goodness she vaunted to everybody, that, wishing to show Catherine a special mark of affection, she offered to lend it to her for the day of her examination. Catherine put it in a corner of her purse with a bit of the miraculous oak of Notre-Dame du Chêne given her by Sister Calixte and a medallion blessed by the Pope lent for the occasion by her mother. But when some days later Catherine returned from the Prefecture and exultingly announced that she had passed, Rosine in her own heart attributed this success solely to the intervention of her little saint.

Next day anybody who knew the everyday appearance of the class would have known at once from a glance at the first row who were the successful scholars. Instead of the loose smocks worn by their companions they now had bibbed and flounced aprons over their

coloured frocks. Their hair, too, was a little different—
some appeared with buns, others had curled their
hair—and made them seem already young women.
Bent over their tapestry-work or embroidery they
worked away placidly, exchanging no more than an
occasional low word or two among themselves, affecting,
now that punishment could no longer touch them, a
voluntary silence out of consideration for the rest of
the class; sometimes, even, unexpected allies for Sister
Calixte, they actually found it necessary to address a
word or two of reproach to the others in grave but not
unfriendly tones.

9

OF ALL THAT LITTLE GROUP of pupils who had been
ten years at the convent only three, who wished to
pass the higher examination, returned for another year:
Catherine, Alice le Hombre, and one of their friends,
Clarisse de Saint-Alban. But since they were too few
to justify the organization of a special course for them
Mother Apolline contented herself with arranging for
them to have lessons with the professor of the boys'
school attached to the convent, the ordinary courses
of which they still continued to follow. In physics and
chemistry on Thursday mornings they now acted as
assistants to the mistress, arranging the instruments,
lighting the alcohol lamp, fetching the flasks of acid,
or turning the great wheel of the electrical machine.
For the rest, they drew plaster figures in the drawing-
class, or strolled about the garden armed with a copy
of the classics. And during the long hours when they
found themselves alone together, busy when the others
were playing, and often outside in the courtyard or
the garden when the others were having classes, they
talked of nothing but secret adventures, their own and
their friends'.

When the present was exhausted they would turn

to the future, for ever discussing what they would do when they were married. But into the programme of entertainments which they imagined for themselves, masked balls and grand dinner-parties where they would all meet again complete with husbands, there always entered an unconscious memory of school festivities.

Often Mother Apolline would take them with her to the Community, or perhaps, escorted by a nun, they would pay a visit to the St. Benoît Orphanage, a little orphanage attached to the Community and now fallen entirely dependent on it since its founder, a devout old lady who for long had assured its existence, had died and left it utterly without means. The Mother Superior had then had the idea of having each orphan adopted by a little group of her pupils, who would partly provide for its wants (a system which persisted right up to the day when, the Sisters having set forty orphans to making linen, the home became a fresh source of profit to them). The girls thus contributed clothing, food, and money. And on top of that candles for the chapel and medicaments for the sanatorium. Some, finding their little charge anaemic, would send quinine or cod-liver oil; and when the fairs came round they would buy spiced breads or sweets to send to them. That would be an excuse for strolling through the fair-ground early in the morning when it was still more or less empty. This year, by a chance which constantly recurred, they would regularly be going down the avenue when Alice le Hombre's young man was coming up it.

Sister Brigitte was always with them, her eyes incessantly darting about from side to side in an otherwise impassive face and seeming to penetrate to the furthest recesses of the avenue, allowing nothing to escape them; thus accompanied the three young girls made their way along the line of booths, examining them as they passed and at the same time keeping a practised eye on the far end of the great avenue, still almost empty. At last in the distance a masculine group would appear, recognizable from afar (for the swain would be accompanied by two friends, always the same two). And at once, without appearing to notice them, there would be a surreptitious nudging of elbows, slow and sustained, a gesture admonitory, explanatory, and expressive of all that could possibly have been said. The two groups met, the young men saluted their acquaintances, the three accomplices bowed very slightly and with perfect indifference, and the Sister herself was obliged to respond with one of those deep bows that nuns accord to all and sundry by reason of the voluntary humility of their state, and now against her will causing her to lower her oblique and suddenly suspicious glance.

During the Easter holidays Catherine, separated from her friends, was suddenly filled with a sense of loneliness, idleness, and boredom. The weather was uncertain, in turn overcast and luminous. And in the

278

variable April sky, blazing for an hour, then almost wintry cold as a great cloud blotted out the sun, Catherine was disturbed to find a sort of reflection of herself. She grew interested in the changes of the wind and would watch the progress of the clouds. And when one day Savine exclaimed: "Ah! The wind's getting round to the south!" she felt for the first time that there was some secret correspondence between the aspect of the heavens and the state of her own heart. But this first conscious contact with the elements filled her heart with sadness. Some curious disorder was rendering her mind lethargic and her movements languid. She felt herself beneath the spell of some strange domination, and feeble, as though sickening for an illness or recovering from one. One morning on the way home from Mass she bought a bunch of anemones, and the air was so soft and mild that she found the flowers a burden; back in her room again she felt suddenly exhausted, as though she had been for a long walk. Oppressed and sad at heart, hardly able to stand, she fetched a vase and arranged the flowers, but mechanically, taking no pleasure in her task, and put them on a little table by the window, which she opened. And just then the little bell of a neighbouring convent began its thin pealing and a long breath of air blew out the curtains, bringing with it a honey-sweet smell of spring. A strange, unanalysable distress came over Catherine: and she began to weep —with a melancholy emotion which she took to be discouragement, but which was really a sense of expectation.

As if a kind of affectionate clairvoyance had brought it home to her—who was now so far removed from all such troubles—that it would not do just now to leave Catherine to herself, Aunt Aurore did her utmost to interest her and occupy her in every kind of way, pretending she simply could not manage without her constant presence or her help. She would give her a piece of work to finish at home, ask her to come and sing at Mass or Benediction, or take her with her in her search for collectors. And several times a week they would go off together to visit the various shops in the rue de Notre-Dame where Mademoiselle de Polyso had dealt for thirty years—to Madame Verpilliat's, the haberdasher's, or to Madame Balavoine-Pincemin's.

But Aunt Aurore was finding now that Madame Balavoine-Pincemin's shop was not so well stocked as it used to be. If, for instance, she wanted some taffeta for her chasubles, or some fine damask, Madame Balavoine-Pincemin, handsome as ever, still with the heavy ear-rings that clicked as she moved, would toss her head and explain with an air of mingled regret and satisfaction that although she had kept such things for many years she no longer did so now. So they would have to fall back on a draper's kept by an old maid in a narrow street not far from the rue Notre-Dame called the rue du Petit-Credo—an ancient, gloomy little shop consisting of several dark, windowless rooms, the air of which was never changed and reeked invariably of tom-cats, wool, and mildew, all mingled with the smell of accumulated stock.

Sometimes when they were sitting there in the silent little shop while Mademoiselle Barbaroux rhythmically unfolded a length of tarlatan or organdie or muslin before measuring it off against the yardstick suspended horizontally on a level with her eyes, suddenly, through the partition which divided the shop into two, they would hear a terrific outburst of invective bellowed out in a voice that shook with rage, followed by incoherent mutterings and sobs, or a horrible rattling in the throat which broke off abruptly. It was Monsieur Félix Barbaroux, Mademoiselle Barbaroux's brother, glover by profession and long-standing villain-in-chief in the dramatic company of the Workers' Circle run by the Oblates; and this would be some part he was learning. If Mademoiselle Barbaroux wanted a length of material from the store-room she would call out to him, the door would open, and on the threshold would appear a tall, dried-up looking old man with a white goatee, a bushy head of hair, and bright eyes set close to the nose in a face which he strove to render fierce. With slow and tragic steps (for in private life he still preserved the gait of crime) he would disappear into the depths of the shop, returning with a bale in his arms for all the world as though dragging in the corpse of his latest victim, throw it darkly on to the counter, and return again to his little workshop and his rehearsal. But now, knowing that people were there, he moderated his effects and his voice was heard only as a low rumbling.

Meanwhile one of Catherine's cousins, Uncle Philippe's daughter, had been married. This provided an occasion for the Comte de Laignes and his brothers and Madame de Villedieu to examine once more the possibility of selling outright what of the property still remained undivided, a project to which they were constantly returning without ever actually doing anything about it, each pretending that he asked for nothing better than to sell, but that the others would not have it. From time to time a prospective purchaser would come forward, and various offers had been made. But to all the propositions put to him Monsieur de Laignes generally returned a refusal; either that, or he demanded so many references, guarantees, and explanations, and raised so many objections, that the would-be purchaser became suspicious and withdrew, and the project came to nothing. But if, later, one of his brothers or his sister happened to ask how far the matter had got, he would still declare that it was not yet abandoned, that he was still busy with it, and that negotiations were continuing; adding that it was impossible to come to any final arrangement until the work he was then engaged on had been completed.

When he had himself taken over the administration

of the family estates he had in fact resolved to clear
up a situation which, ever since his father's death, had
been obscure. Almost at once he had come up against
insuperable obstacles. Numerous title-deeds had been
lost. The reference numbers of the ones he still held
were now as often as not quite different from those in
the local register. And since the descriptions no longer
applied to the actual state of properties which had
been altered by neighbours, and in many places quite
changed in character by the cutting of new roads, it
had become difficult to establish the exact boundaries
of estates. Along the borders of certain woods, moreover, neighbouring proprietors had indulged in un-
warranted tree felling, afterwards selling the land
cleared, which did not belong to them at all. And as
such parcels had later been bought and sold several
times over it was now necessary to work back through
the successive purchasers to the author of the initial
fraud; then the name of someone long dead would
turn up and it would become necessary to sue his
heirs in the courts. Having never returned to Laignes,
and insisting, moreover, that he never would return,
Monsieur de Laignes was obliged to pursue his researches
through Monsieur Hotte, and this further increased
his difficulties.

He spent a large part of each morning in writing
endless letters to farmers, notaries, land-surveyors—
and often the surveyor in question would be retired
or dead, so that here again his successor or his heir

must first be hunted up; he never discussed all this with any of his friends, never, indeed, made the least allusion to it; even his wife never dreamed of asking him what he was so busy doing. He wrote letters, read through title-deeds and deeds of sale, or went through his plans, of which he had several bound volumes; some of these were very old indeed, and in the very oldest the woods were represented by little painted trees like the toy trees of a child's farmyard. And to follow the history of a wood or a plot of land, and to discover its successive neighbours and abutters, he would sometimes have to go through the whole lot of registers, one after the other.

He found there place-names which were still those of his own inheritance. Through the generations a bit of land here would be lost, a bit of land there brought in by dowry or inheritance. Then all at once the sale of land increased, and as the deeds of sale, their margins annotated with the names of purchasers, grew more and more numerous, so the girdle of great woods with which the village had been encircled diminished and receded. What had been sold as woodland soon became arable or pasture; very often, moreover, after the initial sale, it would have been parcelled out and subdivided to form unstable small-holdings which could never hope to serve as the basis for anything enduring. Such pages as these record the end of a story which is spelt out witlessly to-day by the descendants of those who once played so large a part in it;

such pages showed Monsieur de Laignes the slow decline of his own family, a downfall now complete and bringing with it its train of distress and sterility, as if the humble lives so long supported and held together by the de Laignes were, even in estrangement, continuing to follow the fortunes of the family, and, as they had once prospered with it, now declined with it in ruin.

Meanwhile the Comte de Laignes was kept regularly informed by Monsieur Hotte of everything that happened in the district, and in his mind's eye he followed all the changes indicated and worked them in with his immutable memories of the place; he believed, thus, that he had an exact picture in his mind of this village whose fortunes he followed from afar, but actually it was nothing like the reality. He learnt of marriages, births, deaths; was kept informed of the health of those he had once known, told of the coming of a new curé or the nomination of a new mayor (and this was the occasion for much conflict among the country people, divided now into political factions). His permission would be sought to divert a stream or fell timber, lay out a road or repair a roof. And at the conclusion of his letters Monsieur Hotte, carried away by that sense of his own importance which had ended by making him in his own eyes a very considerable personage indeed in whom everyone must be interested, never failed to write a long account of his own doings and to give details of his own and his family's health and of all that had happened to him or his children. And with calm complacency he would always end up with a well-turned compliment to himself, conferring on himself the eulogies which might have been addressed him by a friendly correspondent.

"As for me," he would say, "so far I keep pretty well, and I am the same as ever, always anxious to make myself useful, always working for others as much as for myself."

Sometimes, more simply, he was content to follow his signature with a phrase that perfectly described him:

"Hotte, busy as ever."

10

AT THE BEGINNING of the winter Catherine and
several friends of her own age made their entry into
society. And these young girls, most of whom had
never before in their lives spoken freely with a young
man, now found themselves in continual contact with
them. All that had hitherto made up their schoolgirl
lives now vanished. They were heaped with compliments and tributes; young men flocked round them,
disputing for their favours; and, blossoming out in the
sweetness of this new air, they enjoyed their novel
sovereignty and were prepared to welcome love itself,
which they saw now as the supreme fulfilment of
self-esteem.

At this moment in their lives, a decisive moment,
perhaps, for some, heart and senses alike were dulled
and could give them no guidance. And this double
slumber made them feeble creatures, moved solely by
vanity, so that they no longer experienced the warnings
of that defensive instinct which allows the young girl
whose heart and senses are awakening naturally and
in their own time to wait and to discriminate: their
choice was determined by vanity alone. When they
guessed, and they would guess immediately, that some

young man was taken with them, they were conscious of no delight apart from flattery at this mark of preference: and to think of him was only a way of thinking of their own success and renewing their pleasure in it.

Suddenly, vaguely warned by a sense of shame which they could not have defined, but which was strong enough in some of them to betray itself in a movement of repulsion, they had their first revelation of masculine desire. Little by little beneath its touch they became conscious of a stirring, and their senses were thus awakened before their hearts. And that old sense of physical disturbance, engendered long ago by contact with the older girls and vanishing with the passionate friendships which had succeeded to their cult, was suddenly reborn, applied now to the man they had never ceased seeking through all the divagations of their instincts. In its turn—for the senses cannot act without communicating action to the heart —their heart itself at last awoke. But it was an instinctive and confused sensibility. Not yet contented, they had to know disappointment before finding satisfaction.

Meanwhile the winter belatedly grew cold. The owner of a nearby country-house invited several families to come and skate every day on the ice of a large pond in the grounds; and almost every day for several weeks Catherine met a certain Claude de Brionne, a slender, fair young man of her own age whom she had often danced with at the beginning of the winter and who her friends not unjustly insisted was by no means indifferent to her.

Passing abruptly from the tranquillity of her retired life to this sudden liberty, she abandoned herself to a sort of giddy intoxication. She forgot the past; she never thought of the future: it seemed to her that she had always been as happy as this, and always would be. She did not think how few days had sufficed to illuminate for her, no matter where she turned her eyes, those two opposed and sombre states of man's being, past and future; the whole of life for her was irradiated by present joy, as a child's dazzled eyes see everywhere the brightness of its own vision. At last one morning the rain began to fall. At that, suddenly realizing that there must come an end to this fortuitous interlude, she was filled with a sense of sadness so unexpected and so deep that she wept. What had she done for the last month but look forward every day to the moment she should see him again and look back at that moment when it was gone? This then was love, this feeling which caused her heart to swell at the thought of losing one whom up to now she had thought of as no more than a pleasant companion. She wondered what he was thinking of at that moment, and the reply she gave herself brought suddenly with it the certainty that he loved her.

That afternoon they met once more, as dusk was

falling. Catherine and her mother left the carriage as they always did at the end of the last houses on the outskirts of the town. The whole countryside seemed changed to her. The fields were still white with snow, but on the higher ground the furrows in places were beginning to reappear, large dark smudges in the melting cloth of white. Mud darkened the slippery roads, now slushy as well as hard. At length, behind the line of poplars at the back of the château, a few rare skaters came into view. But the smooth surface over which they skimmed, which only the day before had been glittering with a thousand sparkles, had lost its brilliancy now. And in the thin film of water now veiling the invisible ice on the ponds the changing aspects of the sky were reflected between the trees and rushes of the bank; soon a pair of skaters, sweeping out from the rest, came cutting swiftly through this inverted sky.

Joining hands with Claude, Catherine told herself that surely something would happen now to prolong what otherwise must end. With increasing impatience she waited for the words that did not come. Night came on. The passing of each minute curtailed an hour which seemed very precious to her, short though it was, and although neither of them seemed to have profited by it at all. It was time to part.

From the bank a voice called. She answered. Then slowly, arms still linked, silently gliding side by side, they swept towards the bank. Just before reaching it they stopped. Plainly he realized that never again would he have thus surrendered to him this young girl who stood before him now, so near, and yet already so remote, separated from him by so many obstacles. He trembled, looked at that finely drawn face, and with an effort said:

"When shall we see one another again?"

She murmured, hardly moving her lips:

"Yes, I wonder when."

Then she said:

"We must leave it to chance, I suppose!"

And she was astonished at making such a commonplace remark when her heart was so profoundly disturbed.

He murmured, doubtfully and wistfully, as though he could already see the future:

"What good will that be to us?"

At length, after a good deal of questioning, he proposed that he should lie in wait for her whenever she went to one of the three or four places she regularly visited. To this she agreed; and they drew closer, as though to seal the pact. He took from his pocket-book a pencil drawing of her in the big hat and fur coat she usually wore.

"To remember me by," he said.

She took it, ashamed at having nothing to offer in return, and bowed her head.

"Thank you, Claude; I'll always keep it!" she said.

Next week, making up all sorts of excuses to herself for visiting the most widely separated quarters of the town, she went out with Savine every day. Spring had suddenly arrived. The rainy days of the thaw gave way suddenly to a spell of fine, warm weather. The sky was blue, the air calm. Windows everywhere were flung wide. In the streets people walked less briskly; the gutters were once more filled with running water. Savine, in a seventh heaven of delight, relaxed beneath the rays of this first sunshine, never failing to reiterate at least a score of times in the course of every walk: "Ah! Isn't it beautiful? Such sunshine! And how warm it is!"—But Catherine at her side was sad and troubled; she would have liked to walk quickly, but that was impossible in this oppressive atmosphere, so different from the crisp air of the previous days.

One morning about eleven o'clock, on her way to Aunt Aurore's, she found herself suddenly confronted by Claude. Immediately her heart gave a lurch and for a moment seemed to stop: the ground beneath her feet felt treacherous and insubstantial, and a sort of crimson mist before her eyes and a drumming in her ears quite shut her off from the rest of the world; she smiled, bowed, and passed on. Then, when they were a little way apart, both turned simultaneously, astonished to see such a distance between them and to think of the short greeting exchanged without their even hearing the sound of their own voices. It was only then that she noticed that his whole appearance was different. She, too, in her town clothes, was very different from the girl who only a few days before had agreed to these semi-meetings. Both, despite the memories they held in common, had become quite strangers to each other.

From now on when she went off to her classes— she was taking a course in literature and another in singing—it was unusual if she did not meet him on the way. And so great was her pleasure in these encounters and in this ghost of an intrigue, that she had no wish for anything else, and was reconciled again to the cheerful quietness of her everyday life. One afternoon about this time one of her friends, in dead secrecy, handed her a letter; immediately, before a word had been said, she knew who was writing to her. And with mingled humiliation and delight she took it with a swift, cautious movement that might, it seemed to her, have been habitual, and hid it in the folds of her dress; she did not read it until evening, when the door of her bedroom was safely shut. It was a somewhat awkward and embarrassed letter, breathing tenderness, and really designed to extract an answer from her. Soon it was followed by another, this time containing a sonnet. And the sonnet displayed a greater freedom of expression, the poetic form permitting a certain boldness. The opening two lines, however, smelt so strongly of the author's still recent studies that they rather tended in Catherine's eyes to transform the fine cavalier back into the schoolboy:

> When Nausicaa appears to me in Homer
> Or Virgil makes sweet Amaryllis sing . . .

293

What is more—and this was the outcome of her own studies, also recent—she noticed that one of the subsequent lines had a foot too many. And, somewhat embarrassed at finding herself in the double rôle of preceptor and adored, she could not help being touched by so profound a passion; neither could she help wishing that its expression could have been unflawed.

However, the young man who fulminated thus in verse showed himself timid enough in prose. The greatness of his love was manifest chiefly in the quantity of his letters, which seemed all the same, being nothing but the innumerable repetitions of a single model. They were chiefly remarkable for the amount of information they contained. She was to be met at such and such a place, and the directions which followed would often fill four sheets. Then there would be reproaches if Catherine had failed at a rendezvous, reproaches to which she would reply with further promises and all sorts of excuses. For in spite of the scruples which had long held her back she had at last brought herself to write to him.

In May they met again at a wedding. And two suddenly embarrassed lovers greeted each other with astonishment and distrust: they knew each other very well, but in a different context. And finding each other much the same as ever, but shadowed now by a mysterious couple whose embarrassing and unaccustomed presence they were acutely aware of, they were at once happy to be together again and frightened by a secret which seemed now insupportable. Instead of continuing from the point arrived at in their letters they appeared, spontaneously and mutually, to have forgotten all that had happened, and returned to the tone of their early conversations. By an indirect route, however, they soon returned to themselves, for they fell to discussing other adventures like their own, adventures which were being born and pursued in secrecy all around them; they talked together continually with happy animation, quite unconscious of the friendly, knowing, or inquisitive eyes upon them. Suddenly, although nothing had occurred to warn them, they became aware of the attention focused on them. And it seemed to Catherine then that all the thoughts converging on them were isolating them, pushing them forward, bringing them closer together, and that in spite of themselves they were being hurried several stages farther towards their destiny.

Next day she received a long letter containing all that he had not said the day before, and to this she replied with an even longer letter, full of a new emotion. From then on the character of her correspondence changed. She realized, in spite of her liking for him, that their ways of feeling were different and that he was only superficially interested in those impressions and ideas for which unconsciously she sought a wiser and more serious response in him; she was speaking less perhaps to him than to herself in these letters;

and yet the thought of revealing to a stranger what she alone had known until now was paralysing. And for all her desire to be sincere her meaning was often betrayed by insincere expressions, ill-chosen phrases at once belittling and exaggerating the emotion behind them. But she wrote what she really thought in the diary she kept in secret, where, since she need not think about form, she expressed herself perfectly naturally.

It was quickly noticed everywhere that wherever Mademoiselle de Laignes might be, there Claude de Brionne was certain to be too. It was observed that they exchanged understanding glances, that the flowers they wore were invariably the same. At Mass on Sundays, and from October onwards at evening sermon —those long winter sermons given in a different church every week and not ending until after dark—it was unusual if he was not to be seen standing behind a column somewhere near her or beside the holy-water stoup by the main doors. He followed her to concerts, met her out walking, once or twice even was present at houses where she visited. And once he contrived to gain admittance to the school play, where not even the performers' brothers were allowed in if they were over thirteen; but he came in on the arm of one of the priests.

Some days after this, warned by Mother Apolline, Madame de Laignes' eyes were suddenly opened to what had been going on unknown to her. She demanded

an explanation from Catherine, who, taken by surprise, confessed. But the divulging of her secret, in so
far as it made public a feeling hitherto so well concealed, seemed to her to consecrate it and point to its
natural conclusion, that is to say, to marriage. And
when she finally left her mother's room, after a violent
scene in the course of which, entrapped by her own
answers, she had been led into uttering the words
which had convicted her, she regarded herself as a girl
committed to a long engagement.

Nothing was lacking now from the rôle of romantic
heroine in which she saw herself. The inevitable persecution had begun. She was the unhappy fiancée
imprisoned by inhuman parents. Wasn't she, in fact,
all but shut up? She was forbidden to see Clarisse de
Saint-Alban, whose family knew Claude de Brionne's
mother. Savine too was suspect, and was no longer
allowed to accompany her on her walks. Her least
movement was watched: all invitations were refused
for her. When there was to be a ball she would spend
the afternoon with her friends sadly helping them
dress. And just when she should have been setting out
she would go up to bed instead, and lie and listen to
the familiar sound of carriage wheels rolling through
the silent town.

The more the obstacles accumulated the more she felt
the need to see Claude, and the more frequently they
wrote. Every day, as darkness came on, Claude would
come and find a brief note screwed up in a bit of

hollow wood under the garden gate, containing instructions for the next day prefaced by some tender little phrase which had rather the air of a polite formula. And quite unable to understand how he could have been warned of their plans, Madame de Laignes, who now never left her daughter's side, was sure to run into him no matter where they went. Catherine continued to receive long letters through the intermediary of friends, sometimes even through young girls she scarcely knew, but who were all engaged in similar adventures of their own and all linked one with another by the multitudinous ramifications of this mysterious and extensive plotting, the aim of which was to favour budding intrigue and defeat the watchfulness of parents.

Everyone was pressed into service, younger brothers, younger sisters. Before reaching its final destination a letter might pass through half a dozen pairs of hands. And under cover of their ordinary life these initiates led another life, occult and clandestine. Everywhere, in the most various and unexpected places, letters might have been discovered. As though endowed with cunning and malicious personalities of their own they had a thousand ruses; they slipped beneath doors or through windows, they made their way into a muff in the middle of a room, lay hidden at the bottom of a workbag, in a roll of music, in an umbrella. A girl would bring a whole packet of them to a tea-party and everyone would take her own—an ingenious arrangement which in no way altered the outward appearance of those gatherings, which were perfectly ingenuous and rather austere. And when the mothers came to fetch their daughters in the evening they would see them, old and young together, sitting in a circle in the middle of the room with dozens of paper horns stuck in their hair. They were playing at "My Lord has horns" or "The parson's dog doesn't like bones." To the accompaniment of shouts of laughter a new horn would be stuck in, a forfeit redeemed. And each, in the bodice of her white muslin dress, had a letter from her lover.

Carried away by the contagion of example, it was only because the young men did not ask for more that they were not accorded more. Some were already indulging in hasty meetings. Thus at Alice le Hombre's house, which had a secluded window, Catherine once saw Claude and was able to have a few minutes' talk with him. At another time they had an assignation in a woodshed. Everything conspired to help her, even Heaven, which she tried to interest in her case. Rosine had said to her once: "Why, Mademoiselle, the Sacred Heart would never refuse anything to anyone wearing its image!" And so, to meet Claude, to avoid being caught, to have letters from him, Catherine bought an image and wore it in her bosom next the letter obtained through its intervention and now living under its protection. The leaden saint which had served her so well in her examination was also back in her purse. She had even offered to buy it from Rosine, thereby to secure an exclusive lien on its favours; but Rosine had refused to sell:

"It shows how much I love you, just lending him you for a week! It's a great sacrifice to let him go at all!"

And she proceeded to recount the favours obtained through its intercession by the people she had recently lent it to—favours corresponding astonishingly closely with Catherine's own preoccupations of the moment.

"For instance, I lent him to Mademoiselle Eugenie," Rosine went on, "the cashier at Madame Balavoine-Pincemin's. The poor girl was in tears; her marriage seemed as far away as ever. And would you believe it, a week later I went round to fetch my little saint and there was a bunch of white flowers on her desk. She was engaged!"

October came—long dreaded moment that they had so often tried to convince each other never could arrive—and Claude left for Paris to study law. Once her first grief was over Catherine realized with a somewhat humiliated surprise that she was less conscious of grief than of emptiness and boredom. All that had gone to make up the sole interest in her life of the last two years had simply vanished. Now when she was out her eyes no longer roamed the streets in search of a familiar figure, and the town itself seemed suddenly half empty. Sometimes she tried to visualize to herself Claude's life in Paris. She wondered what he was doing, how he passed his days, and whether he had friends there. And imagining him voluntarily lonely and unhappy she pitied him deeply for being separated from her, without its ever occurring to her that she was not pitying herself for being separated from him.

However, since she had promised to marry him she had come to see him in a different light, more clearly and less exclusively admiringly. In two or three matters he had committed slight blunders, little faults which real love would have immediately forgotten, but which caused in Catherine an involuntary movement of repulsion and summoned up her ironic spirit to the rescue; and this insensibly had allowed her to arrive at a certain detachment from him whom until then she had never dreamt of judging. Once he had sent her a photograph of himself; and, thinking it would be an amusing and pretty thing to do, and one calculated to touch her heart—and also, perhaps, because there was in his present passion an obscure stirring of paternal and domestic instincts—he sent her a portrait of himself as an eighteen months old baby. Catherine, contemplating her lover in the singular guise of a half-naked, chubby infant—the expression of astonishment, the scanty, frizzled hair, the fat dimpled hands, the medallion round the neck, the little bow-legs emerging from beneath the short lace vest—was suddenly reminded of a photograph of herself taken at the same age. She noticed then that both had been taken by the same photographer; and the idea that seventeen years before they might have actually met in the photographer's studio on their respective nurses' knees seemed so ludicrous to her that she felt a kind of resentment against him. On another occasion—it had been her birthday—he had sent her an emerald ring. But this expensive present, clandestinely sent, seemed almost an offence to her, and she returned it with a certain acerbity.

He was now coming home to Saint-Loup on alternate Sundays, and he had arranged with Catherine that on the Monday mornings, before returning to Paris, he would walk past her house just as the cathedral clock was striking six so that she might say good-bye to him from her window. On the Sunday night, before going to bed, Catherine would pray to all the souls in purgatory to wake her at the proper time, and at five to six next morning her eyes would abruptly open. She would at once get out of bed and slip into her dressing-gown—a slim white dressing-gown with wide sleeves made by Rosine to her precise instructions and looking very much like the dress of some Gothic gentlewoman. For a moment she would peer at herself in the glass, hoping to catch an expression of intensity, and repeating to herself:

"He is coming! He is coming!"

By now the cathedral clock would be preparing to strike six. Catherine would listen to the four slow, heavy strokes preceding the striking of the hour, then the six succeeding notes, rapid and shrill, echoed by the beating of her heart.

Cautiously she would open the window a little, and there, looming in the half-light, was the broad grey front of the cathedral, shutting in one side of the empty square. Often it would have been raining during the night, and the air would be moist and soft, with a mild wind blowing, and heavy drops of water dripping one after the other in the silence. And suddenly, as if the very fact of opening the window had wrought some change in her emotions, her exaltation would vanish. No wish was left her, all feeling of being a heroine had gone. And shivering with apprehension, anxiety, and cold, she only felt a great need in that moment of some powerful and persuasive tenderness to succour her weakness and hold at bay the destiny which was sweeping her away. She sighed, "Claude, my Claude"—invoking in her distress the very affection she was trying to escape. In her heart of hearts she almost hoped he would come too late. Who then was she waiting for? Who then was coming to her? And when he appeared in the angle of the iron gates it seemed to her that this was not he for whom she had been waiting. His face was pale and drawn, he looked half-numbed. He waved his arms and said something, but he was too far away for her to hear what he said. Sure, however, that they were words of adoration, she answered with a smile, a sad smile; the sadness could be put down to her grief at seeing him go.

For a moment they stayed gazing at each other from afar; their eyes met with an expression both tried to make ardent but which was in reality compounded of boredom and disappointment. How he was keeping her! Oh that the interview would end, so that reality might become beautified in memory! At last he went, but turned back again, went away once more and returned again, as though he could not tear himself away and make up his mind to leave her; and it was she who finally cut their farewell short. Then, back again in the shelter of her curtains, she fell to considering him. Sometimes even she would shut the window quickly, with a hurried wave of her hand, pretending to have heard a sound in the house; and in her own room, with the curtains drawn so that it might still have been night, she felt restored again, vaguely happy, delivered from the burden which oppressed her: and from the few minutes just past, so recent yet already firmly established in the past by her imagination, she created an idealized image which every day grew to resemble more and more the balcony scene from *Romeo and Juliet*.

The more the passing of time separated her from Claude, the more he for his part clung to her; and the more he clung to her the more his perseverance troubled her and the more she tried to correct herself for feeling as she did. She did not admit it to herself, attributing this deterioration of her feelings, which she thought of almost as a deterioration of herself, to a sort of moral sickness which, she imagined, could not last for ever. Her pride, too, made her most carefully conceal anything that might have revealed the change taking place within her; and the moment of reckoning which every day brought nearer seemed to her so far off that she did not fear it yet. Then, unexpectedly, it loomed suddenly close upon her: Claude made a formal request for her hand in marriage.

Horrified, in the midst of all her romanticizings, by the intrusion of something which would bring her forcibly to grips with a reality she did not in the least desire, she set to work to think up every possible reason for putting off a step whose imminence overwhelmed her. It seemed to her that if her parents consented to the marriage she herself would immediately feel the weight of all the obstacles they had set aside, and that she would arrive at the point where it is too late to turn back only to find that the little love left her had fled. On the other hand, hadn't she solemnly engaged herself to Claude? How escape from that now? And she imagined the stupefaction she would cause if she refused, the questions they would ask her; and she realized too how utterly impossible it would be for her to supply reasons for her refusal, since she hardly knew them herself.

When Monsieur de Laignes told his daughter that Claude's tutor (his father having died some years before) had called on him and been met with a categorical refusal from the start, she received the news with all the outward signs of violent despair; but beneath this manifestation of a grief so intense that her parents for a moment were quite worried by it, there was hidden a profound and secret joy. This was deliverance! Rejoicing that another's will had been flatly interposed between her and that life to which otherwise she would have been committed, she was able, without undue hypocrisy, to write Claude a letter full of regrets and lamentations, shouldering others with the responsibility for a decision which was really exactly what she wished.

Just about this time she was invited to the last ball of the season. As he always did when he was at Saint-Loup and knew she was going out in the evening, Claude brought her flowers, which he left at the garden gate. A bouquet of large roses. But they were already too full-blown, and when she picked them up a shower of petals eddied to the ground. And from the bottom of the garden right up to the front door, the flowers he had given her, shedding their petals at every step, traced a flowery path before her, down which she walked again when setting out.

11

DECIDING THAT SHE no longer had the necessary energy
to run the Tabernacle Charity with effect, Mademoiselle
de Polyso in this same year—she was already eighty—
at last resigned the presidency of it. From one day to
the next the reasons she had given, perhaps without
altogether believing in them, increasingly proved to
have been justified: her health deteriorated, her infirmities increased, her bulk became immense, and she
never moved from her armchair. Enfeebled in mind
and all but impotent in body it seemed as though she
were already beyond this life.

For some little time she continued working for her
Charity; but now she quickly grew tired, and her sight
was failing. The little table with its little tools was
pushed away into a corner of the room; one day it was
found a nuisance and taken away. To pass the time
she started a piece of embroidery which she called her
"rag-bag," a large piece of canvas of no apparent use
which she embroidered with lozenges in different
coloured wools, the remnants of the skeins of earlier
days. Or else she knitted foot-coverlets for the poor
with the wool obtained from unravelling old stockings.

And now increasingly she demanded the presence of

her friends, declaring that their visits were a charity to her. And sometimes she would welcome her nieces in reproachful tones:

"I haven't seen you for three days!"

Everything spoken of nowadays served to recall the past to her; and any little detail or happening, any amusing or painful incident, would remind her of a similar happening thirty or forty years ago: one or other of her two nieces would often figure in these memories, and she would appeal to them for confirmation.

"Surely you remember?" she would say.

And suddenly, after a moment's hesitation, she would murmur, gazing at Catherine:

"But was it you or was it your mother?"

She would be perpetually muddling them up, unable to remember for which of the two this or that present had been made, or whether she had visited such and such a place with Catherine or with her mother. And these two beings, both equally dear, whom at different periods she had known in almost identical circumstances, ended up by being fused into a single person who at the caprice of her memory assumed now the features of one, now the voice of the other; and the objects of her affection came together, as if they had been born together, in a sort of involuntary confusion which she did not attempt to resolve.

Her moods, nevertheless, were by no means always equable: little by little her character was undergoing a

308

transformation. Turning over in her thoughts when alone the same saddening little facts, she had moments of despondency, melancholy, or impatience—to such an extent, indeed, that the Abbé Tourasse, himself soured by age and the mortifications of his career, said to her one day (and she took the words very much to heart, recalling them often with bitterness):

"Illness is not a sanctifying state!"

For all her piety she began to be troubled now with anxieties and doubts. And as the passing of time detached her from life, so she clung to it all the faster, increasingly dreading that moment when she would have to lay it down, a moment, however, which still seemed to her a long way off, though those around her knew it to be very close at hand.

"I have a great fear of kicking against death!" she sometimes admitted to Madame de Laignes, as she might have confessed a weakness.

And then, as though to reassure herself, she would add:

"But I must say, I don't feel very old yet."

On her way to and from her aunt's Catherine had to pass the de Brionnes' house. Surreptitiously, instinctively, her eyes would glance up at the windows, though they hid nothing now that her heart desired. For, if it had not also meant the collapse of a part of her own existence, like the death of a familiar friend, she would have preferred never to set eyes on Claude again and never to hear him mentioned. The sight of him—and his returns to Saint-Loup were already becoming more infrequent—aroused a vague displeasure in her. Under cover of various excuses, now on her part, now on his, the morning encounters had come to an end. They still continued to write, but they were sad letters now because of the effort they entailed; they had all the appearance of being on the same terms as before; but between the lines could be read a slowly increasing indifference. Now, too, there would be intervals of a fortnight or a month during which they had no news of each other at all. They would excuse themselves on the plea of having been ill, declaring that they had nearly died, this both explaining the silences and making it easier to start again.

Embarrassed by everything that reminded her of this adventure which she dragged along behind her, and wishing, consciously now, only to escape from it once and for all, she gradually drew apart from her friends of the past. For these she substituted a friendship with two young girls she had met at her class, two sisters, daughters of a retired officer, who detested society and hardly went out at all, preferring to amuse themselves at home with their mother, whose life they completely shared; attentive students, serious, frank, considerate girls, of an absolute tranquillity of heart.

Catherine was happy in these new surroundings, so straightforward, so free from falsity, glad to feel herself sheltered and far removed from all that had so tormented her during the last few years; she was thankful for the inner stability she found here as well as for the occupation provided for her mind. They played music together or discussed their class. But soon, though quite unconsciously, and as though the disturbance of love had survived love's disappearance, she was heading once more for the reefs she thought so far away, dragging her new friends with her. Thus, though firmly persuaded to the contrary, their interest in literature as such was gradually transferred to its teacher, a handsome young fellow of thirty with regular features and melancholy eyes, who combined with the usual prestige all professors are endowed with in a young girl's eyes the rarer distinction of being a successful author—he had, actually, had a one-act play in verse performed by the Saint-Loup theatre.

They thought of him often, his name was brought up on every possible occasion, and he became to all three girls in their several ways the object of a discreet and passionate cult. The two sisters, brought up in solitude, abandoned themselves to that unreflecting exaltation of mind which marks the beginning of the sentimental period in those who have been held aloof from life by a special education or a retired way of living. But for Catherine, without her at all suspecting it (for she would have considered it impossible to attach her thoughts to any other man than the one she was engaged to), it was a new beginning—that perpetual new beginning of weak natures on whom experience has no effect at all until an alien will or an irrevocable event arrives to pin them down, and who find themselves after each new lesson in life exactly as they were before they underwent it, and ready to go through it again just as defencelessly and as blindly as before.

When they were together they felt that he whom they admired so much was always with them, as assembled disciples feel that their converse is quickened by the breath of their God. He was the inspiration of all they said, and the preferences they defended for such-and-such a book or such-and-such a tragedy were but reflections of his own. If by chance they pretended to disagree it was merely for the thrill of controversy, and all his opinions were discussed at great length. Thus Monsieur Grandidier and the two young Thié- bault girls preferred Racine. Without really knowing why, Catherine defended Corneille; which resulted in his saying to her one day, with that shrewd sense of life and of the human heart which made him so sympathetic in his pupils' eyes:

"I've no doubt that you'll change your mind later on!"

But these literary and moral preoccupations—for philosophical questions also came up for discussion— did not prevent Catherine, when she got home, for instance, after an afternoon of historical reading, from taking as much pleasure as ever in Rosine and her garrulous nonsense. And if now she was slightly less interested in miraculous saints, in spite of all she owed them, it was only because, for the moment, she had no need of their assistance.

Once in a way, yielding to Rosine's entreaties, she would go to the Oblates with her little sister and Savine—their house stood outside the town, on the outskirts of one of the suburbs—to see some play in which the little dressmaker had a part.

There were five or six performances every winter, at seven o'clock on Sundays. The theatre stood at the end of a courtyard enclosed by odd and irregular buildings and entered by a great gate which stood always ajar; the first thing one saw as one approached was its tall and brightly lit ground-floor windows. Already it would be half filled with guests. In the first two rows of empty chairs, reserved for the Oblate Fathers, a few priests would be sitting waiting; behind them, with occasional groups of those colourless females peculiar to all religious gatherings (old maids or widows who seem eternally and universally to be the same age and to wear the same clothes), the young girls of the Charity would be seated, surrounded by their families and sometimes accompanied by friends or employers— a delighted yet circumspect audience, for whom this evening's pleasure was a sort of continuation, a crowning, of the duties of the day.

Several nuns, all young and pretty—their faces

seeming luminous beneath the hoods of black velvet which framed them so closely that only the lobes of the ears could be seen on either side of the face—would be moving about the hall, greeted with unvarying smiles from every row, and never appearing in the least surprised if someone quite unknown addressed them by name; unconstrained and amiable, they answered every greeting with a charming and natural graciousness which blended effortlessly with the clumsy words or silly and affected little jokes thrown at them as they passed. Or, hovering on the outskirts of a little group, they would ask a question, or express an opinion about some matter; then, with a gentle and pious word of farewell that was often a word of encouragement too (the sort of remark one thinks about long after it is made), they would withdraw nimbly in a flutter of long gauze veils and a clicketing of little silver hearts.

When the door opened for Father Jond-Nécan and his train the audience rose to its feet. Pausing in the doorway and repeatedly waving them to their seats he made his entrance with all the airs of a bishop, majestic, dignified, benevolent; beneath the bushy eyebrows which barred with their bristling line the lower part of a full forehead furrowed by responsibility, research of every kind, and mighty enterprises, his small, clear eyes regarded them with a kind of ironic amusement. Immediately after him would enter Father Ganelon, Father Jond-Nécan's right-hand man, and incidentally his rival; a superb figure of a man enveloped in a great Roman cloak. And in the hearts of the members of the Charity these two had an almost equal place, the one as Father Director, the other as the handsomest of all the Fathers. Further, to appear before these two mighty personages was the supreme consecration of a performer's talent.

The most celebrated of all the players, and skilled in comedy as well as tragedy, was an ironing-woman familiarly called *la grande Hermance*, a big built young woman of thirty or so, bony and ungainly; once—for she was consumptive—she had vomited twenty-three pints of blood!—an achievement known to everybody in the hall and always discussed with a certain admiration —this leaving her three parts dead for several days and white as a sheet of paper.

"What will she give us to-night?" was the whispered question in the audience, already excited at the thought of seeing her. Something humorous, it seemed!

The curtain rose and she appeared in man's clothes —in a black skirt, that is to say (for with the Oblates as with the Sisters of St. Benoît decency forbade trousers), a man's overcoat much too big for her, and a tall hat cocked on hair twisted back to make it look short. She regarded the audience for some moments with a sinister air, then announced without preamble (this would be the beginning of a monologue):

"My feet are back to front"—or—"Pity my poor head!"

And everybody split with laughter, from the Oblate Fathers to the old maids in the back rows.

Later she would be seen in a new guise, this time in the big play, which was generally a historical drama: *Raoul du Mont Saint-Jean*, *The Crusader's Return*, or *Jeanne d'Arc*, the work of an Abbé with literary inclinations. In these she would appear in a shining suit of armour which stopped short half-way down her skirt, or dressed as a pilgrim, or as the Jewish virgin in *Jephtha's Daughter*, drawing tears from all their eyes as easily as she had evoked their laughter. Compared with this great leading part Rosine played only very secondary rôles. She would be no more than Joan of Arc's sister, a sort of Watteau shepherdess armed with a crook and wearing a little straw hat trimmed with red poppies. Once, in *The Crusader's Return*, she appeared as an Indian dancing-girl with a tasselled fez and wide Turkish trousers. She was the Sultan's daughter, and the Crusader had converted her and brought her back to France.

At the beginning of summer there was an elaborate celebration in honour of two members who had belonged to the Charity for twenty-five years. These were Rosine herself and one of her friends, Mademoiselle Marie, a daily help by profession, a hunchback notorious for her slanderous tongue and her inquisitiveness.

These two were installed on thrones in the centre of the stage. *La grande Hermance*, in a black dress and white gloves like a soldier on parade, advanced towards them accompanied by two young girls, each bearing a crown of white roses. In the same voice which had unchained laughter and caused tears to flow she now declaimed an immensely long address celebrating their hidden virtues, their humble station, and the glory awaiting them in the next world.

Quite drunk with all this honour, emotion, and fatigue (for this ceremony was the culmination of a long day), the two heroines sat there stiffly in their white muslin dresses and listened ecstatically with tears running down their cheeks. And telling themselves that paradise itself could be no more than this same hour prolonged through all eternity, they took on already something of the aspect of the elect, and the beatific air which would be theirs up there.

At the end of her oration Hermance crowned them with roses. Whereupon, supported by the harmonium, voices arose to celebrate their praises all over again. Each verse ended with a line in honour of the Fathers, and one phrase was constantly repeated in the refrain:

"All these saints are Oblates!"

To right and left of the Father Superior sat the row of Oblates, their eyes half closed, their faces beaming, their heads all nodding in time to the music with palpable approval.

12

THE VICOMTE PHILIPPE DE LAIGNES DIED. He was buried with his wife's family. And, far more than his actual disappearance from their lives, it was this curt rupture of the bond which, in accordance with their frequently expressed desire, was to reunite brothers and sisters in death, that snapped the tie which had bound these four branches of the main stem, a tie which had stretched but hitherto never broken. For a long time past—and it was the only subject on which they were never divided, reproaches and recriminations starting up the moment their common interests came into question—whenever they had happened to find themselves together they had always reaffirmed their mutual intention of being buried at Laignes with their parents. To this end the family vault had been dug deeper and enlarged. And in the course of the long conversations which seemed to take up all their time on the rare occasions when they met, Monsieur de Laignes supplied his sister and his brothers with detailed explanations—explanations to which Madame de Laignes, if she were also present, would listen in silence, feeling like an intruder, her heart filled with jealous melancholy and a sort of involuntary hostility.

The vault, said Monsieur de Laignes, had been re-dug to make room for another four places, and this had entailed having all the coffins out and putting them back again. Some, he had been told, were almost completely destroyed; but their father's and mother's were still in very good condition. He then proceeded to allocate the newly prepared places.

"You," he said to his sister, after reminding her of the layout of the vault, "you will be over Mother, parallel with the altar. I shall be opposite, next to Father; and my wife, if she so wishes, can have a place at my side."

And with no other emotion than a kind of profound satisfaction at the thought that one day they would all be returning home, and in much the same way as others discuss their future plans, so they spoke constantly of burial, sepulture, interment, of that funereal return to Laignes which now, they all knew, would be the only journey they would ever make there—as though realizing that if they wished to return with the dignity befitting their rank and station in life the sole door remaining open to them now was death itself.

Philippe's younger girl not being yet of age, they were now faced with the obligation of doing what they had never ceased meaning to do while Philippe was alive, but had never yet in fact done—that is, sell their joint possessions: but those who were left acted in a sense directly contrary to their long-expressed intentions. On the pretext of waiting for a more opportune occasion or more appropriate moment for selling, they bought in their niece's share of the inheritance; then, the patrimony safe once more, they proceeded to forget all about it again, each telling himself that its dispersal could wait till his own death, that soon enough all this would cease to be theirs, and that to enhance its value now would merely be to labour for the benefit of its future proprietor.

Meanwhile, if they felt that the lands surrounding the abandoned château were already no longer theirs, in the village itself their name, seen only on tombstones now, was already the name of a vanished family. All that it stood for had begun to decay, and in the local people there arose an unconscious compulsion to quicken the destructive work of time. Little by little oblivion settled over that once respected name, which was nothing now but a hindrance to new and very different tendencies. It was scarcely as much as mentioned even, save in church on Sundays when the priest's indifferent voice reading out the Obituary would detail the masses founded of old by past members of the family.

One summer Sunday, a few days after Philippe's death, Rossignol, the old keeper at Laignes, was finishing his dinner when he heard through the open door the sound of footsteps approaching, and a stranger appeared on the threshold. The old fellow stared up in mingled defiance and uneasiness, but his wife, who was carrying the big coffee-pot, hastily dumped it down on the table to throw up her hands and exclaim with petrified amazement:

"Good heavens! Monsieur le Comte!"

Without even untucking his napkin, Rossignol pushed back his chair and stood up, speechless. And there he stood, frozen and dumb, his face below the white hair pale with emotion. Then, as if barely able to grasp such a stupefying situation, he started mumbling broken words of welcome, feeling that each was more inadequate than the last.

When he had come to the end of his stock of phrases, still far too overwhelmed to think of anything but the way in which he had been taken by surprise—the moment was scarcely over, but already he regarded it as firmly fixed in the past—he launched into a detailed recital, continuously interrupted and prompted by his wife, of all that had just taken place, as though Monsieur de Laignes had not been there to see it for himself. At length he returned to his initial amazement with a phrase which seemed to dismiss it but was really only a question in disguise; for, with increasing curiosity and vague apprehension as his emotion calmed, he tried to guess the reason for his master's so unexpected visit. Then Monsieur de Laignes explained that many things had been altered by his brother's death, and that new arrangements would have to be made—all the time concealing from the old man, as indeed he concealed from himself, the sudden irresistible impulse which had come upon him as he waited for a train at a junction on the way home from his brother's funeral—the impulse to revisit the scenes of his childhood.

Rossignol was racking his brains now to remember how many years it was since he had last seen his master. And checking up the various striking events which for him marked the flight of time better than dates or years, he reckoned that it must be twenty-three years. The last time Monsieur de Laignes had come had been just after his marriage, and that was the only time anyone had ever seen Madame la Comtesse. Then, one by one, he asked after all the members of the family. How was Monsieur Bertrand? Had he no sons either? And was Madame de Villedieu just the same, and still as upright as ever? And Mother Marie de Gonzague? And Mademoiselle Catherine and Mademoiselle Françoise—whom he only knew from photographs? Then in hushed tones they spoke about Monsieur Philippe, who had just died. Rossignol's wife explained that they had had the invitation to the funeral and that her husband would very much have liked to go, but just at that moment he had had an attack of rheumatism. And Rossignol himself, displaying his feet in their cloth slippers, added that he found walking difficult even now.

That did not prevent him from going with his master when he asked to see the château, however. Dispatching his wife to fetch the keys from Monsieur

Hotte, whose absence the Comte had been told of on his first arrival at the village, he explained that that very morning Monsieur Hotte had gone off to conclude a sale of wood. And since Monsieur de Laignes several times expressed regret at missing him, the keeper (ready like all peasants to adapt himself to his audience's reactions) started vaunting Monsieur Hotte's industry, ability, and devotion—cautiously at first, then with greater conviction the more his master seemed to approve, yet never saying more than he really meant. For so many years had Monsieur Hotte been charged with the management of the family affairs that now you might say he knew more about them than he knew about his own and that he worked as much for them as he did for himself; moreover, busy as he was kept with the management of the estates he never allowed himself to neglect his own affairs; he had established all his children very comfortably and was acquiring fresh property almost every day.

The keys arrived and they set off together; and since Rossignol's cottage was at the far end of the village they were out in the open fields at once. While Rossignol, already relapsed into the placidity of his everyday life, enumerated the outstanding jobs he had on hand, Monsieur de Laignes, scarcely hearing a word, was taking in all the familiar details of the road. It was with a sort of painful astonishment that he found himself back again in the midst of everything that he had so often pictured to himself, and the difference between the pictured landscape and the real produced a sort of blur in his mind, so that his thoughts faltered between one and the other; and it was with an increasing sense of uneasiness, such as one experiences in dreams without in the least being able to say why, that he felt rather than actually saw the minute changes in everything about him that had altered the whole appearance of the countryside. At last, at a bend in the road, the great trees of the park came into sight. After taking a short cut by a footpath they skirted the walls for a few yards, half covered now by the overgrown branches that hung down, rounded the corner lodge, and in another step or two Monsieur de Laignes found himself gazing through the bars of the iron gates with their coat of arms surmounted by the nine-pearled coronet. Between the two great lines of leafy trees stretched a long strip of meadowland—the avenue up to the château.

One after another, Rossignol tried the various-sized keys in the bunch he held, until suddenly the rusty lock fell back. The gates, entangled in tall weeds, stuck at first, and to move them they both had to push together. And thus it was, squeezing through one half-opened gate, that the Comte de Laignes returned home.

Rossignol went first, trampling down the long grasses to make some sort of path, and explaining as the most natural thing in the world that unfortunately the mowers had not yet come, and would not be able to come for another week; Monsieur de Laignes, following in his wake, made no reply but gazed around him with wild and bewildered eyes that settled at last on the façade of the château, still white, and growing clearer with every step they took towards it.

At the end of the avenue the strip of meadow broadened out into what had once been the carriage-sweep. He looked in vain for the château steps. The trim little rhododendron bushes which had once flanked the terrace (Monsieur de Laignes suddenly remembered how carefully they had been tended every winter) had run riot now and sent up their long and unpruned branches right over the steps, forming a sort of thicket to the height of the first floor. And from top to bottom of the bushes, now in full bloom, a tangle of brambles made an all but impenetrable curtain through which they had to force their way. Rossignol, trying to clear a path with his hands, wished he had brought along a bill-hook.

When at last they emerged on to the terrace, their shoulders covered with leaves, Rossignol discovered that the front-door key was missing from his bunch, and set off back to the village to get it. Monsieur de Laignes, left alone, halted for a moment at the foot of the terrace, trying to reconstruct the place as it had once appeared from this spot. But on every side now it was nothing but weeds, ephemeral growth dying every winter, reborn every spring, tenacious, steadily encroaching—luxuriance triumphing at last over established order, and gradually obliterating the meaning of those neat and sober beds of flowers: here and there in this destructive riot of vegetation a rose gone back to briar flung aloft its tangle of spiny stems, all starred with delicate pink blossoms in the midst of which, here and there, might be seen the broader, shinier foliage of a rose from the ancient garden.

At the end of the avenue Rossignol disappeared from view. The Comte de Laignes, pushing through the weeds and half-concealed by them, wandered about the château out-buildings. Everywhere were broken window-panes; some of the doors had lost their locks; one, warped by the rain, stood half open. This he entered.

A long succession of fortuitous happenings had brought together here the maddest jumble of incongruous articles—broken furniture, gaping baskets, heavy books with leather bindings hanging down in shreds, a cauldron with no handles, a trunk, a bath-tub, odd bits of harness. His footsteps echoing on the dusty tiles, Monsieur de Laignes slowly went from room to room as though half-expecting to find them peopled with phantoms of the past.

Once he stooped to pick up a sheet of paper, coloured by hand, surprised to recognize in it the plan of the château as it stood to-day with all the grand additions that had once been proposed—and his father's ghost seemed very close at hand, but so elusive that though clearly conscious of its presence he could not yet distinguish it. It moved here and there, it was alive and busy, some sort of activity was animating it. It was in the days of the great projects. . . . Then, with no transition—though ten years had slipped by—the shade was suddenly bowed with age. Monsieur de Laignes found a thin little note-book of sewn paper containing the scores of forgotten games of billiards; at first, at the top of every page, below his father's name he read his own name and the names of his brothers. Then on the pages that followed (and here the holidays had plainly ended) the players would be the curé and two or three other village notables.

With these foolish papers in his hand Monsieur de Laignes passed into the adjoining room—the old carpenter's shop—and there he saw the ghost once more, now seated on a chair drawn close up to the bench. How the face had aged . . . and what sadness, what disenchantment must he not have known that he should come here day after day that the noise of plane and saw might help the hours pass by more swiftly? On the far side of the room stood a cupboard with its door ajar, partly exposing its shelves. Monsieur de Laignes opened it fully; and behind one of the two doors of unpolished wood which still seemed quite new he found a long list of dates written in pencil in his father's hand; a list embracing several years and annotated with names and figures indicating weights. One of his father's last distractions, after the acquisition of a very accurate weighing-machine to control his own weight, had been to weigh everyone he met. And Monsieur de Laignes now read that on such-and-such

a day of such-and-such a year such-and-such a vintner
had weighed so much. After that came the weights of
a daily help, all the servants, a laundry woman, the
Abbé Rousselot, and the nurse. And as if reading
through the list had liberated them, a whole procession
of ghosts seemed to appear one after another, each
greeted and named by his father as it passed; the
room slowly filled with forgotten faces. The air in this
little room, so long shut up, was undoubtedly vitiated;
it became unbreathable. Monsieur de Laignes felt
uncomfortable; he went outside.

Quickly and without once stopping he walked past
the stables with their broken stalls, the coach-houses
with doors sagging from their hinges, the orangery
where the roof had fallen in, and made his way back to
the main body of the château; back once more on the
terrace, he stared unthinkingly at the dilapidated
shutters, hanging all askew. But as the discrepancy
between what had once been and what he now saw
grew ever more marked his gaze was turned inwards
and his spirit took refuge in the more lasting image of
the past. And suddenly, in the midst of that inexorable
and frightening silence which reigns in the innermost
depths of the soul, and which no human voice can
ever penetrate, he seemed to hear his mother's voice
calling within the house. His sisters answered. There
was another voice, too, which he recognized less by its
intonations than by its timidity and gentleness; and
this evoked in him a fleeting image of a figure which,

unknown to anyone at all, had once compelled his first adolescent dreams. And then, as much because of what he was afraid of finding on the other side of that door as because of what he knew he would not find, he felt he could no longer cross that threshold, an object, now, of dread. And when Rossignol returned he explained that it was too late now, that it was time for him to go.

But first he wanted to visit the chapel. Telling Rossignol to wait for him by the gates, he made his way through the trees to the mound on which the chapel stood; and having expected to find it completely buried in brambles and weeds, although it was the one place he had still had kept up, he was astonished to see the entrance quite cleared. The grass all round had been mown, and the marks of the rake still showed in the freshly weeded earth before the door. Actually, the moment she had heard of Monsieur de Laignes' arrival, Monsieur Hotte's niece, who was responsible for looking after the chapel, had hurried across the fields as fast as she could go, taking a neighbour with her to clear the chapel approach and sweep out the interior.

After a little, the Comte de Laignes rejoined his keeper, who was waiting for him at the gates. They walked a little way together in silence: then, at the last moment, Monsieur de Laignes stopped. Once more his eyes sought his château. And when at last he turned his back on it and continued on his way Rossignol instinctively kept his head averted.

Meanwhile the news of the arrival of the Comte had spread swiftly through the village; and now at intervals all along the high street, at front doors, at courtyard gates, people stood waiting, drawn by curiosity, respect, or old affection. Suddenly, at the far end of the road, that same road he had traversed so often, first as a child, then as a young man, and which he now trod again as an elderly man with white hair, the Comte de Laignes appeared. An old man standing in a doorway moved out to meet him. And Monsieur de Laignes recognized one of his father's old valets, who had married in Laignes and bought himself a little property. A little farther on was one of the woodcutters; then a servant once employed at the château; then all manner of people—a builder, the wheelwright, a number of small farmers, the baker, an innkeeper. With words of welcome and smiles all ready they approached Monsieur de Laignes with a sort of timid bashfulness which hid their real pleasure. Quickly reassured the moment they saw themselves remembered, and bursting with pride to hear themselves addressed by name, as soon as they had blurted out their greetings and a word or two more of delight and surprise, they would proceed to ask after everybody's health; then, without pause, as though fearing there would be no time to say all they wished, and as much to vaunt their devotion as their memories, they would launch out into some anecdote about the de Laignes, in which, of course, they too invariably had a part. Such vivid memories dwell deep in the hearts of villagers like the holiday clothes in the bottom of their wardrobes, safe from the light of day and all that could tarnish them, almost forgotten, but waiting and ready to be brought out again on those rare occasions when something occurs to open that invisible door so firmly closed upon the past, so rarely opened.

Although they reminded Monsieur de Laignes of a hundred trivial details about himself, his brothers, his sisters, and his mother (whose charity and piety were admiringly stressed on all sides), it was chiefly about his father that their memories lingered, and it was of him that they liked most to speak. One would quote a saying uttered on this or that occasion, another a word of commendation once bestowed by him, another a letter once received from him; and with the passing of time even words of disapproval seemed to have become translated into marks of special favour. He had been part and parcel of that which, even more than kindness or readiness to lend a helping hand, most touches the peasant soul—that is to say, of a common past which makes the same things dear to labourer and master; and thus he remained in their memories as the master, whose task it is to direct and to protect—their natural chief, and very close to them, but one whose influence they would doubtless wish to escape now, and of whom they spoke with regret only, perhaps, because they knew his reign was now no longer possible.

Meanwhile, through constantly saying so, they had

come to regard themselves as happier, richer, freer than in the old days; and yet they all displayed that curious mentality which drives people to deplore a state of affairs they themselves have largely brought about. Wherever he went Monsieur de Laignes was told that the country was greatly changed. It was no longer so gay as it had been, people took their pleasures sadly, disagreement was rife, many people had gone away altogether and left the district. There were seventeen cottages standing empty at that moment. . . . And involuntarily connecting the beginning of this change with the moment when the château gates had closed for the last time behind the last master, they regretted that none of the family had stayed on. Why had they all gone away thus and never returned? They wondered what they could have done to the family to make it—as it seemed—angry with the country. Somebody recalled that when the old nurse had died Madame de Villedieu—and it was the only time she had ever come back, although she lived so near—had arrived just in time for the funeral. She had driven over from Monthuis, and her carriage had waited outside the church door; after the service she had gone off at once without a word to anyone and without anyone's having a chance to say a word to her. And as they said good-bye to Monsieur de Laignes not one of all those who had come to greet him omitted to express the hope that one day the family would come back again; all praying, with a curious mixture of sincerity and unconscious hypocrisy, for a return which they did not really desire.

The cab which took Monsieur de Laignes back to the station that evening followed for a little the road to Fontaines. Along this road in the old days the whole family had journeyed twice a year to Menuls. And suddenly all the incidents of that journey came back to Monsieur de Laignes with extraordinary clarity, as though he were a little boy again in the big old rumbling coach gazing unweariedly through the windows at the unequal jogging of the dappled haunches—every detail of the road came back into his mind, and for a long time he followed it in his thoughts, while every revolution of the wheels bore him farther from it.

They would set off in the morning before dawn, halting only for lunch, which they always had at midday at the same inn in the same quiet, sleepy little village. They did not arrive at Fontaines until evening. The sun would be going down. And here and there on the gentle slopes of the hills, or crowning the little plateau, a solitary wood stood up like an island in the cornfields, breaking the expanse of gold with the double darkness of its trees and its shadow.

If it was late in the year when they set out, and it would often be in the middle of autumn, it would be quite dark when they arrived. And Monsieur de Laignes remembered a time when he must have been quite a child—for his two sisters were not yet born—when the roads round about Fontaines simply did not exist. In the afternoon men would be sent out from the farm to fill up ditches with faggots, and more than once the carriage would have to drive across fields. Often it would be foggy. Far off in the distance they would hear the church-bells ringing the *Berlaude*, something like the angelus, but far more prolonged, and designed to guide through the night shepherds returning with their flocks, or strayed wayfarers. At the entrance to the grounds of the château—at that time the bridge had not been built—they had to ford the stream, and this was sometimes a wearisome business in the blank darkness. But all at once they would catch sight of the château lights through the tall plane-trees of the avenue. And at the top of the steps, framed in the open double doors of the brightly lighted hall—while Porphyre, the old servant, stood at the bottom— Monsieur de Laignes had a vision of his grandmother waiting motionless and erect, her arms folded under her little silken cape, her head held high as usual and crowned with a lace cap from beneath which fell the neatly curled grey ringlets that framed her grave face.

When, an hour later, Monsieur de Laignes' train moved out of the station, the shades which had appeared to him among the ruins of the past and which as he alighted from his carriage he had for a moment imagined he had left behind, returned to people his solitude. Some whispered softly in his ear; others were happy merely to be there. But it was as though in their company he had at last discovered the secret of that mysterious destiny which had attached him so strongly to the scenes of his childhood even as it tore him away from them, and he understood now that the fault was not his, and that they had come to him less to reproach him than to excuse themselves.

Meanwhile the farther he was borne away the thinner became his unseen company. One by one, without a sound, without a sign of farewell save a deeper shadow in the depths of his remembrance, they left him. And when morning came and the cathedral of Saint-Loup pierced the vapours of dawn on the horizon the last of them had long been gone and Monsieur de Laignes was alone.

13

FOUR OR FIVE TIMES a year Catherine and her father went to see her uncle, Major de Laignes, who was at present stationed at Paris; and during her stay there she would be taken to the theatre. The two Thiébault girls, who also had relations in Paris, would always see the same plays, and sometimes they actually met in the same theatre. Then, back at Saint-Loup, they would discuss what they had seen at length, appraising both the acting and the actors' personalities, infatuated now with this one, now with that, and each as proud of her favourite's glory as if she shared it herself. But the fascination of the actual spectacle led to their substituting the interpretation for the play in their memories of it, so much so that they thought they were judging the play when all they were discussing was the players; and thus, in this instrument played upon by another hand, all three saw less the enduring value of the supreme authority expressing himself at second hand through the actor's voice than the brilliance of an exterior at which their judgement stopped short.

In class, meanwhile, Monsieur Grandidier took it upon himself to read a number of contemporary plays, or fragments of plays. And once more they discussed his opinions together, of de Musset and Hugo now, as in earlier days of Racine and Corneille; and they would wonder how he would interpret this part or that, how he would see such and such a character.

"What a fine Hernani he would make! How superb he would be as Ruy Blas!"

And far from realizing that they invariably cast their tutor as the lover, so that in their eyes he soon came to stand for all the romantic junior leads, they still affected in their discussions to regard love as nothing but a poetic fiction with no conceivable bearing upon their own lives—Catherine, subjugated by her admiration for Lucie and Angélique, let herself be so swept away that she blindly adopted all their values and ideas; while her two friends, who had never yet been called upon to defend themselves against an attack which perhaps in the bottom of their hearts they still awaited, found themselves rather in the position of those young ladies at a ball who are not invited to dance and after a time pretend that they do not care for dancing anyway.

Thus, not in the least realizing how essentially sentimental they really were, they sought compensation for the joys of love in the joys of the mind. But they never got beyond the appearances of things, regarding as superior whatever seemed to them real and earnest; and since nothing in the world seemed less real and less earnest than grace, they arrived at the point of aspiring to the higher masculine qualities, as opposed to more peculiarly feminine virtues. And if at this period they had come by a magic wishing-ring they would have wished neither for beauty nor for love but simply to be changed into men, thus attaining at one stroke the supreme goal of their ambition. And if they could have chosen further, their choice would have fallen upon one of the rôles in life that had made most impression on them; that is to say, they would have elected to be a professor, a sailor, or a doctor. Meanwhile, the only means available for attaining their ideal was to join the ambulance society, and this they did, assiduously attending the local doctor's lecture every week at the Charity headquarters.

Gathered round a pink cloth dummy, a figure of uncertain sex with a beardless face and a sad, remote expression, like an enormous bran-stuffed doll with articulated limbs, they learnt how to bandage. Now kneeling at the apparition's feet, now standing at his side, they dressed an arm or wound strips of dry or moistened linen round a foot. Or like Adonis outstretched among the Tyrian women, he would be surrounded by five or six young girls eagerly trying to assuage his pangs. One would fashion him a cap of cotton-wool, another place an imitation poultice on the pit of his stomach, a third fix splints or bolsters to his leg. When the eyes required bandaging they generally took off the head, and sometimes a beginner, turning it round and round on her knees, would end up by turning it upside down in order to finish her task more easily.

After several months of study they were allowed, if they so desired, to act as assistants at the hospital. The ladies were admitted first and only later—after long discussion—the young girls. But on the eve of operating days mothers would anxiously inquire of the doctor whether the place to be operated on was quite decent.

When, however, Catherine was with her two old friends Alice le Hombre and Clarisse de Saint-Alban, the only friends of her schooldays with whom she still kept up, the other side of her nature at once came uppermost. Descending from the heights of literature, love, in this so different setting, was seen as a part of life. They had interminable discussions on passion and jealousy, young men, and the part of love in marriage. But Catherine, although she joined in readily enough, could not help bringing to these discussions something of her new habits of mind, and would consciously assume an air of ironic superiority which seemed to set her apart from her two friends, whose hopes and enthusiasms were really also hers. If they chanced ever to wander away from the subject in hand, a remark about some novel recently read in secret very soon brought them back to it. With music it was the same; for while the Thiébaults only played music of the severest sort, or of that sort where passion is disguised beneath a veil of melancholy, joy, or sadness, here, on the contrary, nobody cared for anything that was not frankly amorous, no matter whether it was good or bad. Thus sentimental waltzes, operatic duets, Italian ballads, surprisingly punctuated by an occasional ecstatic hymn to the Sacred Heart or the Eucharist, took the place now of requiem and oratorio.

To avoid any necessity for comparing the two sides of her nature, between which she would then inevitably have had to choose, Catherine applied herself to the task of keeping her old friends apart from the new, shrinking from the confrontation which would have brought her peremptorily face to face with her own duplicity. She never invited them to her home together and never mentioned either to the other.

The first of them to marry was Clarisse de Saint-Alban. One morning she sent word to Catherine to come at once; and the moment they were together, with a thousand precautions, she took a little square of cardboard from a transparent envelope and showed her friend a portrait. It was her fiancé, Henri de Blaincourt. She was madly in love with him, they were to be married in a month's time, spend their honeymoon in Italy, and then go and live in Paris near her future husband's parents. For a moment Catherine was stupefied. She had a feeling that something unaccountable and immediate had quite cut her off from her friend; but she forced dissimulation on herself, and with little exclamations, cries of rapture, and foolish little jokes tried to conceal the bitterness of the shock it had been to her and her sudden disillusionment. When she left Clarisse the confidences so recently poured out to her came crowding back into her memory; she asked herself if it could really be possible, and how could Clarisse have forgotten all that had been her life for the last few years! But what most clearly showed her that their intimacy was truly shattered was the realization that now she would never dare ask her whether nothing remained of the past which had only just ceased to be.

The first letters she received from the recent bride filled her with astonishment, curiosity, and a sort of shame at the thought that one day she herself, after just such a marriage, might also write like that about it. The letters brimmed over with happiness and love, and were freely scattered with allusions to the husband whose every action she shared and whose name appeared in every sentence: "My little husband is reading over my shoulder . . . Henri, who is with me now"—there were even letters begun by her and finished by him. And moralizings and advice from this old friend suddenly become a wise and experienced senior alternated with details about her own married life and clumsy hints of a wanton suggestiveness. Catherine, who could not always make these out, nevertheless took good care that her mother never saw the letters.

Sister Calixte at the convent had letters from her old pupil too. But if essentially these were much the same as Catherine's, the passionate impetus behind them was veiled in this case by pious turns of phrase. They

341

were scattered thickly with references to the Good God, the secret designs of Providence, and the intercessions of saints to whom the writer vowed distracted thanks. When Sister Calixte, reading one of these letters to Catherine, came upon some such passage she would sometimes smile and sometimes seem annoyed.

The farther Catherine left her schooldays behind her, the more pleased she was to go back to the convent. She would call in the middle of the afternoon and go up to the class-room of the First form, enjoying the sight of all the pupils rising to their feet as she entered and then subsiding quickly at a sign from Sister Calixte; then, as how many times had she not done before, she would instinctively dip her fingers into the holy-water stoup and cross herself as she turned and went over to the high reading-desk, on the steps of which she would come to rest for a chat with her old mistress. And bent over the letter which the Sister would produce from her desk or from a square of cloth pinned to her breast, and reading it half aloud, she would suddenly be aware of broken sentences detaching themselves from the confused murmuring of the pupils busy at their lessons: "The tributaries of the Loire are . . ." or "Charles VIII prepared to invade the Duchy of Milan. . . ." The girls for their part, in spite of their apparent diligence, also caught scraps of phrases, these, however, evoking for them nothing more than memories of other lessons.

"On Wednesday we go to Venice! . . . We went to

see Santa Maria Maggiore. . . . We made the ascent of the Scala Sancta on our knees. . . ."

One afternoon, after saying good-bye to Sister Calixte, Catherine went up to see Mother Apolline. In a corridor on the way up she passed a large, fat woman holding a little girl by the hand and escorted by a nun. They bowed, and Catherine turned into the Mother Superior's room. And there she learnt that the woman she had just seen outside was none other than Julie Chavanges. Deeply saddened both at the thought of such a change and at neither recognizing nor being recognized by her, Catherine stopped for a moment in the chapel on her way out: instinctively her eyes sought out the place that had once been hers. From this place she had seen her adored "big girl" as she sat in the front row, and the contour of her cheek below the mass of golden hair; and she was astonished now to think that Julie Chavanges, who had seemed to her so old then, had in those days been only quite a young girl, younger than she herself was now. She remembered the badges Julie had given her, and the chocolates, which she had never eaten but carefully treasured. And then she saw once more—it was a summer evening in the garden, a little before the annual prize-giving, when Julie Chavanges was going to leave—a tall, slim girl walking at the head of the crocodile on Sister Bonne-Marie's arm. She was smiling. At that moment the little procession was passing a jasmine in full bloom, and Catherine heard her say in

343

a voice whose gaiety seemed to reflect the happiness in her face: "I'm sixteen!" And a moment later, without letting go of the nun's arm—they were turning out of the garden into the courtyard now—she had bent down, humming to herself, and lifted the latch of the gate.

From time to time, on certain feast-days, Catherine still went to early-morning Communion at the convent chapel. On such days she had to get up at six. And always a little late, following the route she had taken every morning day in day out for twelve years, she hurried up the rue Notre-Dame. But since the days when she had gone to school as a very little girl hand in hand with Savine, a slow transformation had overtaken the street; she had seen it happening from year to year; and it was no longer the old rue Notre-Dame of bygone days.

Here and there between the old-established stores little ephemeral-looking shops had sprung up, often nameless, where unknown people sold shoddy stuff at incredibly low prices. Stretched across the fronts, by way of signs, were strips of calico with flashy slogans: "Sale owing to fire—Selling off at a loss—Stupendous Bargains—Going for nothing—Ruinous Sacrifice—50 per cent Discount!" One day a "Closing Down" sale would be announced (and the discount would rise to 60 per cent), but somehow the closing down would be postponed from month to month. Then the shop would

344

shut up, to be reopened later in a similar venture; or the strips of calico would disappear, the jumbled heaps of goods in the doorway would be packed up into boxes, and the business would continue, sometimes in a different shop, sometimes in the same one enlarged.

More often than not these shops would be staffed exclusively by members of the proprietor's family, who between them filled all the necessary rôles. The shop-girls were invariably dark, with glossy hair and rather thick red lips, often quite pretty, and supervised in their evolutions by an elder brother or a heavily bearded father, of whom they seemed to go in awe, and who would call out to them in broad accents and sometimes even in a foreign tongue from among his piles of stuffs at the back of the shop.

These new businesses had an enormous turnover; their stuff, too, seemed good; and, unlike the old shops, they gave no credit and could therefore sell things cheaper. All this made people come again, once they had, tempted by the cheapness, actually ventured into one of these new shops that were so different from the old, and were still regarded with suspicion. And they returned the more willingly in that they came away convinced, so often had they heard it repeated, that they had got a real bargain.

Meanwhile the old shopkeepers lost their customers and no longer dared keep big stocks of anything. Soon they had nothing but samples to show and a proposal to order specially what could be got on the spot next door. Thus business steadily dwindled, and soon they could no longer conceal their anxiety; their former affability gave way to a certain sourness. A dress or a hat bought elsewhere would be received with such disapproving glances, such undisguised reproach even, that the victims preferred not to expose themselves to it again. From day to day their losses increased, until at last, feeling robbed and yet not knowing what to do about it, one after another they retired from business; but often, after a year or two, they would have to take over their shops again from their successors, since these were doing so badly. It became increasingly difficult, moreover, to find serious and solvent purchasers. And since for the most part they had made their children officials, engineers, officers, or doctors, these children were not in a position to take over their businesses for them.

Unimaginative, vengeful, and stupid, many still persisted in waiting in the hope of tiding over the crisis. Others decided to sell up at once; and their ancient shops, which for generations had sheltered their families and seen the accumulation of those unspectacular but solid fortunes which had been the backbone of the town, were now given over to new businesses, which started off with tremendous sales, as many others had done in the last few years.

Only a handful of the ancient merchant houses, like the Balavoine-Pincemin's, seemed capable, after suffering the general malaise which had paralysed and half destroyed the old trade of the town, of defending themselves against the unknown force which threatened them and emerging victorious.

In the nick of time Monsieur Balavoine-Pincemin gathered round him his five sons, one of whom had already begun to study medicine. And although he was known to be very rich everyone was amazed at the amount of capital he was able to sink in his business between one day and the next, allowing him, while other tradesmen were retrenching, to embark upon a radical enlargement of his premises. On the foundations of his own house and two neighbouring houses no sooner bought up than demolished, he put up an enormous new building, all steel, with a ground-floor consisting almost entirely of windows with displays of furniture, materials, carpets—or kitchen utensils, for instance, or stoves of every description. And the departments multiplied to such an extent that the Balavoine sons were now less merchants than financiers.

One last relic of the ancient rue Notre-Dame still persisted, however, in Monsieur Matelin's haberdasher's shop at the corner of the place de la Vicomté. All the way up the street Catherine would have been glancing at clocks to make sure that she was not going to arrive half-way through Mass, and as she passed his shop she would see him standing in his own doorway, as he had always stood, in his black skull-cap and his lutestring sleeves, slapping together the soles of his old felt slippers with a noise like a donkey shaking its ears, and raising a prodigious cloud of dust.

14

SINCE CLARISSE DE SAINT-ALBAN'S marriage Catherine's intimacy with the Thiébault girls had steadily increased. But now to their little group was joined a fourth, a Madame Vianet, whom they had got to know at the meetings of the ambulance society, a widow of forty with a young son; almost entirely alone in this town where her husband, a travelling official, had died, she seemed to have no desire to live in Saint-Loup and only to be waiting for her son to grow a little older before going to settle in Paris.

Disillusioned by a loveless marriage, Madame Vianet concealed beneath an almost repugnant appearance an ardent sentimentality which knowledge of her own lack of charm had rendered defiant: and, although for the three young girls friendship up to now had been no more than a kind of fraud imposed on them by the instinct to love, Madame Vianet began to seek in this intimacy not so much an outlet for her love as a compensation for not being loved. What she had despaired of ever finding now appeared in her life in a guise which allowed her not to name it for what it was, and it was just her artlessness which allowed her to introduce into this high-minded little circle the

ferment of a disorder which little by little changed its
whole nature.

Not a day went by now without their meeting, now
at the house of one, now of another. When Madame
Vianet was away they discussed her in great detail—
what she thought, what she was, what she would
become, what her past had been. And the three friends
would imagine with every kind of romantic embellish-
ment the circumstances of a figure whose prestige in
their eyes eclipsed even Monsieur Grandidier's—he,
moreover, had left Saint-Loup some time ago—and
made them quite forget him.

Through force of always seeing her in so romantic a
light they were soon quite incapable of distinguishing
her real self and personality from the sentimental idea
of her they had created, and little by little the affection
she inspired in them became all-engrossing. She was
admired, and she was pitied. Since many of the families
of the town regarded her with some suspicion she had
to be protected. Without her in the least suspecting it,
fierce battles were fought on her behalf. But their
mutual affection was disguised beneath a continuous
irony, and their ruling passion brought a certain slightly
chilly stiffness into the relations of all four. The irony,
however, was a kind of tenderness, the severity solicitude. And under what appeared to be the most reserved
of friendships there lay hid a growing ferment—which
must be the case when the heart invokes its comple-
ment, the senses; and the senses, with no object here

349

on which to fix, must find their satisfaction in repression, manifesting themselves only in the intensity of the cerebral emotions they provoke. Thus all the elements of love were there, and all its phenomena appeared—desire, that is, and jealousy: but in this case the object was a delusion, the love an abstraction.

If Madame Vianet was travelling they would await her letters with impatience, and when they came hide them, for all the world like love-letters; and the general scorn with which the outside world regarded this incessant correspondence only served to heighten the illusion. The letters were concerned above all with sentimental matters. Conceptions of friendship were gone into at great length; confidence was lauded; they reproached each other ceaselessly—though in veiled terms—for lacking this, for each imagined that the lives of her friends contained some glorious and incomplete adventure on the ruins of which they had managed to build up their lives again, ripened now by suffering.

Impregnated thus all unawares with love, yet truly loving nobody, they came to take an interest in each other so acute that it took on a significance the origins of which their guileless consciences would have been deeply shocked to recognize. Their least words now reflected the acuteness of this state; and to see each other, meet each other, read each other's books, to be parted from each other, were all occasions for joy or grief quite disproportionate to the cause. Far from suspecting that they themselves were victims of that tyranny the effects of which they contemplated in others with a certain pitying contempt, they continued to speak of love, if ever the subject cropped up, with unfailing disdain. With what vengeful energy would not Madame Vianet, strict as a metronome, bang away at her piano while Catherine, Hatred incarnate, sang: "The more one knows of love the more one loathes it!" and the Thiébault girls, like Hatred's hand-maidens, the Furies, improved upon this with:

> Let us shatter love's baneful power,
> Let us break his knots, let us tear off his bandage,
> Let us burn his arrows and put out his fire!

Catherine, moreover, imagined herself all the more removed from its grip since her love for Claude had completely disappeared. But as she had once felt that he could never suffer since she gave him so little, so now she never dreamt that he could love her still, since she no longer loved him: it never occurred to her that two hearts can feel unequally or disproportionately. Had she been told that he was unhappy she would have thought of his unhappiness simply as the expression of the situation in which he found himself, and that would have been a matter of indifference to her.

Claude had been gone two years now; and from year to year Catherine's old friends, her one-time accomplices, were all getting married, one marriage of convenience after another. And it was with profound astonishment, changing soon to bitterness, that this opponent of love beheld them filled with just as much joy and exultation as ever they had found in their first passions, barely concluded but already quite forgotten. Almost immediately after their weddings they would go off for their honeymoons, and on their return a few weeks later they would already definitely be women established in licit bliss, their whole persons blooming in a sort of sober exuberance. And now it was they who, reversing the rôles, affected towards Catherine an air of slightly contemptuous commiseration mitigated by a pitying affection.

Lowering their voices a little, as if speaking of something they hardly liked to mention, they would ask her about her marriage. How was it going? No progress yet? And they would dwell on the difficulty of her situation and on the scant security the future offered her. And they would always end up by saying they hoped it would all come right one day—affecting to regard her rather as a young girl who has been seduced and must inevitably marry her seducer in due course.

On her way home from the Thiébaults Catherine would sometimes call at the municipal gymnasium for her little sister, who was taking gymnastic lessons there with the children of several other families. Opening the door one day into that vast empty space with its clutter of apparatus of every kind, she beheld a thin figure swooping through the air in a great curve that sent a long flutter of flowered stuff flying out behind her, and with amazement Catherine realized that it was a lady dressed in the height of fashion. But precipitated suddenly forward by another will than her own, from the vertical she passed abruptly to the horizontal; and while the iron rings she had let go of swung away and clashed joyously, almost maliciously, overhead, the amateur gymnast measured her length on the tan of the floor, face downwards and arms outflung: but she was on her feet again at once, laughing and sneezing, half-blinded by the sawdust in her eyes.

Very placidly she wiped her face, dusted down her dress, walked past the row of little girls in their grey uniforms without seeming in the least to mind their shouts of laughter, and took her place among the other mothers bent industriously over their needle-work and hardly troubling to conceal their shocked and scornful smiles. It was only then that she saw that a lady was presenting Mademoiselle de Laignes to her; and without further ado, as though it were the most natural thing in the world, she launched into an explanation of how Cécile, her daughter, never seemed able to do that exercise and how she had determined to find out for herself just how hard it was. It was Madame Varambaud, the new attorney's wife.

Shortly after this they met again over a concert given by the ambulance society. The two little girls soon got to know each other, and Madame and

Mademoiselle de Laignes returned Madame Varambaud's call.

Since their sole point of contact was the friendship between the two little girls, conversation centred on Françoise and Cécile. Madame Varambaud was never tired of praising her Cécile. She expatiated on her upbringing and on her successes at the class. She had never had a moment's trouble with her, it appeared; but she claimed no credit for that, since the child's nature was quite exceptional She further politely observed that Françoise was perfectly brought up considering she had been to a convent. At this point in the conversation there was a slight sound from the next room. Madame Varambaud started, got up from her chair, and to the utter amazement of her two visitors, disappeared. Through the door came the sound of keys being turned; their hostess reappeared and, still perfectly at her ease, explained that she had been to lock the larder. And the reason for this astonishing precaution was, it appeared, that her son had just come back from school.

Almost immediately the same door opened again and a young boy appeared in slippers, his eyes wary and defiant. In a tone very different from the one she had employed in speaking of her daughter, Madame Varambaud rather hurriedly explained that this was her son, Michel. He greeted them awkwardly, and went and sat down a little apart, choosing a large arm-chair in the depths of which he lounged without further word; and his bearing was so different from that of the others around him, and his air of rather fierce reserve so far removed from his mother's facile volubility, that it was almost impossible to think of him as the son of so brilliant a woman. And although his slippers, displayed without a trace of embarrassment, gave him a look of being comfortably at home, his shyness and untutored ways gave him something of the air of being merely the tolerated son of an old servant, or the children's foster-brother.

After that Catherine paid occasional calls on Madame Varambaud, and sometimes she saw Michel there too —once she passed him in the hall, catechism in hand; another time he came into the drawing-room to keep her company. Several times she met him almost outside her own house. And he would bow and pull off his schoolboy's beret with a long, embarrassed sweep.

If Cécile had come to spend an afternoon with the de Laigneses he would come with his mother to fetch her in the evening; or sometimes he would be asked to tea as well. And as Catherine still thought of him as a greedy small boy she amused herself by passing him the little cakes more often than she need have done and was surprised when he sometimes refused them. If Catherine asked after him when he was not there Madame Varambaud's comments were invariably unfavourable. It appeared that he was lazy, tiresome, and a great trial to his mother. Yet even then Catherine could not find it in her heart to dislike him.

For Françoise's twelfth birthday Madame de Laignes gave a children's fancy-dress ball, to which Cécile and Michel were invited. Catherine had persuaded Madame Vianet and the Thiébault girls, in spite of their protests, to come too. But on this occasion the little group lacked cohesion. At every other moment, leaving the bay of the window where all four had taken refuge, Catherine would go and greet some lady or introduce a hesitating little couple who had just shyly taken their places in the circle of boys and girls sitting round the room. When the dancing started she went and mingled with the children, under pretext of livening things up, dancing now with the very smallest and now with the bigger ones, and flashing a smile at her friends as the dance brought her close, only to whirl her off again.

And the gayer she seemed the gloomier grew her friends, as if they felt her obvious enjoyment a betrayal of their friendship and in some way a defection from the cause to which they imagined they had won her. Things they had overheard about her sprang to mind, without their knowing why. They remembered allusions they had heard to an affair from which Catherine had emerged engaged to be married. And all at once, their hearts bursting with jealousy and bitterness, they realized the existence of a whole side of Catherine's life and a whole side of her character which until now had escaped them; and with that came a confused presentiment that she had been brought to them more by chance than by a true similitude of tastes and ideas.

All three of them were thinking along the same lines, yet all three preferred to keep their thoughts to themselves; it was only the tone of their conversation that revealed their common preoccupation. They spoke of "society" and those worldly pleasures which leave such irremediable sadness in their wake. When all such charms are exhausted, then at last one sees that friendship alone is solid and will not disappoint. But perhaps, they remarked, some natures are incapable of making port till many storms have swept them, or have such a lust for adventure that, in spite of themselves, they must keep on seeking it. At last, since they all had Catherine in mind, they spoke her name aloud. And moved by a compassion which was not untinged by resentment, they arrived at the conclusion that Catherine was destined to marry sooner or later. Rather as one admits the attraction of the inferior, they conceded that she was made for love. But what disappointments was she not laying herself open to! Besides, whom would she ever meet? It would have to be a man who could appreciate and understand and guide her. Would she ever find such a man?

Meanwhile the dancing, after a short interlude, had started up again, and once more the piano drowned the confused and happy babble of childish voices. Madame Vianet turned her head, and her eyes, seeking her friend, rested unthinkingly on a little harlequin leaning in a doorway: his bat under his arm, his round chestnut head rakishly crowned by the narrow cocked hat, he stood there without moving, watching the glittering whirlpool of oddly assorted pairs as they passed and repassed before him, with mocking, tender, timid eyes.